Praise for the novels of Lee Tobin McClain

"Lee Tobin McClain dazzles with unforgettable characters, fabulous small-town settings and a big dose of heart. Her complex and satisfying stories never disappoint."
—Susan Mallery, *New York Times* bestselling author

"Fans of Debbie Macomber will appreciate this start to a new series by McClain that blends sweet, small-town romance with such serious issues as domestic abuse…. Readers craving a feel-good romance with a bit of suspense will be satisfied."
—*Booklist* on *Low Country Hero*

"[An] enthralling tale of learning to trust…. This enjoyable contemporary romance will appeal to readers looking for twinges of suspense before happily ever after."
—*Publishers Weekly* on *Low Country Hero*

"*Low Country Hero* has everything I look for in a book—it's emotional, tender, and an all-around wonderful story."
—RaeAnne Thayne, *New York Times* bestselling author

Also by Lee Tobin McClain

The Off Season

Cottage at the Beach
Reunion at the Shore
Christmas on the Coast
Home to the Harbor
First Kiss at Christmas

Safe Haven

Low Country Hero
Low Country Dreams
Low Country Christmas

Look for Lee Tobin McClain's next novel
available soon from HQN.

For additional books by Lee Tobin McClain,
visit her website, www.leetobinmcclain.com.

LEE TOBIN McCLAIN

forever on
the bay

ISBN-13: 978-1-335-54078-2

Forever on the Bay

Copyright © 2022 by Lee Tobin McClain

Recycling programs for this product may not exist in your area.

For questions and comments about the quality of this book, please contact us at CustomerService@Harlequin.com.

HQN
22 Adelaide St. West, 41st Floor
Toronto, Ontario M5H 4E3, Canada
www.Harlequin.com

Printed and bound in Barcelona, Spain by CPI Black Print

To My Readers

forever on
the bay

CHAPTER ONE

EVAN STONE TIPPED back his chair in the middle of the Gusty Gull, laughing at someone's dumb joke.

He tapped his thumb on his thigh in rhythm with the music—eighties pop, "Girls Just Wanna Have Fun"—and breathed in the smell of fried fish and crab cakes.

Here in his adopted Chesapeake hometown, he was content. He'd built a life where he could socialize with friends who were drinking without worrying that he'd relapse.

His phone vibrated, and he glanced at the face of it.

Got a minute? Need some help.

He did a double take, stood and strode out into the chill of an early-March night. Cassandra Thomas, his late best friend's younger sister, never, but never, asked for help. Even though she had more reason than most people to do so.

What's wrong, can you talk? he texted back and then, too impatient to wait for an answer, tapped the audio call button.

She answered immediately. "I'm okay. I'm sorry to bother you." Her voice sounded fine, just a little...funny.

His tight shoulders relaxed some, and he leaned against the bar's outside wall. "What's going on?"

"I'm worried about Mom."

"She's gotten worse?" Cassie's mother struggled with

anxiety and depression, and it had gotten more acute since the death of her only son, Cassie's brother.

Cassie sighed into the phone. "Not exactly. It's just, since I didn't get this artist-in-residence job I applied for, she's cancelling her trip. Do you think you could talk to her, reassure her that I'll be safe staying here in Minestown? She really needs to get away, and she might listen to you."

"*Are* you safe there?" Cassie had lived with her brother after college, in an apartment in a half-gentrified area of the city. After he'd been killed four months ago, she'd moved back in to her mother's home on the outskirts of town so they could help each other cope. Minestown was just two hours away from Pleasant Shores, over the border in Pennsylvania, but the depressed community was worlds away from the idyllic beach town Evan now called home.

"Yes. Yes, I think I'm safe."

"You don't sound sure." Cassie was nine years younger than Evan was, but he'd grown up next door. Since Josh was his best friend, Evan had spent a lot of time at their house, and he could recognize the doubt in Cassie's voice.

"No, I know I'll be fine here. And I get it, why Mom's so anxious. She's afraid for me. She only has one child left. But she's not getting better sitting around thinking about what happened."

"Any signs of the guy who…?" He trailed off, not wanting to say it.

"Noooo…" Her voice was uncertain. There was a pause. "No," she said more firmly. "I mean, only in my nightmares."

His gut clenched. "I'm sorry, Cassie."

"I know you are." Her voice was husky now. "We all are. And Mom really needs this trip, but I made the mistake of telling her I thought I spotted the, um, the intruder, once, and—"

"You spotted him?" Evan's hand went sweaty on the phone. "Where?"

"I *thought* I spotted him at a grocery store. I'm pretty sure, now, I was wrong. But Mom's the queen of all worriers, and she's getting worse."

Evan blew out a breath. The last time he'd seen Cassie and her mother had been at Josh's funeral. Her mom had barely been able to stand, even with her live-in boyfriend on one side, and Cassie, looking exhausted herself, on the other.

"Did you tell the police you thought you spotted him?"

She made a disgusted noise. "No."

"Why not?"

"They've basically stopped working on the case. Whenever we call, they just pass us off to victim services."

The idea that no one was trying to find the thug who'd created this misery made a slow, angry fire simmer in his gut, but he'd think about that later. Right now Cassie needed him.

She was twenty-eight, young to him and yet stronger than most women he knew.

"Give Mom a call tomorrow, would you? Not tonight. She's upset."

"I'll talk to her. And…look, what if we could find you a low-cost rental here in Pleasant Shores? It's safe, and I'm here." As soon as he said it, he thought of all the reasons it wasn't a good idea.

"Hmm… Maybe. Josh and I loved it there when we were kids." She cleared her throat. "It would have to be *really* cheap, though, and take dogs. And Mom's just going to be gone six weeks, so I'd need, say, a two-month rental."

"I'll ask around." Really cheap places in a waterfront community were rare, but it *was* the off-season.

"Thanks. Love you. Bye." Her voice was a husky whisper that sent an electrical surge down his spine. Which made him feel like a jerk.

Take care of her if anything happens to me, but don't you dare try to get with her. Josh's prescient words echoed in Evan's mind as he pocketed his phone and turned back toward the door of the Gull.

He would call Cassie and Josh's mom tomorrow, but he doubted he could be convincing. The truth was, *he* worried about Cassie. He'd figured she was safe, living with her mom and her mom's burly boyfriend, but if they left her alone in the family home in Minestown, and if she thought she might have spotted the intruder who'd killed her brother...

Cassie's mom had helped Evan out a lot over the years, before she'd started spiraling into anxiety and depression, and he cared about her. She needed to get away from the site of all her heartache. Cassie probably did, too, for that matter. Evan frowned, thinking. He'd check online tomorrow, see if there was anything vacant near him, cheap and safe. A tall order.

Evan's friend William greeted him when he returned to the table. "You left in a hurry. Everything okay?"

"Yeah. An old friend's sister, having some trouble." Evan sat, but grabbed his coat. "I should take off."

"Want a beer first?" It was a guy Evan didn't know well who'd stopped by the table. He held up a pitcher and a glass.

Evan's friends turned as one and glared at the newcomer.

"What?" the guy asked.

"It's fine. Chill," Evan said to his friends. He was surprised to feel a slight tug toward the beer, more of a dryness in his throat that only alcohol would fix, but it was nothing unmanageable. He gestured at the table. "I'll finish my soda, but then I have to go. Early shift tomorrow." And a cop in a small town couldn't be late to work.

He sat down and the conversation got general, someone continuing a story he'd started, the rest listening and laughing.

"So your friend's sister is having trouble?" William asked, scooting his chair back away from the others.

"Yeah. Trying to find her a new place to stay." Evan debated whether to say more, but only for a minute. In the short time he'd known William, he'd come to trust him as much as he'd trust any man. "She needs to get away somewhere safe, make a fresh start, to get over the fact that her brother, my friend, was killed." He paused, took a drink of soda and forced the memories and the regrets out of his mind. They'd been childhood best friends, and back then Josh had basically saved him. Had tried to save him again when they were older, but Evan had pushed him away and they'd ended up running in different directions. Though they'd reconnected in the past year, they'd never regained their childhood closeness. And now Josh was gone. Evan thought a lot about all the lost opportunities.

"Killed like in an accident, or murdered?" William could ask the question because he was familiar with violence, had lost a daughter to it. He understood that it was okay to bring up a bad experience, because something like that never really left your mind for long.

"Murdered. Shot."

"Sorry, man." They were both silent for a couple of minutes. "Are there safety issues for her? The sister, I mean."

"I don't know. Her mom thinks there are." Add the unsolved murder of her brother onto Cassie's health issues, and Evan totally understood the worries.

Take care of her if anything happens to me.

The noise at the table had risen. One of the guys was leaning in, telling a joke that had the others roaring.

"You know," William said to Evan, "the guy at Victory Cottage is about to move out, and the person Mary had planned to have there next can't come."

"Yeah?" The Victory Cottage program was for victims of violent crime and their families. They came to stay for three months, got counseling, volunteered in the community and generally found healing. William had been a participant and was solid now.

Evan was happy for William, but why had he brought up Victory Cottage when they were talking about Cassie? And then he got it. "You think Cassie could be a candidate for Victory Cottage?"

"Might be. She's a victim, right?"

"Her brother was killed, so...yeah, she is."

"And now that you're living next door, it's more secure. If she *is* at any risk, or feels herself to be, she'd have some protection." Having a local cop rent the place next to Victory Cottage was a recent addition to the program, and a smart one, after the cottage had been broken into by a lowlife from a resident's past. Evan had been glad to oblige, since he was the only single guy on the force. He kept an eye on the place, his cruiser parked in the driveway serving as a deterrent to criminals and a reassurance to residents.

Evan thought about what it would be like to bring Cassie to Pleasant Shores. She already loved it here, based on a couple of childhood visits. It was safe and the location was beautiful, right on the shores of the Chesapeake. It was small and easy to navigate, important since Cassie still struggled with fatigue and other physical issues.

The town wasn't pretentious, but a real fishing village full of ordinary people for most of the year. And sure, the tourists would descend in the summer, liven things up, but it never got tacky-crazy like some of the beach towns over on the Atlantic shore.

Evan could protect Cassie here. He'd felt neglectful of his promise to do that—no surprise; neglect was his calling card—but he hated that he was letting Josh and Cassie down after all their family had done for him.

Bringing her to Victory Cottage would solve Cassie's problems and her mother's, too.

The trouble was, the last few times he'd seen Cassie, before Josh was killed, he'd gotten a *feeling*. She'd grown up, come out of her shell, turned into an interesting woman. And a very pretty one.

Josh had seen what was going on before Evan realized it, consciously, and had called him on it. "No way. I love ya but I also know ya. You're not dating Cassie. Ever." He'd paused, then added, "She's got way too much potential to get tangled up with someone like you. She's going places. Don't derail her."

Josh had been right, of course, and Evan had promised.

Now Josh was gone, and Cassie needed Evan. There was a solution at hand.

But the idea made Evan uneasy for reasons he couldn't articulate, even to himself.

CASSIE THOMAS SET the last carton on the desk of her childhood bedroom and looked out the window for the tenth time. Where was Evan?

And how many times, back when she was a kid, had she looked out this very window, hoping for something to happen, someone to spring her from her soft, comfortable prison?

Ace, her big apricot-colored labradoodle, jumped his front paws to the windowsill beside her, standing like a person to look out.

"We're going on an adventure," she whispered into Ace's shaggy ear, and he nudged her with his nose as if to say he was excited, too.

She'd longed for independence to chart her own course practically since childhood, but her health, and Mom's needs and Josh's protectiveness meant she'd never lived alone. The fact that she was about to do it almost made her giddy. Finally, she was going to get unstuck, spread her wings.

She spun away from the window, straightened the cover on her single bed and put the packing tape and scissors into a neat stack on her desk. She'd replaced her childhood posters with good nature paintings, had brought the neutral comforter and pillow shams from Josh's house, but the room still felt like it belonged to a kid. She'd packed up her dolls and supplies, but she wondered if her passion for dollmaking—a child's pursuit, according to most—was what kept her feeling stuck in the past.

After opening her laptop, she double-checked the lists she'd made: routines that kept Mom calm and steady on one, activities that helped her stave off depression on the other. She emailed the list to Donald, Mom's boyfriend, even though he was here in the house, downstairs, and knew her mom's routines as well as Cassie did, if not better. You couldn't be too sure.

She picked up her phone and scrolled. Was there time to call Mom's therapist and remind him that today was the day Cassie was leaving?

"We can all back out," Mom said from the doorway, her voice catching.

Cassie turned. "No way. You're doing that trip, Mom." She worried about her mother traveling far away from her therapist, but going back to Ireland would fulfill a lifelong dream. Cassie and Donald had strategized about ways to help Mom stop spiraling into darkness, and that was what they'd come up with. The counselor had agreed, and just looking at brochures and websites had gotten Mom more energized than she'd been since Josh's death.

Now she seemed to be backsliding. "I feel better when I can see you."

"I know you do." Cassie crossed the room and reached up to hold Mom's shoulders and look into her face. "You're going to have such a good time." She pulled Mom into a hug, and Ace came over to lean against the pair of them.

"Yes, but I'll worry about you." Mom stepped back, her chin quivering.

Cassie forced confidence into her voice. "I'm excited about this Victory Cottage program, and with Evan living next door, you know I'll be safe. He's just as protective as…" She trailed off, her throat tightening. "Anyway," she said, "if you don't feel ready, it's not too late to change our plans." She wanted to go, wanted independence in the worst way, but Mom came first. Cassie might have more physical issues, but Mom was fragile, emotionally and mentally.

If Mom couldn't handle being apart, Cassie was ready to cancel her dreams in order to stay with her.

Mom stepped back, drew herself up and patted Cassie's shoulder. "No. You've sacrificed enough. I know you'll be safe. And it'll be good for you to get away, too." She straightened her shoulders. "We can do this."

A car door slammed outside. Ace barked, and Cassie moved back to the window. There was Evan, climbing out of the driver's side of a pickup truck and going around to the passenger side.

Cassie fanned herself with the brochure from Victory Cottage. Watching Evan move was always a pleasure.

He opened the door and helped a slender, white-haired woman climb out. Who was that?

Cassie's friends had always thought Evan was hot. Short hair befitting a veteran and cop, broad shoulders, his weathered face reminding her that he was thirty-seven—Josh's age—and had already lived a life full of action and ups and downs.

Mom came over and stood at her side. "He's a good man in a lot of ways," she said out of nowhere. "But he's not for you. Dating-wise, I mean. You know that."

"Of course." She glanced over at her mother, puzzled. Why would Mom feel the need to tell her that? Evan was Josh's friend, not hers. He thought of her as Josh's annoying little sister, the one with all the health problems. Right now he was being kind, because she'd asked for help. But once she got on her feet again, once the three-month Victory Cottage program was over, their relationship would go back to the occasional text or phone call.

The doorbell rang, and Cassie turned to go downstairs, but Mom put a hand on her arm. "I mean it," she said. "Evan's a recovering alcoholic, and kids of alcoholics can get drawn into the same patterns. You need to be cautious."

"I'm not going to fall for Evan Stone."

Mom put a shaky hand to her throat. "That's what I said about your father."

"I'm not in the market for romance," Cassie amended. Her childhood illness had pushed her toward being quiet and quirky, not to mention her nonsexy aches and pains and frequent need to rest. Men weren't interested. Which was a good thing, because relationships meant dependence. Cassie had had enough dependence to last a lifetime.

She had things to do, a business to run.

"Good. You'll be better off single. And you'll always have a place with me and Donald."

"Right." She and Mom went downstairs, Ace running ahead of them, and there was a flurry of introductions. The white-haired woman turned out to be Mary Rhoades, who'd started the Victory Cottage program, and she somehow herded Mom and Donald into the kitchen so Evan and Cassie could carry her things out to the truck.

"Mom, take Ace," Cassie said, and Mom called the big dog. He trotted into the kitchen. He'd comfort Mom by his loving presence, help her keep it together.

"That was brilliant, bringing the Victory Cottage woman along," Cassie said to Evan once they were upstairs.

"I know your mom will like her," he said. "And she'll offer a little more reassurance than I could provide. Mary's great."

"Thank you so, so much for this. It's the only way Mom would agree to the trip, and she really needs to go." She wrapped her arms around Evan in a big hug, just like always.

Just like she'd always hugged Josh.

A heavy feeling settled behind her eyes and made her throat hurt. She'd never feel her brother's embrace, never hear his ready laugh again.

Evan tightened his arms briefly around her as if he could read her thoughts and then let her go quickly, half pushing her away. "None of that. We've got work to do."

He tested the weight of a carton before letting her carry it, waved away her protest that she could carry more as he picked up three of her actually heavy boxes and started downstairs.

She needed to make sure he didn't expect to keep her in bubble wrap, even though he had a point regarding her ability to lift and haul heavy boxes. "You know I'm healthy now, right? Stronger all the time. I lift weights at the gym." She flexed her arm to show her decent biceps.

He raised an eyebrow, one side of his mouth quirking up. "So now you're Wonder Woman?"

"I could take you," she said, the words coming out automatically before she could even remember why: she'd used to make that threat to him and Josh, back when she was a little kid trailing after them.

Then, though, it had been "I could take you both." Now there was only one of the duo to joke around with. That heavy feeling settled behind her eyes again.

Evan must have had the same thought, because his smile slipped away. They walked through the living room and he stopped before a family picture: Mom, Josh and Cassie. "Hard to believe he's gone." She saw him swallow hard.

"Yeah." Her eyes strayed to another picture, pushed to the back. It was a rare whole-family picture taken when Cassie was a baby, before Dad left and Cassie got sick and

Mom got depressed and Josh... She swallowed. "We should get on with it."

As they headed through the house and up the stairs, he kept looking around, and it hit her: he hadn't been here for years. He had to be remembering all the days he'd spent hanging out with Josh in their living room. They'd been as close as brothers at one time. She wrapped an arm around him as they reached the top of the stairs. "It's hard, I know."

"Yeah. Let's go." He extricated himself, and they grabbed the last load of boxes.

Cassie closed the bedroom door behind her, the quiet click resonating. Despite what Mom had said, she had the feeling she wouldn't be coming back home, not as the same person, anyway, and not to stay.

She closed her eyes for a fraction of a second, then turned and followed Evan downstairs.

They loaded the last boxes into the truck, and then he looked over at his old house. "Who lives there now?"

"A nice family. They have a couple of young kids."

"Good." He laughed, but it sounded forced. "About time your mom had some decent neighbors."

"Oh, Evan." His parents had continued to live there until a couple of years ago, when they'd moved south. They'd slowed down their drinking, Mom had told her, because both of them had developed some health problems.

Unfortunately, they'd never been the nurturing types, and that hadn't changed when they'd sobered up.

Evan was looking over at his old house, his eyes far away, and she figured he was seeing into the past, a difficult childhood where he'd had to fend for himself.

Mom, Donald and Mary came out the front door, Ace pushing his way past them to run to Cassie.

Mary followed the dog and put a hand on Cassie's arm. "Your people are delightful, and I've promised to keep them updated on your well-being, within the bounds of your privacy, of course," she said. Something in her wise blue eyes told Cassie that she'd gleaned some knowledge of the issues in their family, just in that short time she'd spent with Mom and Donald. Or maybe Evan had filled her in. "I'll let you say your goodbyes. We'll have a good opportunity to get to know each other during the drive to Pleasant Shores." She opened the back door of the truck and climbed easily into the backseat. From her face, Cassie would have guessed her to be in her sixties, but she moved like someone significantly younger.

"I'll sit in back with Ace," Cassie protested.

But Mary scooted over and patted the seat beside her. "Ace, come here, boy," she said, and Ace jumped readily into the backseat of the truck. "You sit in front. Ace reminds me of my doodle, and I'll enjoy his company on the way to Pleasant Shores."

"If you're sure." Cassie liked Mary already.

Mom was crying a little, and Cassie went to hug her, her own eyes brimming. She turned toward Donald, wanting to tell him to take care of her mother, but he had Evan off to the side of the driveway, talking seriously to him. Evan was nodding, rubbing the back of his neck.

They turned and started toward the truck, and Cassie caught the end of their conversation: "Don't take offense," Donald was saying. "But you know what I mean. She's young. Inexperienced. Not strong. She couldn't handle someone like you. She's just not cut out for—"

"Donald!" Cassie's face went hot. "I don't need you to..." She broke off, not even knowing what to say. Donald had managed to insult both her and Evan. How was she supposed to fix that?

"I get it." Evan shook hands with Donald. And then he said something about traffic, managed to help her into the passenger seat while keeping her at arm's length and climbed into the truck.

As they headed out of Minestown, Cassie looked over at Evan, who was staring straight ahead. There was an awkwardness between them that had never been there before. "Look, I'm sorry about Donald," she said. "Every now and then he decides he needs to be my overprotective father figure and throws out something ridiculous like that."

"Don't worry about it," Evan said.

"Parents have trouble letting their nestlings fly," Mary said, and the conversation got general as they cruised onto the highway. The awkwardness passed, although Evan didn't do much of the talking.

Underneath her and Mary's getting-to-know-you chatter and the quiet music Evan had turned on, though, Cassie kept wondering.

Why would both Mom and Donald emphasize that Cassie and Evan weren't right for each other? Wasn't that obvious?

CHAPTER TWO

AVERY SANFORD TOOK a deep breath and walked into Goody's Ice Cream. It was the second-to-last business on her list.

The shop wasn't busy midafternoon, but Goody still frowned when Avery asked if they could talk. "I got a lot to do before the after-school rush, kid," she said without coming out from behind the counter. "What's up?"

Avery glanced around the shop and leaned closer. "I'm looking for a job."

Goody narrowed her eyes. "Not going back to college?"

Considering that it was March, halfway through the spring semester, that ought to be obvious. "No."

Curiosity flared in Goody's eyes, which surprised Avery. She didn't know? Normally, gossip got around; most people in town would already have heard the reason she hadn't headed back. But Goody tended to keep to herself. "I'm pregnant," she said, keeping it short and sweet. "Need to save up."

The whole range of reactions passed over Goody's face. Avery could predict every one, because she'd seen the same movie on the faces of multiple people in town. First, shock. Avery had been what the older folks called *such a nice girl* in high school. Second, disappointment, because Avery was supposed to do the town proud. Third, *I told you so*, because any dock kid, but especially a girl, who tried to rise up above the rest was opening herself to a put-down.

Goody's face went into the fourth emotion Avery some-times saw: pity. "I'm real sorry," she said, "but I won't have extra work for anyone until the season starts. It's hard enough keeping my long-term employees busy during the winter."

"I understand." Avery turned to go. "Thank you, any-way."

Goody cleared her throat. "Heard there are some open-ings picking crabs at the processing plant up shore."

Avery stopped. No way. No *way*. She turned back to thank the woman, because the suggestion, however awful, was kindly meant. But her throat was too tight to force the words out, so she just gave a little wave and turned to hurry out of the shop.

At least Goody hadn't asked any nosy questions, like "who's the father?"

She also hadn't questioned Avery's decision not to go back to school. The baby wasn't due until August, so Avery could have finished her sophomore year at least.

Avery didn't want to explain to anyone that, once you were carrying a baby and responsible for it, you couldn't feel the same as the other college kids. All the parties, the impromptu TikTok dance sessions at the dorm, the résumé-building activities offered by the various clubs, seemed ir-relevant. How was a single mom from a poor family going to get through four years of school and then find an im-pressive job?

Her folks were being great about letting her live at home, but they were disappointed.

One last place to check before she gave in to the ultimate fate of a dock kid, the seafood processing plant. She walked across the street and down the block toward the Gusty Gull.

The breeze off the bay had picked up, and the midafternoon sun wasn't warm enough to counter it, not in late March. Avery wrapped her jacket tighter and walked faster.

There were a few tables of people, late lunchers or early drinkers, scattered around the big, dark restaurant. She made her way to the bar area, cleared her throat and spoke to the bartender, thankfully someone she didn't know. "Hi, I'm Avery Sanford. Looking for a job. Do you have any openings?"

The woman didn't stop polishing glasses, but she did look Avery over. "How old are ya, honey?"

"I'm twenty."

"Too young. I need waitstaff who can make the drinks as well as serve them."

With the image of picking crabs eight hours a day in the back of her mind, Avery pushed the matter. "I haven't had a restaurant job before, but I've done catering work. I know how to serve food and bus tables and act nice with people. And I'm good at math. I won't make mistakes at the cash register." It wasn't what she'd expected to use her math skills for, but she had no one but herself to blame.

The woman, who was about her mom's age, tilted her head to one side and frowned.

"I'm a hard worker," Avery said. "I won't call off and I won't be late."

"Let me think. Maybe we could use some waitress help on Friday and Saturday nights. You up for something like that?"

Anything that can keep me out of the plant. "Sure. I mean, it's not like I have a real active social life."

"You will if you start working here. You're cute. But don't get involved with the customers or coworkers." The woman fumbled around under the bar and came up with an application form, crookedly photocopied. "I'm Darcy, by the way. Fill that out, and I'll talk to the owner, but I'm pretty sure we can use you part-time."

"Great, thank you so much!" Avery took the form and sat down on a bar stool to fill it out.

Darcy walked from table to table, refilling drinks while Avery whipped through the form.

The group of ladies who'd been lingering over their lunch were starting to leave. Avery recognized them and ducked her head, but she was too late. One of the women, Mary Rhoades, came over. "Avery Sanford. How are things going?"

"Hi, Ms. Rhoades." Avery couldn't look her in the eye. Mary was one of the benefactors of the scholarship fund that had sent her and her twin brother, Aiden, off to school with such high hopes a year and a half ago.

"What are you doing?" Mary glanced at the paper Avery was filling out and then back at Avery's face.

Avery sighed. There was no keeping a secret in Pleasant Shores. "Applying for a job."

Unlike Goody, Mary usually knew what was going on with the people in town. Case in point, she knew that Avery had slunk back into town and was staying, and why. She'd even asked Avery to help with the dog training kennel in town, while she decided whether to keep it going or phase it out. Avery was grateful for that little trickle of income and hoped it would continue, but it wasn't enough. "I can still help at the kennel, if that's what you're worried about. I love taking care of the dogs."

Mary frowned distractedly. "Of course, dear. But I'm

concerned. The Gusty Gull is no place for a young girl to work, especially late at night. I've heard it's a tough crowd."

But Avery wasn't a young girl, not anymore. She'd stopped being one when she'd seen the double pink line on the pregnancy test. "It's just a couple nights a week. I need the money. Besides, I grew up on the docks. I can handle people getting rowdy."

"I'm sure, dear, but…" Mary frowned. "I could use some part-time help at the bookstore. Would you be interested?"

"I'd love to work at Lighthouse Lit." Respect for Mary compelled her to add what she hadn't mentioned to the bartender here: "My baby's due in August, though. I'd need some time off then."

"Let's take one thing at a time. August is a long time away."

"Really, you're hiring?" The thought of working at Mary's wonderful bookstore was amazing, even if it was temporary.

"Come over when you're done here and we'll figure out the technicalities and hours." She smiled. "Maybe you won't need to work here at the Gull for long. And while the baby's small, you could bring him, or her, to work. We love kids."

It sounded too good to be true. "You shouldn't be so nice to me, especially when I messed up on the scholarship."

Mary shrugged and lifted her hands, palms up. "Life doesn't go in a straight line, and there are some things you can trip on over the way. I'm old enough to know that. But I also know you're a smart, goodhearted young woman. I want to help." She turned away, then looked back and smiled. "It's not unselfish, either. You'll be a real asset to the bookstore."

"Thank you?" Avery couldn't keep the question out of

her voice as she watched the woman leave, and then turned back to finish filling out the job application.

Did Mary need the help, really, or was she just being kind to a poor kid in town? That would be like Mary. Avery hated people feeling sorry for her; hated the thought of charity.

But she had no business acting too proud to accept help.

With two jobs—three, actually, including the kennel—and if she could make good tips at the Gusty Gull, she could save up some serious money. Maybe enough to rent a little place for her and the baby, so she didn't have to mooch off her parents.

"It'll be hard," she whispered, patting her stomach, "but I'll take care of you. I promise."

EVAN HELPED CASSIE move her things into Victory Cottage. Then, because he felt obligated to help her settle in—*not* because he wanted to spend more time with her, he assured himself—he offered to bring over some takeout from the new Chinese place. As the sun set over the bay, they sat in the kitchen, eating Moo Shu Shrimp and drinking iced tea. Cassie's labradoodle flopped down onto his side with a loud sigh.

"Thank you for this," Cassie said, indicating the food. "It's ridiculous that I'm twenty-eight and don't even have a car. Well, not one I can drive."

"But you do have a car?"

She nodded. "Yeah. Josh's. But it's a stick, and I never learned to drive it. He was going to teach me, but…" Her voice cracked on the last word, and she bit her lip.

He reached out and squeezed her hand. So many things she wouldn't get the chance to do with her big brother now.

She sucked in a breath and spoke again. "Anyway. In the middle of Minestown where Josh and I lived, driving didn't seem important. I always used Uber and Lyft, or Josh drove me. Once I moved home with Mom and Donald, in the suburbs, I realized I needed to learn to drive Josh's car. I just didn't get around to it."

He could imagine why. Only four months after Josh's death, her grief, and that of her mother, was fresh and raw. He imagined them barricading themselves in their house, wrapping their arms around each other, eyes closed, trying to shut out the ugliness that had taken Josh away.

She cleared her throat. "I know I could trade it in for an automatic, but I hate to do that. He loved that car." She raised a hand like a stop sign. "And before you ask, yes, I'm strong enough. My legs are only weak when I'm over-tired, and my doctors say the more I use them, the better." Cassie had had cancer as a kid, and there were lingering aftereffects. Not so much from the cancer as from the chemo, from what Evan understood.

He couldn't bring Josh back, but maybe he could help Cassie with this one practical thing. "Do you want me to teach you to drive it?"

The moment he said it, he second-guessed the offer. The last thing he needed was more reasons for him and Cassie to spend time together. She was young and grieving and he'd promised Josh he'd protect her, not hit on her. But he couldn't deny the visceral reaction he felt when she was nearby.

It was just that she was so pretty. That easy smile, the wavy blond hair that always seemed to resist her efforts to tie it back, the depth in her eyes that hinted she'd seen too much sadness for how young she was.

She *had* seen too much sadness, and getting involved with him would only add to it. If she was even interested, which she wasn't.

He was a substitute big brother to her, and that was best.

"*Would* you teach me to drive it? Mom and Donald could bring it when they come. They want to visit once before they head overseas." Then she paused and a frown crossed her face. "But never mind. The truth is I've already relied on you way too much."

Time to clear the air. "And your mom and stepdad cautioned you about me. I understand that. Believe me. I won't make a move on you."

"I know, I…" Her cheeks flushed pink. "I'm sorry about how they are, Evan. I know you'd never… I know you're a good guy."

"Not that good." He wasn't sure how much she knew about his past, how much Josh or her mom might have told her.

"Besides," she added, "I'm not in the market for a relationship. Any relationship." She smiled, but it looked a little forced. "I'm all about independence. 'I buy my own diamonds and I buy my own rings.'"

"What?" Cassie didn't seem like the diamond jewelry type. Though inevitably, someone would put a ring on her finger someday.

The thought disturbed him more than it should have.

"You know, the old Destiny's Child song? 'Independent Women'?" She nudged him, smiling. "Oh, wait, I forgot. You're too macho to like a girl group."

"I'm into country." And he enjoyed her teasing him a little too much. "Think about the driving lessons. It wouldn't be a problem for me to teach you."

"I will. Thank you."

While she took Ace outside for a bathroom break, he looked around at Victory Cottage. The place had pine floors that seemed to have been recently refinished. Bright-colored rugs matched the pillows scattered on the couch and chairs. The place was meant to hold a family if needed, he guessed. He'd seen the child-friendly bedrooms upstairs when he'd carried up her boxes.

Cassie came back in and closed the curtains, blocking out the view of the dark water, rippling with lights from a few boats.

"Sorry," she said, "I know the bay's pretty, but it's getting dark and I still get a little spooked at night. Because of…what happened."

"Makes sense." He'd talked to an officer he knew on the Minestown Police about the case, but he'd never heard Cassie's side of the story. "You don't have to talk about it if you don't want to, but someday I'd like to hear what happened. What your role was. You were there, right?"

She glanced over at him. "Yeah. I was there."

"How much did you see?"

She nodded. "When the guy started pounding and kicking on the door, Josh yelled at me to hide upstairs, and at first, I did. But I couldn't stay crouched in a closet while Josh was being attacked. I sneaked back out, and when the man pulled a gun I couldn't help it. I ran down."

Worst thing she could have done, but he understood it. "So the assailant knows you saw him?"

"Yeah." She sucked in a breath. "Actually, after the guy… After he shot Josh, he seemed almost confused. He kept looking at the gun and then looking at Josh. That gave Ace time to run down and jump him, and I called 911. The neighbors heard the commotion and came in yelling, but they didn't see much before the man took off out the back. The police came, and I ran to Josh, but it was too late."

He put an arm around her and pulled her to his side, fuming. Why hadn't Josh let Evan know his private detective work had led him into something dangerous? Why hadn't he, Evan, followed up on Josh's vague hints, like that night he'd told Evan to take care of Cassie if anything happened to him?

Questions filled his mind—what had the guy looked like? Had he seemed to be acting alone? Did he and Josh have words before the shooting started?—but Cassie was in no state to answer them; not now.

He had to worry about her safety, though. If the guy had seen her, and he hadn't yet been apprehended, she was at risk. He hated that.

She pulled away, got up and grabbed tissues from the kitchen. She came back, blowing her nose and wiping her eyes.

He felt a strong urge to hold her, to offer comfort, but it wouldn't be right. He stood. "It's been a long day for you already. I'm going to take a walk. I usually do before bed." It was his substitute for a nightcap. "You're welcome to come, but don't feel obliged."

"No, I'll go. I'd rather do that than stay here alone."

That might end up being a problem for her. "As far as being here alone, remember, I live right next door. You can call me any time you get spooked."

"I know. I'm glad."

She hooked Ace's leash to his collar and the three of them headed out of the cottage by the back door, Evan pushing aside a big box that hadn't gotten unpacked yet. The label on the top of it said "dolls."

He tilted his head to the side, confused, flashing back to her childhood years when she'd been so sick. She'd often been on the couch under a blanket, playing with dolls, when he and Josh would burst into the house for food and supplies. "You still, um, have your dolls?"

She whacked his arm. "I don't play with them, I make them, remember? In fact, I'm hoping to get a lot done while I'm here. I'd better. They're my livelihood."

Then he did remember. She had a small business making lookalike dolls for kids with serious illnesses. A growing business, actually, from what Josh had told him; apparently, she had more orders than she could fill, mostly from non-profits that worked with the families of sick kids.

"You want to be that busy?" he asked as they walked down toward the street. Even though she seemed perfectly healthy, he couldn't help thinking of her as fragile.

"I like being busy. It beats being bored." She clicked her tongue to Ace as they walked out and locked up the place. "Believe me. I had *years* of being bored. Enough for a life-time."

"Yeah." When she'd first been diagnosed with cancer, her mom had freaked out and overprotected her. Josh had, too.

"Plus," she added, her voice matter-of-fact, "I get tired easily and probably always will. Long-term side effects from the chemo. Since I'm my own boss, I can take breaks when I need to."

"That's good, then."

They walked across the yard and down toward the bay, Ace trotting along at Cassie's side. Crickets or cicadas, he never knew which, made their rising and falling call, piercing the near-darkness. The smell of new-mown grass filled the air.

They stood looking out at the bay, and he pointed out landmarks. Talked a little about volunteer possibilities in Pleasant Shores, since volunteering was part of the Victory Cottage program. After a loop around a couple of blocks, they strolled back and stood by the gate of the little picket fence in front of Victory Cottage.

Cassie was easy to talk to, and easy to be quiet with, probably because they shared so much history.

Down the street a car door slammed, and Cassie jumped. Automatically, Evan turned toward it, stepping in front of her. He watched as two shadowy figures moved toward a front porch, triggering an automatic light.

Then he could see that it wasn't a threat. He watched as the pair plopped down on the porch, heard their too-loud laughter. "It's okay. Just a couple of folks who've probably been drinking."

"Oh. Good." She was jittery, and understandably so.

Evan decided he'd take a stroll down there when he left Cassie, check the license, give them a warning about driving drunk. Prevention was always better than punishment; at least that was his philosophy.

Thinking about prevention brought something else to mind. "Did Mary tell you about the local program for at-risk teenagers? That's a group you could potentially volunteer with, if you'd be interested."

"I would." She looked up at him in the moonlight. "I've taught art to kids and adults, but never to teenagers. I'd enjoy giving it a shot."

"I'd be glad to help." He *wanted* to help.

Her eyes were soft, curious, almost a little shy, as she tilted her head to one side and gazed at him. Wispy blond hair blew across her face, and she pushed a lock of it behind her ear.

Cassie was just the right height to pull into his arms.

She looked away. "I'll think about it, talk to Mary about it. There's no need for you to help me with the volunteer stuff. You've already done too much for me."

"Look," he said, "I work a lot, as a small-town police officer, and I do some community stuff when I'm not on duty. I don't have a lot of free time. If anything, I'd be more of a consultant."

She nodded. "I should go inside. I'll call Mary in the morning."

"I'll see you in." He walked behind her to the door, waited while she unlocked it.

"Thanks for everything, Evan," she said once she was safely on the other side of the screen door. "Really. If it weren't for you, I'd still be stuck in my childhood bedroom listening to my mom cry downstairs."

"Glad to spring you," he said. "And her."

And he was. He was glad to help Cassie, because it was what he'd promised Josh he'd do, and because Cassie was a sweet girl and deserved it.

And he needed to keep thinking of her that way, as a sweet girl. Not as a mature, beautiful woman.

He'd keep his involvement minimal, make sure that was clear to both Cassie and Mary. And he'd keep it to daytime.

Late on a moonlit Chesapeake night, he really, really needed to stay away from Cassie Thomas.

ON HER FIRST night in Pleasant Shores, Cassie was so tired that she fell asleep instantly.

Her second night was a different story.

She'd unpacked and stowed all her practical necessities, stocked up on groceries, talked to her mother on the phone twice. But now the sun was setting and she was alone in a strange place.

Alone. Living alone for the first time in her life.

Don't be a wimp. You have Ace.

But could she count on him to challenge an intruder, after what had happened?

She'd stored the few remaining boxes in one of the spare bedrooms, and she climbed the steps and went in, the big labradoodle following her. She dug through a box, found Ace's wire brush and knelt beside the dog, detangling his thick fur. Usually, she groomed him nightly, but it had been a couple of days and it showed. Fortunately, Ace was patient as she worked through the knots.

She glanced out the window toward Evan's place, wondering whether he was home and what he was doing.

He'd been a rock yesterday: driving her, loading and unloading, calm and steady. He'd kept her company when he'd probably rather have gone back to his place to get some rest or watch a game on TV.

Except...he'd seemed to enjoy the walk they'd taken together. And when they'd parted at the door, she'd gotten the strange feeling that he wasn't thinking of her as Josh's little sister. It had felt a little bit like someone dropping her off after a date.

Had the idea of a good-night kiss flashed into his mind the way it had flashed into hers?

A creaky sound started up, seeming to come from the yard. The gate, maybe.

She put the brush aside, hurried to the window and looked out through the old-fashioned blinds. In the deepening twilight she could see that it *was* the gate, simply blowing in the wind. She should go out and close it. That was what anyone would do.

But she wasn't anyone; she was a big chicken.

Ace cocked his head and studied her. He wasn't barking, so it probably wasn't an intruder.

He would warn her if it was.

He'd warn her, but could he protect her? He hadn't protected Josh.

Everything's fine.

She turned to her last two unpacked boxes. She needed to get busy; that was the best way to deal with silly fears. Besides, she had plenty of work to catch up on. She pulled out cloth and yarn, needles and thread. Then she checked her computer for the picture of the little girl who'd be the recipient of the next lookalike doll in her queue.

Absorbed in studying the photo and planning how to create a doll that matched the child's coloring, she forgot about the creaking gate. On some level she noticed the wind picking up, whistling around the eaves of the place, but only in passing. She sketched out a pattern on graph paper and looked through her cloth supplies.

The little girl who was to receive the doll had a rare kind of cancer that might not be curable. She was only six, so she couldn't possibly understand her situation, what that meant. But she could undoubtedly feel the worry radiating from her parents. Cassie remembered that, more than any physical pain or weakness.

Worry about Cassie—or not wanting to worry about Cassie—had sent her father running for the hills. That, in turn, had damaged her mother's mental health.

Serious childhood illness wreaked havoc on kids and

families. Anything she could do to help—even just giving a kid a smile—she wanted to do. She looked again at the young patient's information and learned that she was into princesses. A crown, then, or a sparkly tiara. A pretty ball gown.

She thumbed through her fabrics and found a blue satin that would be perfect for a princess.

Crash! The sudden noise jolted her, and her heart pounded as her muscles froze her into place.

Something clattered in the back of the house. Then she heard another loud, metallic bang. Ace barked, sharply. Once, then twice more. He stood and trotted to the top of the stairs, then looked back at her.

She heard another crash.

Whoever had been in front, opening the gate…was that person now in back?

CHAPTER THREE

TERROR GRIPPED CASSIE as she forced herself to move. Ace had loped to the window, barking, gruff and loud. That would scare off any intruders, wouldn't it?

It didn't before.

She flicked off the light and tiptoed to the window. Cautiously, she moved the edge of the curtain and peered out.

The lawn was dim, shadowed. The sun had gone down, but purple, orange and pink streaks remained, casting a little light.

No one was in the yard. Or...was that a movement?

She heard a thump and a thud and sweat formed on the back of her neck as she flashed back to the worst night of her life.

It had started with a strange crash, too, like something had hit the door. Josh, who never got scared, had looked alarmed. He'd started for the window, and then there was a heavy pounding on the front door, again and again.

"Go upstairs. Hide," he'd ordered. "Take Ace."

"But—"

"Now." He'd glared at her until she'd grabbed Ace's collar and reluctantly climbed the stairs, urging the dog to come along with her.

Just like it had back then, her breathing quickened. Ace whined. He jumped his front legs to the windowsill, person-like, and she put an arm around his comforting, bulky neck and peered out.

Nothing. *It's nothing.* Probably a garbage can or some trash blowing around.

She looked across the yard toward Evan's place. There was a light on now. Thank heavens. Maybe he heard the noise, too. Maybe he'd come out.

But he didn't. She slid her phone out of her pocket, scrolled to his number. Fingers poised over the screen, she closed her eyes and stopped herself.

He'd said to call him anytime, but she wasn't going to do that. She wasn't much of a strong, independent woman, not yet, but she wanted to be. That was her goal. So maybe she was shaking a little; that didn't matter. She needed to overcome her fears and get on with her evening.

"Come on, let's go downstairs," she said to Ace. Her voice sounded loud in the quiet house. She walked across the room, out into the hall, down the stairs. Ace stayed at her side.

That awful night, the big dog hadn't wanted to stay with her. He'd strained toward the downstairs and Josh. She'd barely been able to hold him back.

The intruder had come in—Josh must have opened the door—and started yelling. Josh had called to her to stay upstairs, to hide.

But she hadn't been able to wait in a closet while Josh faced danger alone. She'd ordered Ace to stay and then, when he kept straining toward the noise and shouting downstairs, she'd gripped his collar and crept with him to the top of the stairs.

That was then; this is now. Stay in the moment; live in the present. The grief counselor's words echoing in her mind, she got a cup of water, plunked in a tea bag and set it heating in the microwave. Tea, that was the right idea. Chamomile, to help her sleep. Everything would look better in the morning. She'd laugh at her fears.

That was what she'd thought on that terrible night, too. She'd figured it was some drunk friend of Josh's. Maybe a former client. In his detective work, he'd gotten the information that had helped to convict some lowlifes, but he always said his work wasn't truly dangerous.

She'd gripped the banister, watching as Josh and the man argued. The man was older, maybe in his forties, with a clipped beard and a slim build. He didn't look scary, until she saw the totally irrational expression on his face.

The argument had gotten heated. And then he'd pulled out a gun.

She jumped when the microwave timer pinged, once again yanking her back to the here and now.

It was only the second night she'd spent alone since the crime, she realized suddenly, and last night she'd been too exhausted to pay attention. Of course she was nervous. But what she needed to do was distract herself from the nightmarish memories. She blew on her hot tea and headed toward the living room, thinking she'd watch some TV.

She wouldn't call Evan, wouldn't act like a child afraid of the dark. She needed to grow up. Women lived alone all the time, in far more dangerous places than a sleepy little beach town.

If she didn't learn to be independent, she'd be doomed to live with Mom and Donald all her life. Or to glom on to some protective man, never managing through her own strength.

On the wall by the door, a pretty painted sign read *Thrive*.

Cassie wanted to thrive, wanted it more than anything. She wanted to conquer her fears and build up her business and find a place for herself in a community of friends. Right now, though, she'd be satisfied with just getting through the night.

She looked around the living room for the remote, and then shivered and clung on to Ace, stroking him.

Ace would protect her if he could, but still, she'd feel safer upstairs. Yes, she'd go upstairs.

One more loud bang from behind the house, and then a series of small crashes that seemed to be coming closer and closer.

She grabbed her phone and called Evan.

"Hey, how's it going?" he asked, his voice relaxed, a little sleepy. "I was dozing off in front of the TV. Glad you woke me up."

"Do you hear anything outside?" she asked.

"Why?" His voice went alert. "What's going on? I'll be right over."

"Be careful." She of all people knew that a man, no matter how strong and protective, wasn't bulletproof. But he'd already ended the call.

Seconds later she heard more noise outside, and Ace let out a warning bark.

"It's me," Evan called. "Checking around."

A minute later he knocked on her back door, identifying himself again, and she rushed to open it and usher him inside.

"Raccoons knocked the garbage can lid off. Looks like they were having a party out there. The wind picked the metal cover off and blew it around, I'm guessing." He smiled at her. "I put a couple of bricks on top of the lid. It should keep them away for tonight. Tomorrow we can get you a raccoon lock."

She backed away from him and sank into a chair, her knees unable to support her. He came in, and Ace made happy circles around him, his big tail wagging.

Cassie couldn't get over the fear that easily. She wiped her hands down the sides of her jeans and took deep breaths. *It's okay. It wasn't a killer; it was raccoons.*

She nudged out one of the kitchen chairs with her foot and gestured for him to sit.

"I'm fine." He remained standing, leaning back against the counter.

"Thank you for coming over. I'm sorry, I feel like a wimp. It's just, me and Ace are jumpy ever since…"

"Don't apologize. That's what I'm here for."

"It's kind of you, but I won't do it again." Her breathing was steadier now, her heart rate coming back down.

"I'm serious, it's not a problem," he said.

"It *is* a problem. Calling you out at night for raccoons!" She puffed out a breath, disgusted with herself.

"I get a rent reduction for living next to Victory Cottage, just because of situations like this." He flashed another reassuring smile at her.

He had such a great smile.

"People come to stay here because they've experienced trauma," he continued. "I provide some security. And sometimes something from their past comes back to haunt them." He shrugged. "I can use the money. Glad to do it."

He turned as if to leave, and she didn't want him to. She

stood and hurried over to the fridge. "Can I get you something to drink? Glass of wine?"

"No, thanks. I'm fine."

"Oh, I'm sorry." What was she thinking, offering wine
to an alcoholic? She was an idiot. "I have soda. Pretzels,
veggies, chips…"

He studied her face like he was trying to read her.

She couldn't look away.

I need you. Please stay.

Only she wasn't sure exactly why. For protection, sure,
but what else?

His eyes were trying to communicate something, too,
something dark and a little dangerous.

He looked away and the spell was broken. "Thanks, but
as long as you're okay, I'll take off. Call me if you hear
anything else."

He spun and headed for the door. "Later," he said over
his shoulder, and then he was gone.

She was left wondering what had just happened.

What had it meant, the way their eyes had locked, that
strange flippy feeling she got in her stomach from it?

It didn't matter. She'd made a fool of herself. She'd given
in to her fears.

Her goal was to gain true independence. Tonight she'd
gone in the wrong direction.

She marched to the living room and studied the book-
shelves. She picked out a nice long novel—one with pink
flowers all over the cover, telegraphing that it was sweet,
not scary—and headed upstairs, snapping her fingers for
Ace to follow her.

She'd read herself to sleep, and if there were any more

noises outside, she'd deal with it herself. She wouldn't call Evan.

He was reassuring, but she was getting strange feelings around him, and she didn't want to freak him out. Didn't want to let him see her attraction—because she did feel it, she had to admit—when there was no possibility of them getting together.

Her mother had warned her about the whole codependence issue for kids of alcoholics, had even recommended a book about it. Maybe her slightly electric feeling around Evan had to do with that.

But it was no good to focus on something that could never come to fruition. Mom had warned her about it often enough. She'd never have a family. Men didn't want to be around women with issues. They'd leave, eventually. Just like her father had left when she'd gotten sick.

"It takes a very special kind of man to handle women like us," Mom had said.

Logically, Cassie knew Mom was wrong. For one thing, Josh had told her that their father hadn't left because of Cassie's illness, at least not entirely, but for other reasons that had nothing to do with her. Which might have just been Josh being kind, but might have been true. For another thing, there were plenty of inspirational stories about husbands standing by their wives through all sorts of difficult health crises. For that matter, Mom had a lot of issues herself and had found Donald to love her despite them.

But Cassie didn't want a Donald. She didn't want a man; she wanted independence. She had to learn to stand on her own two feet.

AVERY NOTICED THE kid at the end of the bar right away—he was her age and her type—but she couldn't focus on him. It was only her second night of working at the Gusty Gull. Managing her tables and keeping her orders straight, especially as people had more to drink, was all she could handle.

Last night she'd followed an experienced waitress around and learned the ropes. She hadn't expected to be waitressing on her own so quickly, but she was game. She'd seen what kind of money the other waitress had made, and she was glad to have a chance to earn tips for herself.

That was the whole point, she thought, letting her hand rest on her apron-covered, slightly rounded belly as she hurried to refill water glasses.

Being at the Gull on a Friday night showed her a side of Pleasant Shores she hadn't seen before. There were Mr. and Mrs. Turner, dancing surprisingly well to a fast song even though they were what Avery considered old. A couple of kids she'd looked up to when she was younger, star baseball players, were at a corner table, dressed in handyman-type uniforms, drinking hard. Erica Rowe and her sister, Amber, were apparently having a girls' night, talking and laughing, ordering appetizers, desserts and fruity drinks.

Avery liked it. She felt grown as she carried trays of drinks and bar food to the various tables.

"Hey, Avery!" The call came from a table of dock kids just a little older than she was. They waved her over. "Come sit with us."

"Can't. Working." She was glad it was dark so they couldn't see her flushed face. In the space of a few months, she'd gone from promising college sophomore to waitress in a bar. Her mom's lips had gotten tight when Avery had come home and told her about the job, and even the promise that it was only part-time, and that she'd start at the bookstore next week, hadn't lightened things up. Mom had been super tense lately; Dad, too, and some of the things she'd overheard had made Avery realize, for the first time, that Mom had gotten pregnant with her and Aiden before marrying Dad.

Apparently, Mom was reexperiencing the difficulty of an unexpected pregnancy through Avery. Which was pretty mind-blowing.

But in Mom's case, there was a man who loved her to help shoulder the burden.

In Avery's case, no marriage was going to happen. And although she loved *being* a twin, she prayed she wasn't going to *have* twins. One baby was all she could manage.

"Do you guys need anything?" she asked the kids gathered around the table.

"Nah. Marty's bringing our dinners." It was nice that they didn't rub her failure in her face. They suggested getting together, asked after her family. Dock people stuck together, and anyway, she wasn't the only one working; all of them had been out fishing, trying to get in the last good catch before oyster season ended.

"Hey! We need refills!" The voice behind her was irritated, and she turned to see a table of middle-aged guys. When had they become her table? But then she remembered the other waitress, Marty, saying something about it as they'd passed each other a few minutes ago.

"Sorry," she said, rushing over. "I'm new. What can I get you?"

They ordered pitchers and aside from one grumpy guy, assured her it was fine; they weren't in a hurry, glad to see a new pretty face.

"Flirt with the guys a little," Darcy, the bartender, told her when she went up to get their drinks. "Better tips that way."

"Those guys are old enough to be my father!"

"I didn't say marry them. I said flirt. Your call, though."

Avery didn't feel right about it. She looked over at the guy her age at the end of the bar. He was watching her, and apparently listening, too, because he gave a little smirk.

He was cute. It figured she'd think so. He wore the kind of on-purpose ragged clothes rich kids wore, and when he'd gone to the men's room earlier, she'd noticed a swagger in his walk.

Just like Mike Miller. Arrogant rich boys: her kryptonite. She turned away from him, delivered the pitchers and gave the older guys an extra-friendly smile.

The Mike lookalike was back in his seat now, trying to get Darcy's attention, but she was busy. So Avery pulled a beer for him. Then she went to look after her tables.

It took all of her focus, and that was just as well. She got into a rhythm: check with each table until someone wanted something, go get it or put in the order, take it back out and check the rest of the tables, carry away empties. Once a guy put a hand on her butt, which was annoying, but her dock friends called him on it, whooping and shaming him until he threw enough money to pay his bill on the table and slunk out.

The night went by in a fast blur until most patrons emptied out after midnight. The rich kid at the end of the bar stayed.

"Go see if you can nudge him along," Darcy said. "Find out if he's local, where he's staying. I want to close down and get out of here."

Avery hadn't intended to talk to him, but now she'd been ordered to do it by her boss. She went down and leaned on the bar. "Never saw you in town before."

"Just got here," he said. "But if all the ladies are as pretty as you, I might stay."

She rolled her eyes. "How many girls have you said *that* to?"

"A few," he admitted, "but none of them minded." He gave her another one of those cocky grins.

Again, she thought of Mike. Mike, who'd come on so strong, promised her things, not that she'd needed that. She hadn't been looking for a husband. But she *had* expected him to use a decent condom or to stop when his crappy one broke.

Her mom was after her to let Mike know she was pregnant, get him to pay child support. Avery couldn't stomach it. She didn't want him to be a part of her child's life. Of *her* life. Somehow she'd manage on her own.

"Last call," Darcy said at a volume that wasn't really necessary because the kid was the only one still drinking. At the couple of remaining tables people were gathering their things, waving, laughing, heading out.

"Where are you staying?" she asked the kid.

"Get me one more beer and I'll tell you."

"Only if you drink it fast."

"That I can do." He proved himself by finishing his half-full glass in one long drink, so she pulled him another. He was as good as his word, draining the glass without taking a breath.

She leaned on the bar. "Impressive," she said, letting her sarcasm show. "What are you, a frat boy?"

He glanced away. "Not anymore."

"I did my side of the deal. I got you a beer. Where are you staying?" She was really curious.

"My car. Or I could stay at your place," he said.

She nearly spit out her ice water. "I live with my parents in a trailer. We don't have room for guests." That wasn't true; her twin brother's room was empty. He was still at college, doing well. He hadn't screwed up like she had.

Should she offer this kid Aiden's room? Nobody should have to sleep in their car. She opened her mouth to do it, the courtesy of the docks overriding her skepticism about him.

"I could sleep with you." The kid waggled his eyebrows and grinned like he thought he was cute.

"Dream on." His remark changed her mind about inviting him to stay. But she could see something vulnerable in his eyes. "Are you really sleeping in your car?"

"Yeah, but it's fine. It's an SUV. Plenty of room."

Plenty expensive. "There's a little motel just across town," she said. "I'm sure you could afford it."

"I'm fine."

"Police here don't like vagrancy." The truth was the police department here generally nurtured the few homeless people into either getting their lives together or leaving.

"You know the police? Is there an Officer Stone?"

"Sure."

"Where's he live?"

She thought a minute and then wrote down the address of the kennel. "He's in the little white cottage two doors down from this place. I don't know his street number."

"Nice guy?"

"Yeah, he is."

"Hey, I could use some help here," Darcy called, pointing at a mop and broom.

"Sure! Sorry!" Avery hurried over and, after a quick lesson in how to operate the big commercial bucket, started mopping the floor Darcy had just swept.

When she looked up again, the kid was gone. Gone to sleep in his car?

There was something that didn't add up about his story, but Avery wasn't sure what it was.

And it wasn't her business. She had plenty to worry about without getting involved in some rich, troubled kid's life, no matter how cute he might be.

BERTIE HAD MADE *a mistake. He'd lost control and shot the detective. Worse, he'd left a witness, and now, disastrously, he'd lost track of her. When he'd spied on her family home, he hadn't seen her, early morning, late at night, even looking in the windows.*

His worst fears were true. She'd moved away.

Where had she gone? What was she doing? Was she going to find him and turn him in?

Since this last catastrophe, his heart raced all the time and he couldn't sleep.

He'd broken the fifth commandment. Punishment was coming if he didn't do something.

He shouldn't have even gotten a gun, but he'd needed to practice for his stage role, didn't he? Being in productions was part of his job as a theater professor.

His counselor would have said all of it had to do with going off his meds, but he was way off the mark. The things the man had hinted about regarding Mother...no. Bertie had been right to quit therapy and the antianxiety medication.

He could solve it himself, he mused as he drove by the apartment where it had happened for the tenth time. Maybe he'd even rent out a place here, the better to examine all the angles. There was a for-rent sign on the end unit, and he snapped a photo so he'd have the number.

When he'd lost control as a child, Mother had taken care of the punishment. It had been severe, always, but afterward, he'd felt cleansed. Forgiven.

He needed to figure out how to get that feeling again, on his own. Deliberately, he slowed down his breathing as he parked across the street from the row house where it had all gone down.

Think. Be logical. You know how to do that. *He'd always been smart, the smartest kid in the class. He could solve any problem, including this one. His research and technology skills were stellar.*

He breathed deeply, in and out, and though he still felt panicky, a plan began to form.

Step one was finding the girl he'd decided on to impress Mother, bringing her home. Step two was finding the witness to his foolish mistake—and making sure she didn't tell anyone about what he'd done. Either by scaring her into silence, or...no. He didn't want to think about the alternatives; not yet.

CHAPTER FOUR

THE PING INDICATING a text message early Sunday morning brought Evan out of a sound sleep. He was off today, but you were never truly off in his line of work.

He expected—almost hoped, in a weird way—that the text was from Cassie. He hadn't talked with her since that night she'd gotten scared of the raccoon noise outside. He'd wanted to give her space. Give himself space, too, since he was having trouble remembering that she was off-limits. But it was strange to be so close to her and not be in touch.

He looked at the face of the phone and groaned internally when he saw his ex-wife's name on the screen. He threw off the covers, washed his face and went downstairs.

As he put on coffee—he couldn't deal with Kelly without coffee—he reviewed his checking and savings account balances in his mind. It had to be a money issue; it always was. He'd never been a real father, hadn't seen his son since Kelly had moved him out of state when he was three, but he always kept up with his child support payments and then some.

Evan didn't blame her for taking Oliver and leaving. He'd been no use to either her or his son at that point.

Kelly knew he was a soft touch when it came to money for Oliver. It was how he overcame his guilt. And she played on it, sure, but she had a right to. She'd raised the boy alone.

He poured himself a cup of coffee, took a scalding, for-
tifying gulp and read the text.

Call me.

Evan's heart pumped a little faster. She never wanted
him to call her. Had something happened to Oliver?

He placed the call and tried to calm himself by looking
out across the bay, where morning sunshine was trying to
peek through the cloud cover.

She took the call right away. "Hey."

"Kelly? What's up? Is Oliver okay?"

"I don't know. He's missing and I can't find him at his
usual hangouts or with his usual friends."

"Missing?" Evan's palms went so damp that he almost
dropped the phone. "Do you think he's hurt? Or…" He
couldn't say his worst fear.

"No, no." She sounded impatient. "He must have left of
his own free will. He took his stuff."

"Isn't he at college?"

"No. He dropped out."

"What?" Evan put the phone on speaker so he could
pace. "Why did he drop out? And when were you going
to tell me? I know I paid this term's tuition." Kelly was
pretty well-off and had been for years, ever since she'd
remarried, but she'd still seized on Evan's offer to pay for
Oliver's college and came to him for all the extras Oliver
needed, too. Which was only right. It wasn't her husband's
responsibility.

"Yeah, well, he conveniently waited until the drop/add
period was over before getting in trouble." She paused.
"For drinking."

Evan frowned. "Is that a kick-out offense? He's of age, right?"

"Right, but apparently he broke into a school-owned van and tried to drive a group of his friends to a casino. Didn't get far, and no one was hurt, but the school booted him." There was a pause, then: "He drinks altogether too much, and when he does, he doesn't think."

She didn't say it; she didn't have to. Like father, like son.

"He needs someone to talk some sense into him," she went on, "but I can't anymore. He tunes me out. I think he needs a man's guidance, but of course, that's not happening."

Shame slammed Evan. He *hadn't* given his son any guidance, and although that was by Kelly's choice, he regretted it every day of his life.

It was weird to be talking to Kelly. He hadn't heard her voice for several years. She must be more upset than she was letting on.

"What do you need from me?" he asked. "How can I help?"

"I thought maybe with your police access, you might be able to get some information. See if he's been picked up." She sounded cool, but he figured she wasn't, not that he knew her that well these days.

"I can try," he said. "Any clues on where he's going?"

"I have no idea. No idea who he is anymore."

"I'll do my best," he promised.

Tires squealed outside, and Evan went to the front of his place and looked out. A lanky kid—scratch that, a lanky *man*—scratch that, Evan's younger self—half stumbled out of a late-model SUV, grabbed a duffel and staggered toward the porch.

Evan stared.

"Okay, thanks," Kelly said.

"Hey, don't hang up." He felt like his knees were weak, so much so that he put out a hand to steady himself on the kitchen counter. "I, uh, I think I found him."

"What? He came there?"

"Pretty sure it's him."

"Wow," Kelly said, and then after a pause, "Well, good. I took the first twenty-one years. You can deal with him for the next." She paused, then added, "Have him call me," in a choked-up voice.

"Will do." Evan's heart pounded. He ended the call and walked, as if through thick mud, to meet his adult son for the first time in eighteen years.

"IT WAS GREAT to see you," Cassie said to Mary on Monday morning, giving her a firm handshake. They were standing outside the door of Mary's bookstore, Lighthouse Lit, so named because it was built in the shape of a lighthouse. "I can't wait to get started."

"I'm so glad you're going to work with the teenagers, making dolls," Mary said. "Do you need a ride home, dear?"

"No, I'll walk. It's a nice day."

"But Evan said…" Mary trailed off.

Cassie narrowed her eyes. "What did he say?"

Mary looked sheepish. "Truthfully, it was your mother as well. They both mentioned that you're easily fatigued and have to be careful about physical exertion."

Cassie stifled her irritation. "I mentioned that I might need to take breaks while working with the kids. I'm fine walking home, but thank you for being concerned."

Mary shook her head. "What am I thinking, trying to tell an adult woman to take care of herself? I know you'll be fine. We'll talk soon."

After Mary had gone back into the shop, Cassie drew in a deep breath and started toward home. It wasn't as if people acting overly protective of her was something new, but she'd hoped to escape that when she'd come to Pleasant Shores, to make a new start.

Ah, well, she'd just have to prove herself.

She walked briskly, thinking about all she and Mary had discussed. The idea of working with teenagers was in equal parts exciting and terrifying. Cassie had struggled in high school until she'd learned the social ins and outs. It was a product of her years of illness; she'd had little experience with other kids. Mom had tried, but she'd been busy scrambling to earn a living.

Josh had come to the rescue, coaching Cassie on how to navigate the cliques and high school banter, and things had improved as high school went on. Teens were a wildcard, though. She wondered how they'd feel about making dolls. She'd have to present the concept carefully, that was for sure.

It would be fun, if nerve-racking. A new project, and she was ready for one.

Clouds and fog pressed in, but it wasn't actually raining. On impulse, or maybe to prove to herself that she wasn't the physically weak person Mary, Evan and others supposed her to be, Cassie turned toward the bay. There was a bike-and-walking path that ran along the shoreline, she'd heard, but she hadn't yet explored it.

She reached the path and started walking. Out on the bay, a couple of fishing boats were ghostly shapes in the fog, their lights making stretched-out diamonds, their motors muffled. Up ahead the shape of a squat lighthouse jutted, surrounded by plumes of vapor. The water lapped against the shore.

No one else was on the path. It was as if she were alone in the world.

Alone.

Anxiety clutched at her stomach, something that never would've happened before Josh's death. She'd generally welcomed the chance to be alone, especially after her overprotected childhood.

Not anymore. She wished she had Ace with her, but it hadn't seemed appropriate to bring him to a professional meeting.

She should have gone back home to get him before venturing out.

Up ahead, a shape loomed in the darkness. A lanky man coming toward her. Her heart thudded, but she forced herself to keep walking, keep breathing. She couldn't let herself fear every random jogger, or she'd never get over her nerves and achieve the life she wanted.

She strained to see the guy as he got closer. His form seemed familiar, the way he moved.

He was bundled up, a scarf around his face. It wasn't that cold, was it?

That ropey body, the near lope, and now that he'd nearly reached her, that furrowed forehead. The ice-cold eyes.

It was *him.* Josh's killer.

She screamed and ran off the path and into the deserted street.

CHAPTER FIVE

EVAN DIDN'T KNOW much about raising kids, but he'd been around a lot of twenty-one-year-old men in the military, and he knew discipline was important. So when Oliver hadn't awakened by noon on Monday, he knocked on the door of the spare room where Oliver was sleeping. When there was no answer, he went inside.

The alcohol smell was overwhelming.

Oliver was sprawled in the bed, head thrown back, snoring. Evan looked around and saw a bottle of whiskey, half hidden in the bedding Oliver had thrown off. Half full, too.

It felt like there was a magnet in the bottle, drawing his hand. He could practically taste the strong, cheap brand, could feel the burning as it went down.

His fingers had nearly closed around the bottle when he came to himself. He shoved it out of sight with his foot. He'd envisioned lots of complications since his son had arrived on his doorstep, but this strong of a desire to drink hadn't been one of them.

He'd have to lay out some ground rules with his son.

His son. The fact of him being here still stunned Evan.

They'd tiptoed around each other yesterday, been polite. Oliver had said he was visiting mostly to avoid his mother's anger about him dropping out of college, but they hadn't discussed it deeply. Evan had ordered pizza for dinner and they'd watched a basketball game. Talked a little, not much. Like strangers. Oliver had turned in around eleven.

Apparently, he hadn't gone directly to sleep.

"Hey, wake up." He shook Oliver's shoulder.

Oliver snarled and turned away.

"Come on, we have stuff to do." He'd taken the day off, but he needed to figure some things out, get errands done, because tomorrow he'd be back to work.

Should he tell his son he couldn't have liquor in the house?

His AA sponsor would say *definitely*. But Evan had failed Oliver for so long, and it was like a miracle that he was here. He hated to start their relationship with a bunch of rules and regulations.

"Come on," he said, shaking Oliver's shoulder again, "we need to get groceries and figure out your next steps. I'll buy you lunch." Did you say that to a kid or was it assumed? Was Oliver a kid or an adult, at twenty-one?

There was so much he didn't know about parenting.

Oliver sat up, looking how Evan could remember feeling. He glanced around and Evan knew, without Oliver's saying it, that he was looking for the whiskey bottle. "A hair of the dog is a myth," he said. "You'll feel better if you have breakfast. Coffee at least. I have some downstairs."

"Yeah." Oliver rubbed his face. "Give me ten minutes."

"Sure." Evan walked downstairs.

Were you supposed to feel an automatic connection to your kid? When he looked at Oliver, his emotions were all over the place. On the one hand, he didn't even know Oliver. What he liked on his pizza, whether he was into sports, whether he could take a joke.

On the other hand, he'd been receiving pictures and brief reports once a year since Kelly had taken their son out of state. That was his one condition for not reporting her for it, because in their custody agreement—which had never been fulfilled—a stipulation was that neither parent could move more than 150 miles away without agreement from the other.

So he'd watched Oliver grow, in pictures, had received a few notes about a good report card or a success on the soccer field. He'd been proud when Oliver had been accepted at the University of Illinois.

He had the chance to know Oliver now. Even if his son only stayed a few days, it was more than Evan had ever had, and he needed to take advantage of the time.

He poured a mug of coffee for Oliver—didn't know whether or not he took cream and sugar or liked it black, as Evan did—and looked around the kitchen. Should he fry up a couple of eggs?

The carton in his hands, movement outside caught his eye. He walked over to the window and saw Cassie. Running toward Victory Cottage, her gait as awkward as a runner in the last stages of a marathon. She stopped for breath, hands on knees, looked behind her and took off running again.

Had something happened to her? He put down the eggs and strode outside. "Cassie! Hey, Cassie, what's wrong?"

CASSIE LET EVAN lead her into his cottage. She was breathing hard as she eased herself down into a chair in his living room.

"Wait right there." He walked back to the door and scanned the yard and street.

Then he closed and locked the door and turned back to her, looking her up and down and zeroing in on her face. "What happened? Are you hurt?"

"No, I'm okay." She could barely gasp out the words. Her muscles quivered with the exertion, her joints already aching. She'd pay for that wild run tomorrow.

"Was someone following you?" He walked back to the door and, once again, looked out the side panel, scanning the area in front of the house. "I don't see anyone."

"I...don't...think so."

"I'll get you a glass of water."

"Thanks." Her breathing was getting back to normal, but her mind was racing. Had it really been that awful man?

She hadn't been able to see him clearly. He'd seemed to be coming right toward her, but when she'd taken off and then looked back, he'd disappeared into the fog. She wasn't fast; far from it. If he'd wanted to catch her, he could have.

Evan came back in with a glass of ice water and handed it to her. When she lifted it to her lips, her hand shook. She took a few sips and then set it carefully down on the table beside her.

"Thanks, Evan," she said. "I'm really not sure what I saw, but I thought..." Her voice trembled. *Stop it*, she scolded herself. She sucked in a deep breath and went on. "The guy looked a lot like Josh's killer. Same build, same eyes. But he had a scarf up over his face, so I couldn't tell for sure."

He pulled up a chair and leaned forward. "Tell me every detail. Where you were, what you saw, what he said, if anything."

So she recounted the episode, feeling more and more foolish as she did. "He was probably just some guy," she said, although the uneasy feeling in her gut wouldn't go away.

"You said you thought you'd seen him once before, back in Minestown. Tell me about that."

"I thought I did, once, out shopping." She'd panicked, left a full grocery cart in the aisle and rushed out of the store. "Mom was waiting in the car outside, and we got the security guard and went back in. It turned out to be nobody. Just some dad doing the shopping for his family."

Evan nodded. "That's a common phenomenon among crime victims, thinking you see your attacker everywhere. But that's no reason to let down your guard. We know that Josh's killer saw you, and it's possible he would come looking for you."

Hearing Evan say the words out loud made her stomach lurch. But at least he wasn't treating her like some flighty, delusional female.

There was a sound above them, then footsteps coming down the stairs. She tensed, looking at Evan. Did he know someone was up there?

But the young man who appeared looked almost exactly like Evan had looked as a teenager.

"Your son," she said, glancing at Evan as her heart rate settled.

"Yes. Cassie, this is my son, Oliver. Oliver, Cassandra Thomas. We grew up together."

"Nice to meet you." He turned to his father. "You said there's coffee?"

"I poured you a cup. Granola bars in the cupboard."

Cassie raised an eyebrow as soon as he'd left the room.

"A day of surprises. I didn't know you had company. I'm fine now. I'll leave."

"No, don't." He called into the kitchen, "Hey, Oliver, can you come out here a minute? Change of plans." Then he said to Cassie, "We'll drive down to the path and look around. Then I'll call Minestown and see if there are any updates on the case."

She knew she should protest. His son was visiting, and from what Josh had said, they hadn't built much of a relationship in Oliver's younger years. She didn't want to interrupt their time together.

But the thought of having Evan at her side for a bit, now when she was still hot and breathless from running scared, was incredibly reassuring.

Oliver came in and leaned against the doorjamb. "What's up?"

"Groceries will have to wait, unless you want to get them yourself."

"I can, but I need cash." Oliver reddened slightly.

Evan reached for his back pocket. "Forty enough?"

"Not really."

"How much, then?"

"At least sixty," Oliver said.

Evan looked like he wanted to protest, but then he glanced over at Cassie, pulled out his wallet and handed some bills to his son. "List is on the fridge," he said. "Come on, Cassie, let's go take a look while we can."

She climbed into Evan's truck and directed him toward the spot where she'd seen the man. "I'm sorry to take you away from your son."

"It's rough going between us," he said. "I don't mind taking a break and doing something I know something about. Unlike parenting. How's your dog for protection, by the way?"

"Ace?" She blinked at the change of subject. "Ace would do anything in his power to protect me, but he's older, with some orthopedic problems." She puffed out a breath. "We're quite a pair."

"Your dog, or Josh's?" He steered toward the bay.

"Ours. We rescued him together." She pointed. "That's about where I saw the man."

The bay sparkled in the late-March sunlight, and there were two joggers and a bicyclist out on the trail. Everything looked normal, and so open. "It was foggy," she explained, feeling sheepish. "Maybe I just got spooked. It looks like a totally different place now."

"We have to take every possible related thing seriously, if we want to find Josh's killer." He pulled into a little parking lot that faced the bay and stopped the car. "Anytime anything like this happens, you come directly to me. Or call me, or 911."

"I really appreciate knowing you're nearby, Evan." She reached over, intending to pat his arm or some such thing.

He grasped her hand in his and didn't let go. "I'm serious, Cass. I can't let anything happen to you."

She must be an emotional mess, she decided. His callused hand felt so strong, so good.

"Look," he said, "I promised Josh I'd take care of you, and that's what I'm doing."

Of course, he was just helping out Josh's little sister. She pulled her hand away, nodding.

"I'm going to call a guy I know on the Minestown force, try to find out where they are in the case."

"I'll call my contact, too." Evan was the cop, but Cassie

had been in touch with the police at least weekly since Josh's death.

"You stay here and talk. I'll get out." He did, jumping down with easy grace.

Cassie had always admired that grace. She admired it still.

On the phone, the officer in charge of victims' families greeted her, listened to what she said and started in with the placating remarks. "It's very common to see the person who hurt your family everywhere," the woman explained. "How are you doing otherwise, Cassie?"

"I'm fine." She gritted her teeth. "Any new developments on Josh's case?"

"We're doing the best we can with our limited staffing. I'll call you and your mother the moment we make progress."

Cassie ended her call and sat back, wanting to scream. She just had time to get control of her frustrated emotions when Evan returned to the cab of the truck.

"Anything?" he asked.

She shook her head.

"Me either," he said, "except my contact let me know they've put the case on the back burner."

"For good?" Cassie asked, her fists clenching.

"They may just be going through a crime wave or a phase of low staffing." Evan's voice was soothing, just as Officer Shelton's had been. "I'm sure they'll get back to it."

Heat rose in her. "You know that once they stop investigating, they'll never pick it up again without some big, new evidence."

He nodded, tight-lipped. "You're not wrong. That's why—" He cut himself off.

"What?" When he didn't answer, she pulled her legs under her and turned toward him. "Tell me!"

He drew in a breath and let it out in a sigh. "I'm going to look into the case myself, see what I can find out. Like you say, if new evidence is uncovered, the police will re-open the case. I want to try to find that evidence."

"How? You have a full-time job and your son is here. You can't go sleuthing around in your spare time. You don't have any." She'd heard through Josh that, since getting sober, Evan had become a workaholic.

"Yes, I'm busy, but Josh deserves justice." He met her eyes again. "And you deserve safety, which you'll only have for sure when the perp is behind bars."

"Tell me how I can help." She saw him start to deny her request and narrowed her eyes. "I mean it. I can research, I can take you back to Josh's place, I can show you where he hung out. Tell you more of the details about that night."

"I'm glad to see any sights or hear any details you think are important. I can't let you put yourself in danger, though."

"And yet you can put yourself in danger? I want to work with you on this."

He took her hand, his thumb brushing over her knuckles. "No. Uh-uh. I'll do the legwork myself."

She wanted to argue, but his featherlight touch on her hand had made her lose her train of thought. She sucked in a breath, staring at him.

He knew what he was doing, touching her hand with that tenderness. Maybe he meant it, or maybe he was just trying to distract her from trying to help him seek justice for Josh.

Whatever he intended, it was working—and she had to fight it. Fight *him* and his appeal.

If she was to establish herself, gain her independence so she wasn't a drain on others—so she wasn't as dependent as his son appeared to be—she had to stand on her own two feet. Stop thinking about Evan as anything but Josh's friend and a cop who could help get justice for her brother.

Because in addition to his tendency to overprotect her, Evan had a drinking problem. Cassie had grown up with an alcoholic father, and she knew better than to repeat her mother's mistake.

And men ultimately didn't want a woman like her. They wanted someone strong, healthy, easy to be with. Fun.

She shook off the oddly romantic feelings she was having and pulled her hand away. "I want you to keep me updated on everything you find out. And I want to go with you to Minestown. Like it or not, we're in this together, and I'm not backing out."

Again, he pulled in a deep breath and let it out in a sigh. "All right, Cassie. We can go to Minestown together and we can share information. That's as far as I can go. Deal?"

She shook his hand formally. "Deal," she said.

AFTER A HARD day's work, Evan got home on Tuesday night, starving.

In the living room, Oliver was laughing at something on the TV. Evan knew he should greet his son, ask him about his day, but he'd get dinner started first. He filled a big pot and turned on the gas burner, then opened the cupboard.

No pasta, no jarred sauce, even though those had been on the grocery list Evan had told his son about. In fact, the cupboard looked pretty much the same as it had before Oliver had gone to the store.

He walked through the kitchen, opening cupboards. The

food must have been put away somewhere else. After all, Oliver was new to Evan's kitchen and his routines.

He didn't find the spaghetti fixings, so he went into the living room. "Hey."

"Hey." Oliver glanced away from the screen and gave Evan a little wave.

"Where'd you put the pasta?"

Oliver pulled a beer from a twelve-pack on the floor beside him. "Want one?"

"No." He'd definitely need to have that "no alcohol in the house" talk with Oliver, no matter how brief his stay, because a cold beer sounded way too good to him. "Where's the pasta?"

"I, uh, I couldn't find it at the store."

That was so ridiculous that Evan almost laughed. "That grocery's a quarter of the size of a city one. Why didn't you ask?"

Oliver looked away.

"In fact, did you think about starting dinner, since you're here watching TV while I'm out working?" As soon as he said the words, Evan regretted them. Oliver was here for a short time, and if he wanted to be waited on some, Evan guessed he could do that.

"Whoa, man, chill." Oliver took a long chug of beer, his throat working. He wiped his mouth with the back of his hand. "I'm not much of a cook. Mom always cooks for me."

Evan felt the remark as a blow, a reminder of all the things his ex had done for his son, all these years, while Evan had done nothing but pay child support. "Fair enough, but your mom's not here now." He sighed. "Pizza again, or Chinese?"

"Chinese." Oliver's eyes strayed back to the TV screen.

"I like moo shu pork. Maybe some General Tso's chicken, too." He crushed the empty in his hand and then pulled out another beer and cracked it open.

Evan frowned. "Do you drink every day?"

"It's light beer!" Oliver held up the can.

"And it's five o'clock. How many have you had?"

"A couple." The words were a mumble.

Evan knew how alcoholics tried to fool themselves and others. Knew, because he'd done it many times himself. He walked around to where he could see the area in front of the couch. "I count seven empties," he said.

Oliver sat up. "Geez, I didn't know it was a police state here." Then his frown turned into a silly smile and giggle. "Get it? Police state? 'Cuz you're a cop." He swung his legs to the floor and pushed himself to his feet. "Listen, I'll just head out to the Gusty Gull. I don't want to put you out, ordering food for me."

Evan opened his mouth to ask Oliver to take the rest of the twelve pack with him, but his words died unsaid. What kind of selfish father encouraged his already-tipsy son to drink more?

Oliver stretched. "Need to fill the tank with gas, too." It almost sounded like he wanted Evan to foot the bill for that.

"You're not driving. You can walk to the Gull."

"No way!" Oliver looked down at the coffee table.

Evan did, too, and his reflexes were quicker than his son's, which said a lot about Oliver's state of intoxication. He grabbed the car keys just as Oliver made a dive for them himself.

Evan pocketed the keys and started to turn.

"Give them to me!" Oliver skirted the coffee table and came toward him.

Evan turned back, unhappy to realize that he didn't want to turn his back on his son, any more than he'd turn his back on any perp. "I'm not letting you drive drunk."

"Who do you think you are, telling me what to do? You were never there for me. For Mom, either."

The words hit their mark, but Evan maintained his composure by looking at the man—kid, really—in front of him as if he were just any teen Evan was trying to keep out of trouble. "I'm ordering Chinese. You can stay for it or not."

Please stay, his heart said, but his mouth couldn't force out the conciliatory words.

Oliver stood, and Evan realized for the first time that his son was taller than he was. Skinny, but tall.

Oliver shoved past Evan and went to the door. "Don't wait up," he said. Then he added, with heavy sarcasm, *"Dad."*

CHAPTER SIX

AVERY WAS SETTLING into her job at The Gusty Gull and to her surprise, it wasn't boring. Waitressing was a challenge, and she was proud of herself for catching on quickly. She'd even gotten called in for an extra shift tonight, Tuesday, after just two nights on the job.

The place was dim, even though it was still light outside, but that was just the way the Gull was. The cooking smells were delicious. At least for now. She'd already discovered they weren't so great when she got home with clothes permeated with the odor of fried food. The place was half-full, a mix of couples and families, older and young. For dinnertime, they were playing a country soundtrack, but she already knew they'd put on more contemporary music as it got later. She was starting to catch the rhythms of the job.

She stood at the pass-through, sneaking a fry that had fallen off a plate. Hot and crispy. Yum.

"I saw that," Darcy joked. "Don't start eating the food here. You'll be doomed." She looked Avery up and down. "Of course, you're so young and slender, you've got nothing to worry about."

Avery washed her hands and then grabbed the plates of food that had just come up. She wasn't going to be slender for long. In fact, underneath her loose shirt, she already had a little baby bump. She'd looked at online pictures and knew her pregnancy would be obvious soon.

Four months. Almost halfway.

She got busy with her tables and blessedly, forgot her worries, until her parents came in. The hostess showed them to a table in her section, of course.

Emotions churned inside her, just at the sight of them.

She had that kid-like happiness at seeing her parents, and in addition, a sense of pride that they could see her working, starting to earn her own living. At the same time she wished she were just a college kid, emphasis on the *kid*. Able to come home on school breaks and sleep in and get special treatment, like her twin, Aiden, did, instead of helping with chores and facing her parents' disappointment on a near-daily basis.

She took menus over, and Dad's eyes welled up with tears.

Mom whacked him on the arm. "Stop it. I'll have sweet tea and he wants a beer. Light. You're doing a good job, honey."

For some reason Mom's kindness made her feel worse. She saw the Gull through her parents' eyes: the scuffed floors, banged-up tables, the faint smell of beer that lay under that of the fried food. There was a reason her folks didn't come here often. Not that they ate out much, they couldn't afford to, but when they did they preferred one of the bright chain restaurants up the coast. Cleaner, Mom always said.

They had to be stretching the budget to come here on a Tuesday night. It was sweet of them, but maybe misguided. She wished they'd stayed at home.

She continued attending to her tables, but she was conscious of Dad's eyes following her around. It made her more careless, less friendly, and she got a couple of point-edly bad tips.

Waiting tables, you were dependent on people's whims. You had to fake a smile whether you felt it or not. She wished she could go back to school, study, go to parties where people saw *her*, not just a role.

Mom went to the ladies' room, and on the way back out she beckoned to Avery. "Dad will come around," she said. "It's just hard for him. He pinned his hopes on you."

"It's not like I died." Avery flushed. "So I'm not in college anymore. It's not the end of the world."

"I know it." She patted Avery's shoulder. "Carry on. We'll be okay. See you tonight."

Mom headed back to the table. Just before she got there, she straightened her shoulders.

It was like a lightbulb went off inside Avery's head: this was hard for Mom, too. Mom was always supportive, had been there to talk everything through, told her about check-ups and prenatal care, came with Avery to her first embarrassing pelvic exam.

She was the one who waited up when Avery got home late. She smoothed things over with Dad.

Still, she realized now, it might be hard on Mom, having her pregnant daughter home.

As her parents left the restaurant, Avery studied her mother's face and noticed there were bags under her eyes, more so than normal. Dad put an arm around Mom, but he didn't speak. Dad had worked hard all his life, been so proud of his twins for going to college. And Avery was the one who'd always been the stronger, more serious, student. Now, Dad must be thinking that only Aiden would escape the hard life on the docks.

She went to clear their table and teared up when she saw the twenty-dollar tip.

Mom was trying to have healthier food for her, which meant that groceries were more expensive now that she was home. They really didn't have twenty dollars to spare.

Her pride at working, earning part of a living, had totally dissipated in the forty-five minutes her parents had been here. She couldn't stand facing their disappointment every day, *being* a disappointment every day.

"Hey, step it up." Darcy was frowning at her. She gestured toward a table that was waving for their check.

Great. Avery was disappointing her boss, too.

She got the table their check, went around to make sure her remaining customers had everything they needed and then stepped into the ladies' room. She dabbed at her tears with toilet paper so as not to get raccoon eyes. Her feet stuck to the floor; someone had spilled a drink.

She went out and got the mop and took it into the ladies' room to clean up the spill. There was a full-length mirror and she paused and smoothed down her shirt and apron. When she stood sideways and looked for it, the bump was definitely visible. She was going to be a mom.

"I'll never be ashamed of you," she whispered to the baby. "I'll be proud, whatever you do."

She finished mopping and pushed the bucket out and back to the kitchen, thinking. She needed to get out of her parents' house. It was next to impossible to become an independent adult, which was what she needed to do, when she felt like a young, naughty kid at home.

Even more than how she felt about herself, she needed to stop making Mom and Dad's lives miserable.

When she came back out from the kitchen, there was that kid, Oliver, sitting at one of her tables.

He cough-talked into his hand as she walked by. The word *hot* was in there somewhere.

She didn't mind the ancient cook calling her *sweetie*, but no way was she taking cute remarks from a kid her age. She turned back. "What was that?"

"I said you're hot," he said with what he probably thought was a winning smile.

She leaned over him, into his face. "I. Don't. Care. What. You. Think." She spun away, knocking against his shoulder, hard.

When she got back to the pass-through to pick up her last order, Darcy was frowning. "You picking up an attitude?" she asked. "Because I could give this job to someone who wants it. I wondered if a college kid would fit in here. Shoulda listened to my gut."

Panic squeezed Avery's stomach. "I can do it. I'll be nice to everybody." She grabbed the hot plates of food and hurried away before Darcy could make a decision against her.

She had to make this work.

And she could do it.

She was a dock kid who'd gotten straight As, had shoved her way into leading the science club when the privileged boys who populated it didn't think her worthy, had earned a scholarship to pay her way through school. She could handle being a waitress.

It was her parents' visit that had upset her. She needed to break free of them, for her own sake and for theirs.

And just like that, an idea of how to make that happen bloomed in her mind. If only she could afford it.

EVAN WAS SITTING on his front porch, watching the sun set over the Chesapeake, when a car pulled up and Cassie hopped out, calling her thanks to the driver. She half walked, half bounced toward the door of Victory Cottage, looking energetic and pretty in her shiny workout tights and hooded sweatshirt.

She was taking care of herself. She wasn't Josh's sick little sister anymore; she wasn't fragile. Physically *or* emotionally, because she was integrating into the community faster than he ever had, if she was already joining classes and getting rides.

"Hey," he said to let her know that he was here.

She gave a little shriek and jumped backward.

"Sorry, sorry, it's Evan," he said, standing. "Didn't mean to scare you." Man, did she look good in the spandex.

"Whoa." She laughed a little, waved away whoever had dropped her off and took a few steps toward him. "It's okay. I'm jumpy." She fanned her face. "Coming back from yoga class."

"I can see that." He gestured at the car. "New friend already?"

She nodded but didn't elaborate.

A surge of emotion rose in Evan. Did men take yoga? "You need to be careful who you befriend," he said.

She tilted her head to one side, frowning. "Why's that?"

"You never know. You've had some scary things happen to you. Plus, are you sure you're up for yoga? Don't you have to be a little careful?"

"Stop it. You're not my doctor, and it's not your business, but exercise is really good for me." She socked his arm, gently. "C'mon, Evan, lighten up. I'm starved. Gonna go make myself a PB&J." She turned toward Victory Cottage.

She was right: he needed to lighten up. To realize that although he would always want to protect Cassie, she was strong and independent in her own right.

She was a woman.

Evan suddenly realized that he'd never ordered that Chinese food and that he was starving, too. "Want to grab dinner at the Gusty Gull?" he blurted out.

She turned back to study him. "Why?" she asked bluntly. "Are you trying to take care of me? Because believe me, I've been there, done that. I want to be on my own here. I don't need another big…" She trailed off and swallowed hard.

She'd been about to say *big brother.*

He put a friendly arm around her, just a little squeeze, and then backed off. There. Brotherly. "I know I can't replace Josh. But let me take care of you just a little, okay?"

She let out an exasperated sigh.

"Besides, I have an ulterior motive. My son went down there and I wouldn't mind checking on him. Without looking like I'm checking on him, you know?"

"So I'm a prop, huh?" She smiled as she said it, and it was like the sunshine coming out from behind a cloud. "Sure, then. Let me change into jeans and I'll be right out."

Fifteen minutes later they were seated along the wall of the Gull, as far away from Oliver as possible. Most tables were full, and the loud music competed with laughter from the Gull's patrons. It was getting to the time when the restaurant vibe flipped over to a bar one. More Oliver's speed.

Evan was pretty sure his son hadn't seen them come in. He seemed occupied with Avery, newly working as a waitress. And with his beer. He was very occupied with drinking beer.

"Is it hard for you, coming to a bar?" Cassie looked over the top of the menu at Evan.

"Not usually." He rubbed the back of his neck. "Been a stressful week, though. I can't let down my guard."

"I admire that you got your life straightened out." She gave him a brilliant smile, then turned her attention to the menu.

Why did admiration from Cassie feel so good? Was he really that needy?

He already knew what he wanted to eat, so he watched Oliver as he got a little louder, talking with other patrons at the bar.

Evan didn't know what to feel. He loved his son and was glad he seemed to be the outgoing type, making friends easily. He wanted to cut him a break, but he also felt ashamed that his own genetics and neglect had contributed to his partying behavior.

"He's not going to like you spying on him," Cassie remarked.

Evan snorted. "Just like I didn't like him spending my grocery money on booze."

"Uh-oh, that doesn't sound good. How long is he in town?"

"No idea."

"Do you think he might stay?"

The idea had been creeping into Evan's mind. He hadn't managed to talk seriously to Oliver, to find out whether he had a plan. He hated to get on his son's case about it, but it would be good to know. "I just don't know. I don't think he knows," he added so he wouldn't seem like the worst father in the universe, having no idea of what his son was doing.

Avery took their order, less talkative than usual, but

after all, she was a new waitress, learning the job. Doing well with it, from the looks of things. He wished life hadn't gone this way for her, wished she could have stayed in college, but it happened. He had the feeling Avery would land on her feet.

Soon after, they were consuming the Gull's trademark fried seafood platters. Heaps of golden fries, along with oysters, shrimp, rockfish and crab cakes. Generous cups of tartar and cocktail sauce. The Gull made no claims to gourmet status, but the portions were large and the seafood was fresh.

The only thing missing was an ice-cold beer, Evan thought ruefully as he sipped his soda.

"Heaven," Cassie said. "I love fried clams." She held one up, waved it around to cool it and then popped it into her mouth.

Watching her do that made his own mouth go dry. He swallowed hard. *She's off-limits.* "My favorite's the crab cake. Try it."

She cut hers open and dipped a steaming bite into cocktail sauce. "Mmmmm," she said. "Ecstasy."

He sucked in a breath. Deliberately looked away from her.

He focused on his food—he really was starving—and she did, too, and the energy between them went back to normal. The fact that they'd known each other forever made it feel acceptable to be silent rather than chatty, to use wads of napkins, to make a bit of a mess. Cassie was comfortable to be with.

That was something he hadn't known to value as a younger man, but he valued it now.

And he didn't need to think about that, either. Getting

emotional about Cassie, thinking about any kind of deeper connection with her, was far more dangerous than the physical attraction that kept pulsing between them.

Fortunately, a couple of his friends came in, and he introduced them to Cassie, and everything got less personal. He was a little surprised that she could comfortably joke around like one of the guys. But then again, wasn't that what she'd always done with him and Josh?

When they were ready to go, Avery brought over the tab. Her shoulders sagged a little and her smile looked forced. Which made sense. Waitressing was hard work, and Avery wasn't used to it.

There was a shout from Oliver's side of the bar. Oliver had moved to sit with some other guys his age, who also seemed to be drinking a little too much. Evan didn't know whether to be glad about the friends, or worried about their habits.

"Is he your son?" Avery asked.

"How'd you know?"

Avery and Cassie looked at each other and laughed. "You look pretty similar," Avery said.

"Oliver *is* Evan, a few years ago," Cassie said, adding, "I knew Evan growing up."

"Ah." Avery took Evan's credit card. "Not into father-son bonding tonight?"

Not sure how to respond, Evan settled on the simple truth. "We're not exactly close. Hate to admit it, but it's true."

"I'll keep an eye on him," Avery offered. She sounded way older than the twenty-year-old she was. She headed for the cash register.

An idea flashed into Evan's mind. "I wonder…" he said, and trailed off.

"Wonder what?"

He watched as Avery walked back toward the bar, speaking to Oliver and his group, making them all laugh. "Avery said she'd keep an eye on him," he said. "What if I pay her to keep an eye on him, kind of babysit him, let me know if he gets into trouble?"

"No. Not a good idea." Cassie shook her head decisively.

"Why not?"

"That's no way to connect with your son. Keeping secrets, overprotecting him."

Evan frowned. "I'm not… Look, that's your issue, Cassie, but it's not mine. I just want to make sure he's safe, that's all."

She looked offended for a few seconds, then shrugged. "Maybe it *is* my issue, but that doesn't mean it's not yours. Anyway, it's not my business to decide. Except…" She trailed off.

"What?" He found he really wanted to know, valued Cassie's perspective. She had a lot of Josh in her, and Josh had never steered Evan wrong. In fact, Evan wished he'd listened to Josh a little more often. It might have saved him some heartache.

"What if he finds out you're spying on him?" Cassie studied him. "He's going to be mad."

"That's true." He frowned. "But I don't know how else to keep him safe. He's too big for me to tie down. He's a legal adult."

"Which means he can make his own decisions, right?"

"Right, but…" Evan shook his head. "It would be just between me and Avery. She can call me if he's in trouble here at the Gull. Maybe if they're out socially. I know she needs the money." His mind made up, he beckoned the young woman over.

"Don't say I didn't warn you," Cassie murmured.

Evan pulled out a chair and explained the proposal to Avery. "Just think about it. I don't mean you have to follow him everywhere. Just, if you see something tell me." He avoided looking at Cassie's frown, focused on Avery. "You don't have to decide now."

"I've already thought about it," she said promptly. "I'm looking to make extra money. I'll do it."

They agreed on the particulars, Cassie sitting off to the side, looking out over the bar, checking her phone, ignoring him.

He was just trying to be a good father, wasn't he?

Of course, what did he know about being a good father? Cassie was right, most likely. If Oliver found out, he wouldn't be happy. Evan had the feeling that going behind Oliver's back would turn his son off in a big way.

Evan had grown up with benign neglect from his parents, and it hadn't served him well. Still, he'd gone on to neglect his own son.

Having Oliver here seemed like a chance for a do-over, and he didn't want to make the family mistakes all over again.

He just hoped he wasn't making a different kind of mistake.

CHAPTER SEVEN

"THANKS FOR DRIVING ME," Cassie said to Evan as they headed toward the dockside area of town. "I could have walked, but I would've had to use one of those grocery pull carts or a little red wagon for all my supplies."

"And Uber hasn't made it to Pleasant Shores," Evan said.

It was the Thursday before Easter, and at Mary's suggestion, Cassie was holding an after-school meeting with the at-risk teens before some of them scattered for Easter break. The meeting would be held at the home of the two people who ran the program, William and Bisky Gross, who lived down by the docks, and Evan had offered to drive her before she'd thought to ask.

"I'm not just driving you, by the way," Evan went on. "I'm coming in."

"Are you now?" Cassie's stomach tightened in a strange mix of happiness and annoyance and nerves.

"Just for this first time," he said. "The kids can be a little rough, and they know me. I want to make sure they're not more than you can handle."

Cassie looked up at the ceiling of the truck and prayed for patience. With herself as well as with Evan, because the thought of having him with her really did calm her nerves, even though it was directly opposed to her goal of gaining independence, standing on her own two feet.

"I can handle a group of teenagers," she said, pretty sure

that it was true. She'd been a straightforward art major in college; she'd loved her art classes; they'd set her on fire and introduced her to a whole new world of color and perspective as well as all kinds of new modalities and materials. She'd wanted to teach, planned to do it eventually, but her health issues had forced her to take it a step at a time rather than overloading herself. "I was taking classes to get my teaching certification. Didn't get as far as student teaching yet, but I loved my practicums."

"The truth is Mary asked me to participate and I couldn't say no. Don't worry, I won't try to take over. I'm crap on making dolls." He half smiled at her.

That made her smile back. Made her stomach flutter, too, if she was being honest. And while she wasn't afraid of the kids, it always helped to have an insider from the community on your side. Josh had always said so, and it held true for teaching as well as for detective work.

So she appreciated Evan's presence. She even told him so.

And then she changed the subject. "How's it going with your son?"

He glanced over at her. "Thanks for asking," he said. "It, um, looks like he'll be staying for a while."

"Oh yeah? How do you feel about that?" She still had a little trouble believing that Evan had a son, a son who was an adult, or technically so. She'd done the math as soon as she'd met Oliver and realized that Evan must have been seventeen or eighteen when he was born. Nobody was ready to be a parent at that age.

Evan rubbed the back of his neck. "I've never had a chance to know him, so in that regard, it's good. Really good."

"Why didn't you get visitation rights? I mean, if you don't mind talking about it."

He turned the corner, and they were on a little road that ran alongside the bay. Docks and small piers pushed out into the water, most with weathered fishing shacks and boats clearly made for serious fishing, not recreation. Evan raised a hand to wave at a couple of white-haired men who stood talking beside one of the shacks.

"It's pretty here," she said. "And seriously. That was a nosy question, about visitation, and you don't need to answer."

He glanced over at her. "I didn't visit because I was a drunk. By the time I got sober, my ex had left the state and taken Oliver."

The flat words made her heart hurt. He'd married so young and then, in all likelihood, caused the end of the marriage through his alcoholism. "I'm sorry," she said, knowing the words were inadequate. "But after you got sober, didn't you want to see him?"

"Of course I wanted to." His voice had a sharp edge to it. He paused, blew out a sigh. "But my ex wouldn't have it, and she was probably right. Better for him to grow up without me."

"No, Evan." She didn't know everything about Evan's life, but she knew he was a good man now. "You could have been a first-rate father. Can still be," she added firmly, because she didn't believe in closed cases. There was always hope. She had to believe that.

She thought they were done talking about his son, because Evan looked out over the bay where a couple of boats were visible. Then he said, "Oliver is plenty mad at me for my shortcomings as a father. But he has nowhere else to go."

What could you say to that? She kept quiet, giving him space to talk more if he wanted to.

"He also seems to be following in my footsteps, with the drinking." He pulled into a driveway that led to a two-story frame house on a rise above the bay. "So there's that."

She patted his arm. "That must be hard to deal with."

Inside, she felt somehow honored. He was treating her like a real friend now, not just Josh's little sister.

She shouldn't find it so pleasing, because it meant they were getting closer, a dangerous thing. A wiser person wouldn't have asked such personal questions in the first place.

But having Evan treat her like an adult and a friend, a close friend, made her feel like a woman. A woman he took seriously. A woman he might come to care for, apart from their history, right now.

As they parked she looked at the house and imagined they were a couple, visiting friends. Which felt dangerously, alarmingly good.

"Let's focus on these kids, where we can maybe make a difference." He got out of the truck, and before she could gather her things and open the door, he was there to help her.

She took his hand, letting him grab her heavier bag and help her down even though she was perfectly capable of climbing out of a pickup by herself. He had enough on his plate without her getting all prickly about accepting his help, so she just smiled and thanked him.

They walked into a noisy gathering that spilled from the kitchen to the screened-in porch. A tall, striking woman stood at the stove, stirring a big pot of something that smelled like chili. An even taller man in dress pants and shirt pulled corn muffins out of the oven. Both of them carefully dodged an active toddler who seemed intent on twining herself around their legs.

A couple of teenagers sat talking at the kitchen table, and the sound of music and loud talk and laughter came from the porch.

"Welcome to the zoo," the woman said, wiping her hands on a dish towel and holding one out to shake Cassie's. "I'm Bisky, the good-looking guy is my husband, William, and this—" she bent down and swooped the toddler up in the air, then nestled her in her arm "—this is Harper, the reason we need some help." She nuzzled into the little girl's neck and blew a raspberry, and the child squealed. Then she set the girl on the floor. "Go play with Charlee and Saul," she said, pointing to the teens at the table.

The little girl ran to the teens and hurled herself into the girl's lap. The girl cuddled her and didn't even pause in the story she seemed to be telling the boy.

William, the husband, greeted Cassie and Evan and took their coats, then beckoned Evan over to help pull things out of the refrigerator.

"Could you help me get this into bowls?" Bisky asked Cassie as she removed an assortment of crockery bowls from the cupboard and handed a ladle to Cassie. "One thing I've learned, working with teenagers, is that it's best if we feed 'em first."

Obediently, Cassie started scooping chili into the bowls. Bisky walked out into the porch full of teens, and Cassie heard her ordering someone to set the table, someone else to get drinks from the refrigerator. Then she came back into the kitchen. "Scoot," she said to the two teenagers at the kitchen table. "Tell everyone to come and get it, and then you kids can eat out on the porch while William and I explain things to our new helpers."

The pair of teens did as they were told, taking the little girl with them. Soon the kitchen was full of teenagers, jostling each other.

It was fun, comfortable chaos. The teens grabbed bowls of chili, doctored them with cheese and sour cream, chose drinks and scooped up salad. Bisky and William assisted, the toddler ran wild and Evan handed out corn muffins. Cassie perched on a stool and watched the action.

She'd wanted something like this for herself. Had wanted a man who'd help in the kitchen, who'd put a hand on her shoulder like William did when he walked past Bisky, who'd help serve the guests. She'd wanted a little girl who'd run up and hug her: a fun, lively child she could lift high in the air.

A little girl who'd rather play with trucks than dolls. That was what she'd probably get, considering that she made dolls for a living. She'd lean back against the man, her husband, and he'd put his arms around her and they'd have a laugh about it.

"Help yourselves," Bisky said to Cassie and Evan, jolting Cassie out of her real-seeming daydream, and they followed William, carrying steaming bowls of chili and a plate of corn muffins to the table.

While they ate, Bisky and William explained that the program provided the teens with volunteer experience that could give them a leg up on college applications or finding jobs.

"And as a bonus, they stay out of trouble," Evan added. "Some of the kids are at risk of going the wrong way. They need something constructive to do."

"Got it." Maybe Evan was good with these kids because he'd gotten in a fair amount of trouble during his own teen years.

"Having something new to keep their attention during these last few months of the school year will be a godsend," Bisky said. "Harper keeps us busy, and—" she glanced at her husband, smiling "—we're expecting another kiddo in the fall."

"That's great news!" Evan reached across the table to fist-bump William, then Bisky. "Congratulations. Boy or girl, or do you know?"

"It's a boy." William put an arm around Bisky, pulling her a little closer.

She smiled up at him. "We're excited. Also frazzled," she added, looking over at Cassie and Evan. "So thanks for helping out. You guys are lightening our load."

Cassie felt a little flutter of something. If William and Bisky were leaving the program to her, she'd need help. Bisky seemed to assume that she and Evan were in this together going forward.

Doing this work together fit in with her persistent daydream that she and Evan were a couple. Was that a good thing for Evan? For her?

There were all kinds of reasons it wasn't a good thing. But right now, in this friendly kitchen, talking and laughing and planning with warmhearted people, Cassie couldn't quite remember what those reasons were.

As THE KIDS, Bisky and William cleaned up after dinner, Evan helped Cassie pull out and set up her supplies and samples.

Dolls. When he'd heard about her idea for working with

the teens, he'd been skeptical. Admittedly, they weren't just baby dolls or Raggedy Ann and Andy; they all had distinct faces and hair and clothes, some with hats or glasses or dog companions, one with her own stuffed balance beam. A couple of them, made to look older, even sported tattoos.

The fact that she had a business making them, earned a living doing it, was impressive.

But they were dolls, and Evan was pretty sure the kids would make fun. "Look, don't be hurt if they don't take to this," he said, wanting to cushion the blow.

She laughed and waved him off. "I know what you're thinking, but it'll be okay. You'll see. Everyone loves dolls."

He was skeptical as he unloaded more supplies from the box and handed them to her for her display. What would his old drinking buddies, let alone his cop buddies, say if they could see him now? Making dolls, of all things.

And not even minding it. Which meant he had it bad.

The kids came in, and she was half right about everyone loving dolls: most of the girls immediately clustered around the table where she'd put out the samples, exclaiming about how cute they were, admiring the outfits and shoes. "Can we pick the dolls up?" one of them asked.

"Of course! They're sturdy, made for kids."

So the girls were fine, but the boys sat down, crossing their arms or checking phones, clearly uninterested.

"Okay, everyone," she said, "have a seat, and let me tell you what this doll-making thing is all about." She pulled out her laptop and a little projector, and an image appeared on Bisky's wall. "This is a presentation I show to the non-profits I work with, basically selling them on ordering dolls for their clientele."

She flipped past the title to the next slide. It was a little girl in a hospital bed, with an IV pole, looking small. But she was smiling and holding up a doll like the ones Cassie had displayed.

"It matches her," one of the kids said, and that was true. The doll's brown cloth skin, multiple braids and hospital gown were an almost perfect match to the little girl's.

The image made it real to Evan, and apparently to the kids, too.

"This is for kids who are in the hospital?" Charlee asked.

Cassie leaned forward. "Yes, some of them." She clicked to the next image, which showed the same little girl's arm, close up. There was a white patch and some tubing attached to a small device. The child had pushed up the doll's sleeve, and it had the same apparatus in miniature.

"That's an insulin pump!" one of the boys exclaimed.

Cassie gave him a warm smile. "Bingo. Do you know someone who wears one?"

"My little sister." He frowned. "She hates it."

"That's too bad. I've heard it's hard to get used to at first, especially for a kid. That's part of the point of the dolls. Kids can practice with them, and they don't feel quite so alone." She flashed to another image, this of a girl without hair, an IV in one arm and a doll in the other. Cassie held up a doll with an IV. "This doll's getting chemo."

You could almost hear the wheels turning in the kids' heads. Most of them, at least.

"They're cute," Sarah, one of the older teens, admitted. "But I doubt a doll, even a lookalike doll with an IV, would make a kid with cancer feel better."

"Maybe not." Cassie didn't push it or get defensive. "But I had cancer growing up, and it was boring to go through chemo, plus you feel alone. I think I would have liked a doll to keep me company."

Several of the kids' eyes widened. "Are you okay now?" the boy whose sister had diabetes blurted out, earning an arm punch from the girl next to him.

"I am. I was lucky." Rather than commenting on her ongoing health problems, she handed one of the dolls over to him. "Do you think your sister would like something like this?"

"She'd love it," he admitted.

"That might be a first project for several of you. Make a lookalike doll for...what was your name?"

"Alex."

"Alex's sister. Anyone interested?"

Several of the girls immediately raised their hands, and Evan started to relax. Cassie knew what she was doing, how to connect with kids. She was probably going to be fine.

Maybe she didn't even need him to be here.

"So what happens to the boys who get sick? Do they get a *doll*?" That came from Callum, a skinny redheaded kid whose family had moved here recently. Evan had noticed him in town, alone most of the time, with a perpetual sneer on his face.

Cassie looked at him, her face thoughtful. "That's a problem," she said, "and I don't really have an answer. Younger boys tend to like the dolls, but those who are diagnosed at, say, seven or eight or older, most of them don't."

"Or they don't want to admit it," one of the girls said. "Maybe teddy bears? I happen to know a male in this room who has one."

The boys looked at each other, and then one, Owen,

laughingly raised a hand. "It's me," he said sheepishly. "I sleep with him most nights, too."

Good-natured ribbing followed, but Owen's confession worked in Cassie's favor, getting some of the boys on her side. "We can try a few teddy bears," she said. "I've never made one, but we can learn together. Then we can take them to a couple of kids as a trial and see how they like them."

A lively discussion of toys and gender ensued. William and Bisky drifted in and got in on the conversation. "I didn't like dolls," Bisky admitted. "I preferred trucks and boats."

"And you fish for a living now," Evan said. "Makes sense."

He was pretty sure he wouldn't have been allowed to play with dolls, even if he'd wanted to. Maybe if he'd been born in a more progressive time and place, where kids played with all different toys, he'd have gotten better at the caring, nurturing side of life, the side he was so terrible at.

"I wouldn't have minded a teddy bear," William said, which made the kids laugh, probably because William was such a giant. "But my dad would have beaten me for it. He was very much into stereotypical gender roles."

Callum nodded in understanding, and Evan, who'd been keeping an eye on him, got a little insight into what might have put the sneer on the kid's face and made him a loner.

"I think all kids should be able to play with whatever kinds of toys they want," Cassie said firmly.

As if on cue, little Harper rushed in, adorable in pink footed pajamas, pushing a big toy dump truck and making beeping noises. The truck had a doll in the back.

"What if your new baby boy wants a doll?" one of the girls asked Bisky and William.

"He can have it, of course," Bisky said.

"It's fine," William said at the same time.

The two of them looked at each other with a flash of shared understanding and love, so warm and intimate that it made Evan jealous. Bisky and William had known each other in childhood and reconnected later; maybe that childhood friendship was what made everything seem so easy between them now. It hadn't always been smooth sailing for them, but they'd come through their troubles deeply in love.

Cassie got into the details of doll making and sewing then, inviting the kids to come up and gather around her, try things out. She forked her fingers through her hair, her face glowing, and spoke intently with the kid whose little sister was sick, then another girl who was studying the dolls with tattoos.

She had a passion for her craft, and it looked like she'd be great at teaching, too.

When the kids started leaving, it was with a commitment to come back the week after Easter ready to work.

Bisky and William came over to help Cassie pack up her things. "That went really well," Bisky said. "I'm so glad you're here. And you, too," she added to Evan. "Those kids are a handful for anyone alone, and with William's new job and my work and the baby—and expecting another—well, we're glad you can both participate."

"Much appreciated," William added, clapping a hand on Evan's shoulder.

"Glad to do it," Evan said, even though he hadn't known he was volunteering for the whole next three months.

Judging from Cassie's raised eyebrow, it was a surprise to her, too.

But it was true; despite how busy he was with work and, now, with Oliver, Evan relished the thought of doing something good in the community and spending time with Cassie, working together.

"Sounds like everyone's interested in participating, so order all the supplies you need, and the program will pick up the tab," Bisky said to Cassie.

Cassie's smile was wide and warm. "I'm glad you think it'll work. I'll get shopping. In fact, maybe a few of the kids would like to come along."

"YOU DID GREAT," Evan said as they drove through town toward Victory Cottage.

"Thank you! Thanks for driving me, and for being my backup in there. I think your presence helped get the boys on board."

"Glad to do it," he repeated.

He pulled into the driveway between their cottages and turned off the car. In the moonlight he could read her skeptical expression. She'd always been a little insecure, covering it up with a touchy attitude. "I like the idea," he said, meeting her eyes. "I have no problem spending time with you, Cassie. I want to."

Her own eyes darkened. She pushed back her hair and drew in a breath. For a long minute they just looked at each other.

Evan knew the next move, knew it by heart. He'd gone through the steps of romance many times. It was his chance to kiss her.

But this was Cassie, and he'd made a promise. He needed to ignore the tightness in his chest, the tingling sensation in his arms, that told him what it would be like to reach for her and pull her close. The vivid images of touching and kissing and holding her that kept playing out in his mind.

He tore his gaze away and looked out over the moonlit bay, trying to cool down.

"Well," she said, "I should get going. Thanks again for the ride and the help. Don't worry, I can carry everything." She practically fell out of the car in her haste, grabbing bags haphazardly.

Okay, then. That answered how she felt about the idea of kissing in the moonlight. He wasn't the only one who thought it was a bad idea; clearly, she did, too.

Which was for the best, Evan reminded himself as he climbed out, carried the remaining bags to her porch and dropped them off.

He definitely had some cooling off to do.

HIS FISTS CLENCHED. *His brother, the younger brother who'd displaced him in Mother's heart, was getting married.*

Charles had already surpassed him by getting a degree in ministry, like his father, Bertie's stepfather. Bertie's own degree in theater didn't compare. No telling what Mother would think if he failed to get tenure.

The thought of that horrible possibility made his stomach churn, so he shoved it away to focus on the problem at hand.

Recently, Bertie had told the family he'd met a woman. Mother wanted grandchildren more than anything. He'd known that showing her he had the potential for a family would make her happy.

But Charles had surpassed him, like always.

His mind journeyed back to childhood, when he'd been the unwanted child from a previous relationship. Once Charles had been born, everything had been labeled as Bertie's fault. He remembered the dark closet, the days

*without food, hearing the family talking and laughing out-
side the closet door as they ate a wonderful-smelling dinner.*

   If he cried, Mother would be angry, and he'd be beaten.

   *Fortunately, he had a plan to make everything right.
Once he took his beautiful new bride to Mother, once they'd
settled nearby and started producing the grandchildren
she craved—and when he told her he'd made sure he'd
never be caught for his little mistake—she'd love him. Finally, he'd have the status he deserved as her oldest and
favorite son.*

   *He just had to make it all happen faster than Charles
did.*

CHAPTER EIGHT

AVERY WAS ALREADY sweating and impatient by the time she'd walked all the way from her parents' house to Evan's. It was Saturday morning, and she had a lot to do today. She'd gotten quick agreement from Mary about moving into the place next door to Evan, providing dog care and upkeep in exchange for free rent. Then, when Oliver had shown up at the bar last night, she'd hit him up for help moving. He'd promised to be at her parents' place at nine o'clock sharp, but she wasn't surprised when he didn't show. He'd been pretty trashed last night when he'd agreed to help her move.

It had been a brilliant brainstorm on her part, or so she'd thought: she could get help with her move *and* babysit Oliver per Evan's wishes, thus earning her paycheck from him.

The temperature was in the low sixties, warm for the beginning of April, and the sun sprinkled glitter on the water of the bay, visible between the houses. A beautiful Chesapeake day. But Avery was too stressed to truly enjoy it; her stomach was churning. Was moving out of the home she'd grown up in the right thing to do?

She tapped on the front door, but there was no response inside. On a hunch, she walked around to the back of Evan's place. Sure enough, the man was on his deck, drinking coffee and reading the paper, alternately looking out over the bay. Seagulls swooped and cawed, and a pelican cruised low over the water, fishing. Back here there was a breeze that cooled her sweat, and she shivered. "Hey, Evan."

"Avery." Evan stood. "You just passing by? Want a cup of coffee?"

It always kind of freaked her out when men did that, stood up when a lady entered the room, or in this case, stepped into their yard. Nobody her age had that kind of manners. But she had to admit, it made her feel special.

"No coffee, thanks." She walked up onto the deck and leaned against the railing. "I'm moving today. Oliver said he'd help, but he didn't show up."

"He's still asleep. You're moving out of your parents' place?"

"Yeah. Mary's letting me live in the blue house in exchange for taking care of the dogs and doing some yard work." She gestured to the place next door where she'd been visiting twice daily to feed and play with the dogs.

"That's good. The dogs will be better off with someone living there."

"I think so, too, and Mary agrees."

"Hey, listen." He lowered his voice. "We never talked, the other day, about how I'd get money to you, so I got you cash for this first time. I can send you the money electronically, PayPal or Venmo, if that works better."

She took the envelope he was holding out to her, feeling stealthy and weird about it.

"We need to keep it aboveboard, report the income."

"Sure. The truth is, though, I like cash. I'll report it same as I do with my tips."

"Great. I really appreciate this. He's a work in progress, and anything I can do to keep him safe, I want to try it."

"I'll do my best."

"Good." He shook her hand, which made her feel professional and adult. "Welcome to the neighborhood," he said. "Let me go wake up Oliver."

"Thanks." His lack of surprise about her moving in next door made her feel better, like what she was doing was normal and made sense. She walked to the side of the deck closest to the blue house and looked over, let herself feel excited.

Her own place. *Our place*, she said, patting her belly. Away from her mom's anger and her dad's sad eyes. She was so glad she'd gotten the brainstorm to ask, and to offer up extra work around the place. Mary had been concerned that she was taking on too much, what with the bookstore and the Gusty Gull, but Avery knew she could do it.

Honestly, figuring out how to manage her own life was more challenging than any college class, but more worth it, too. The stakes were way, way higher than a grade on a test. She found she didn't mind. College had been more complicated than she'd expected, with weird social stuff to navigate, not just with other students, but with some of the professors. She hadn't grown up hearing stories about college days, since her parents hadn't gone. It was an alien world to her.

At least earning a living was straightforward.

From upstairs she heard male voices. It sounded like Evan and Oliver were shouting at each other, and pretty loud, since she could hear it through the closed windows. When it escalated, she felt bad that she'd caused a fight.

She went inside and up the stairs. She'd tell them there was no need for Oliver to help, let him off the hook.

Although the last thing she wanted to do was ask her parents to help her move. They'd done enough for her already, and besides, it was bound to get way too emotional if they helped.

"Treating me like a kid," Oliver was yelling. "You have no right."

"If you made a commitment, you keep it."

"That's rich, coming from you."

Avery knocked hard on the doorjamb, peeked to make sure Oliver was decent and walked in.

Oliver's gear was spread all over the room, dirty clothes on the floor, the wastebasket spilling over with empties. Oliver was propped up on his elbows, shirtless but wearing sweats.

He had nice muscles. Clearly, he was cut from the same cloth as his dad, who was also built, to the point where girls her age speculated about him. He was a dad, but younger than her own father and the dads of her friends.

Now, though, he looked just the same as any frustrated father.

Oliver's sneer had died when she walked in, but not quickly enough that she didn't see it. "I was expecting you at my house this morning," she said.

Oliver frowned. "How come?"

That was what she'd been afraid of. He'd made the promise while drinking, and he didn't remember it. "You said you'd help me move today. You don't remember?"

"Nope."

Avery glanced at Evan. Concern was written all over his face. "He really did promise me," she said.

"That's what bothers me. Blackouts mean your drinking problem's getting worse."

"Says the expert."

"Don't start." She sat down on the foot of the bed. "Your

dad has coffee. That'll help you wake up." She didn't have a problem bossing him around, because he reminded her a little bit of her twin, Aiden.

Although Aiden had never looked *this* hungover.

"I'll fix you a travel cup." As Evan left, Avery could see he looked relieved that Oliver was now in her hands.

Well, he *was* paying her to babysit him.

"Be right back," Oliver said as soon as his dad had gone downstairs. He sprinted out of the room and down the hall, and she heard him throwing up in the bathroom.

Again, nothing she hadn't seen from her brother and her college roommates. Nothing she hadn't done herself, before she'd been forced by the baby to grow up.

Still, she didn't exactly want to listen. She went down and stood outside the bathroom. "Clean up and come down. I'll be out by your car. And hurry. We gotta do this fast."

He mumbled something that indicated he'd heard, and she went downstairs. With a wave to Evan, she headed outside.

HALF AN HOUR LATER they were at Avery's house. They lived in a double wide set on a patch of land on the bay. Things were a little brown now, but shoots of Mom's daffodils pushed up all around the house. Dad had built a little front porch, where you could sit and talk to anyone who walked by. Out back was the dock and their fishing boat, and to one side, blocking the view of the next trailer down, was a big apple tree she and Aiden had climbed as kids.

She'd never thought twice about her home, but now she saw it through Oliver's eyes. He looked from it to her like he'd just realized they didn't have a whole lot.

How had Oliver grown up? she wondered. She'd figured

he must be struggling like everyone else, since his parents were divorced and his father didn't live fancy. Come to think of it, he had a nice, expensive car. Not much cash, though.

It didn't take long to load her boxes into Oliver's SUV. When they were finished, she left Oliver drinking coffee and leaning back in the driver's seat with his eyes closed, and she went in search of her mother.

She found Mom out back, digging in her flower garden. Avery stood and watched her for a minute, feeling like she wanted to memorize her. Mom wore her Saturday jeans, holey but not in a stylish way, her old Nike sneakers and a red T-shirt from the restaurant up the shore where she used to waitress. She attacked a clump of zebra grass with her shovel, viciously.

"We're taking off, Mom," Avery said.

Mom went still for a minute, then jammed the shovel into the ground and came over, peeling off her gardening gloves. "Okay. If you need anything, you know where to find me."

Avery *did* need something. She needed Mom to fix her problems, make things easy for her.

The trouble was the size of her problems was bigger than when she'd been a kid. Not fixable by a mom.

Still. "Are you sure this is the right move? I can stay."

"No." Mom shook her head back and forth rapidly. "No. You need to get on your own or we'll strangle each other. And it'll be easier on your dad. Speaking of which, he'll be back soon, so…"

"Tell him I love him." Geez, she felt like she was moving halfway around the world instead of halfway across town.

"I will. Now, scoot."

But instead of scooting, she walked forward and pulled

Mom into her arms. Her mother was stiff as a board, until she loosened and hugged back, and when Avery stepped back, she saw that Mom's eyes were watery. Mom, who hadn't cried a tear when she and Aiden had moved into their college dorms last year. That made Avery tear up.

They looked at each other. "Shoot," Mom said, "you're walking distance away. And you're coming home tomorrow after church, for Easter dinner. Right?"

"Right." But even that wasn't going to necessarily be easy. She dreaded seeing Dad, who didn't yet even know about the move. Maybe that had been cowardly on Avery's part, but she hoped he'd handle it better after the fact and with Mom's soothing way of presenting things to him.

Moving out was the right thing, but it felt really, really scary.

CASSIE WALKED BACK home from the bookstore at midday on Saturday, swinging her heavy shopping bag. She couldn't wait to dive into the eclectic mix of books she'd purchased, particularly the one on enhancing an online business.

That was actually why she'd gone to the store. Mary had ordered the book for her and it had just come in.

Since Mary's bookshop did a brisk online business, in addition to the storefront, she knew a lot about attracting online customers, and Cassie had hung out awhile talking to her. Mary had terrific ideas about ways Cassie could expand. And Mary, good bookseller that she was, had suggested several more books Cassie might find useful, as well as the novel they were reading for the store's next book club meeting.

Mary hadn't just tried to sell her books, though. She'd

gotten Cassie a cup of tea and they'd sat down together for a good half hour, talking.

She'd keep an eye on the teenagers here as they worked, see if any of them showed an interest and a knack for sewing work. If they did, Mary had suggested that she set up an internship. Good for the kids, good for her. Someone else might be enlisted to help with the accounting side of things, and yet another to do social media. It was a way to expand the dolls project into something bigger, something that would benefit not only the doll recipients, but also the teens of Pleasant Shores.

Cassie was feeling better all the time, she realized. Not exactly getting over the loss of Josh, but starting to live again alongside the grief. Working with the teens, and now thinking about building up her business, all of it was making her see the future in a positive light.

She came around the corner and stopped.

There was Evan, and he was talking to…Mom and Donald? They weren't supposed to arrive until tomorrow. She quickened her steps. "Mom! Is everything okay?"

"Surprise!" Donald said when he saw her.

Mom spun around and opened up her arms. "Hi, honey!"

Cassie's anxiety lightened. Mom didn't look bad. "I thought you were coming tomorrow, that's all. But I'm glad to see you now." Over Mom's shoulder, she raised an eyebrow at Donald.

"Your mom was so eager to see you, we decided to come early," he said.

Immediately, Cassie understood. When Mom got anxious, it was best to do something rather than sit around. As Mom's counselor said, distraction was often the name of the game.

"And we brought the car," he added, gesturing to Josh's vehicle and his own, parked right behind it. "When we head back on Monday, we'll pack and then leave on our trip."

"Perfect." Cassie could only hope it would all work out as planned. "I have to warn you, I don't exactly have Easter dinner ready to go."

"We do!" Mom opened the back of their hatchback to reveal grocery bags, as well as two overnight bags. "We didn't want you to overexert yourself, honey. I know how tired you get."

"You didn't have to do that!" Cassie looked from Mom to Donald, who was sliding an arm around Mom, his expression worried. "But I'm glad you did. You're a much better cook than I am." And the truth was she'd been planning to buy most of the stuff already made.

She glanced at Evan and found him looking at her. One corner of his mouth quirked up as if he knew there were undercurrents, even if he didn't know what they were. "Can I help you carry things in?" he offered.

"That would be great." With all of them helping, they made short work of hauling food bags and suitcases inside.

While Mom and Donald settled into the guest room, Cassie walked Evan out. "Thank you for helping," she said.

"Of course." He turned toward his place.

And she didn't want him to go. Didn't want to sink back into her role as the supposed invalid in Mom and Donald's world. She wanted to stay the adult, the independent individual, the woman who felt like a woman. She was starting to find all those sides of her, with Evan's help.

She reached out and touched his sleeve, so softly she wasn't sure he noticed.

But he must have, because he turned back.

Some of what she felt must have shown in her eyes. His expression softened. "You okay with…all that?" He nodded sideways toward the house.

"Yeah." She swallowed. "They're great. They want the best for me."

"They do." He reached out and caught her hand in his bigger, callused one. "So do I, Cassie."

His eyes were locked on hers.

He started to let go of her hand, but she wouldn't let him. She clasped his fingers and, when his gaze darkened, looked out toward the bay to dodge it. She swallowed and sucked in a too-loud breath.

He stepped closer, and his other hand, the one she wasn't holding, touched her face with featherlight gentleness. "You'll be great," he said, his voice husky. "You'll have a good time with your family this weekend."

A breeze blew the fragrance from a flowering tree their way, deliciously light and sweet. She could hear some little kids down the block, shrieking joyously at a game they were playing.

She wanted, so badly, to turn her lips into his cupped hand. Wanted to kiss it. But there was a reason she shouldn't.

Evan couldn't possibly handle her issues; no man could.

But did that mean she couldn't ever explore this breathless longing?

His thumb stroked her cheek like it was precious. Like *she* was precious. "I should go in," he said. "See what Oliver's doing." But his hand stayed close to her face, stroking.

"Don't."

His thumb went still. "Don't what?"

"Don't go." She dared to look up at his face, and then

wished she hadn't, because there was something there, some intensity in his eyes that burned like a hot coal. "Don't go, because I..." She had no idea how to finish that sentence.

"Ah, Cass." His voice had a little bit of a smile in it, but not like he was laughing at her. More like they shared a funny secret. "This is tough."

"It is. I don't know why, but it is." Neither of them named what they were talking about, but they both knew.

What she didn't know was why. This was Evan, whom she'd known since she was a child. Josh's friend. She remembered him playing cowboys with Josh. Remembered how, once, Evan had stopped in the middle of a game to pick up one of her dolls and tuck it into her arms, when she'd been too tired and out of it to know she'd dropped it.

She remembered him staying for dinner, too, night after night, and that made her think of a way to change the subject. "What are you and Oliver doing for Easter?"

He shrugged, glanced toward his house. "I don't know, I guess I'll...cook something?"

"If you don't have plans," she heard herself say, "would the two of you like to join us for Easter dinner?"

CHAPTER NINE

HAD IT BEEN a mistake to invite Evan and his son for Easter dinner? Cassie wondered as she and her mother made up the guest bed in the spare room.

It might be asking for trouble, especially with Oliver joining the group. Donald had frowned when she'd told him and Mom about the invitation; he was undoubtedly planning his next speech about how Cassie was too young and inexperienced for a man like Evan.

Mom's mouth had tightened, too. She hadn't said anything more about it to Cassie, not yet, but Cassie knew her mom. The wheels were turning, and she was planning how to frame her objections.

The trouble was Cassie *knew* it was a bad idea, but it was as if her mouth had a mind of its own, and once she'd said the words, she couldn't take them back.

"It's a cute place," Mom said as they pulled up the comforter and spread the throw pillows. She walked over to the window and looked out. "Nice views from up here."

Cassie went to stand beside her mother. You could see Pleasant Shores's downtown from here, though once the trees came into full leaf, that wouldn't be the case. For now, though, the little shops and a few pedestrians were visible. "There's Lighthouse Lit," she said, pointing to the lighthouse-shaped shop that anchored the little row of retail and dining establishments. "That's the place Mary owns. Mary Rhoades, who came with Evan to pick me up?"

"I remember. She was lovely." Mom looked over at Cassie, thoughtfully.

Cassie wanted to postpone the inevitable discussion of Evan. "Come into my room, and you can see my view of the bay," she said.

Mom complied. "Very pretty place," she said. "I didn't expect to see so many boats this early in the year."

"Some are fishing boats, like those two," Cassie said, pointing. "I'm surprised to see the sailboats, though. Doesn't seem quite warm enough." They talked on a little more and then Mom headed downstairs, saying she needed to help Donald with the food they'd brought. Cassie had the feeling they were skirting the surface, but she wanted to keep it that way.

Ace padded into the room and stuck his nose in her hand, and she knelt to give him a chest rub, then leaned her head against his. "You're my pal, aren't you? Maybe we'll take a little W-A-L-K in a bit." With that in mind, she put on her Vans and tied back her hair in a high ponytail.

On the way downstairs, Ace beside her, she heard Donald's rumbling voice. "You need to talk to her. It's better coming from you."

Uh-oh. What did Mom have to tell her? She didn't want another lecture about Evan being inappropriate, but that would be way better than bad news about Mom, or a cancellation of their trip.

If it *was* about Evan, better to get things out in the open so that they didn't emerge in the middle of Easter dinner.

"There's the big boy who needs a walk," Mom said, holding out her hands to Ace, who ambled over to her. She knelt to pet him and then looked up at Cassie. "Want me to come? Have some girl talk?"

No. "Sure, Mom," she said.

They walked outside to see Avery standing at the curb by the driver's side of Oliver's SUV. He was inside, and they seemed to be having a heated conversation. Cassie waved, and Avery said something into the car, slapped the hood of it and walked toward Cassie and her mother. "Guess what? I'm your new neighbor now," she said. "Don't worry, I'll be quiet and keep to myself."

"You moved in here? That's great!" Cassie really liked the young woman.

Avery smiled at Cassie's mom, and Cassie introduced them.

"You seem so young to be on your own." Mom looked worried.

"My parents live down by the docks," Avery said, waving a hand in that direction. "They're close. We just needed a little space."

Cassie glanced sideways at Mom to see how that struck her. Cassie had needed space, too, more of it, but it had taken her a lot longer than Avery to seize it. And for Mom to accept it. "I'm glad you're my neighbor," she said. "Let me know if you need anything."

"Same." Avery headed into the little blue cottage. "Nice to meet you, Mrs. Thomas," she called over her shoulder.

They turned and started walking toward the water, but as soon as they were out of Avery's earshot, Mom nudged Cassie. "I think that girl is pregnant," she said.

Cassie nodded. "She is."

"Is she on her own?"

Even though Cassie knew it came from a place of concern, the question made Cassie uncomfortable. "I don't know, Mom. I didn't ask if the father was involved."

"Well." They walked a few minutes, and Cassie was opening her mouth to tell Mom about some of the things they were passing when Mom said, "You know, seeing that girl brings up something I want to talk with you about."

Please don't let this be a sex ed talk. She and Mom had never been the "talk openly about everything" types. Mom had done her best to make sure Cassie knew the right facts at the right time, but mostly by sharing informative books and booklets. Talking about it directly would have been too embarrassing for both of them.

Mom's pace picked up. "I'm concerned about your getting involved with Evan Stone," she said. "You don't want to end up like that young woman back there, pregnant and dealing with it alone."

The leap Mom had made was so ridiculous that Cassie laughed. "Evan's my friend, Mom," she said, even though a tiny part of her brain reminded her of the vibes that had been passing between them. "He's been kind to help me get settled here, but believe me, he has plenty on his plate. He's not thinking about me that way, and I'm not thinking about him in any other way than a friend." Not to mention that it was unlikely Cassie could even get pregnant, given the chemo and radiation's effect on her body. Mom didn't like to talk about that, though. For that matter, neither did Cassie.

"You were quick to invite him to Easter dinner."

"He and his son are alone—"

"His *son* is here with him?"

Might as well get everything out in the open. "That kid

Avery was talking to, in the SUV, that was Oliver. Evan's son. He's staying here in town for a while."

"Well." Mom looked almost relieved. "Seeing his son, seeing how old he is, that ought to cure you of any romantic feelings you might have about him." She shook her head. "I'll never forget the disaster that was."

"Disaster what was?" Cassie asked, although she was pretty sure she knew.

"Now, mind you, I like Evan. But he was always a little advanced for his age, if you know what I mean." She glanced over at Cassie. "It was his parents' fault. He saw too much when he was small."

Cassie nodded. She hadn't known Evan's parents well, probably because Mom had sheltered her from them. But Josh had told her how Evan had to help them to bed, clean up after them, even talk to the police when they'd gotten into trouble. That was probably why he'd ended up becoming a cop.

"But even for Evan, having an affair with a *teacher* was beyond the pale."

Cassie's jaw almost dropped. "A teacher? I never heard that."

"Well, a student teacher. It wasn't commonly known. Her family and Evan's hushed it up, because of course, she'd very likely be liable for what happened."

Cassie was still reeling. "She took advantage of him! How old was he, anyway?"

"Evan insisted he was the aggressor. I do admire that about him. He took responsibility, even though he was only...sixteen? Seventeen?"

Cassie kicked a stone and tried to remember, or imagine, Evan at that young age. But although he and Josh had been so close in childhood, they'd parted ways in the later years of high school. Evan, she now remembered, had moved away.

Had he done that because of getting a *teacher* pregnant?

She didn't have to wonder long, because Mom took up the story. "Apparently, the young woman was on probation with her teaching, anyway. She'd squeaked into the education program and it didn't shock anyone that she quit, although the reasons for it would have been shocking, had they been known."

"They must have gotten married," Cassie mused, "because he's mentioned his ex-wife. At least, I assume he's talking about Oliver's mom."

"Yes. They would have had to get parental permission, given Evan's age, but that wouldn't have been a problem."

Cassie looked over at her mother. "Why haven't you ever told me this before?"

"It seemed like gossip. Nothing you needed to know about."

"Protecting me again?"

"Honey, I know I'm overprotective. Donald and I have talked about it, and the counselor has helped me to see it. But now—" She broke off.

"Now what?" They'd gravitated toward a bench that looked out over the bay, and both of them sat.

"Now," Mom said, "it seems more protective to tell you the truth about what you'd be managing, if you got involved with Evan Stone."

"I see." And she kind of did. But as they moved on to chat about the boats on the bay, and Cassie's doll project and, inevitably, her health, Cassie continued to think about what she'd learned.

She didn't think less of Evan, exactly. He'd been young, full of hormones. And clearly, he'd paid the price for what he'd done, with an early marriage, early divorce and years of child support to pay.

The whole thing just seemed to put him more out of her league, though. While she'd been literally playing with dolls, he'd become a father.

When she'd been seventeen, she'd been so backward that she'd barely had friends, let alone dates, let alone heavy involvement with a teacher, of all things.

Cassie almost wished she could un-ask Evan and Oliver for Easter dinner, but she couldn't.

She just hoped it wouldn't be an embarrassing disaster.

AGREEING TO COME to Easter dinner with Cassie and her family had been a mistake.

Evan had to admit that the ham and potatoes smelled awesome, as did the home-baked pie and cake. Oliver would love it, if he ever got here.

Cassie and her mother were putting the finishing touches on the meal. The family had invited him to join them at church, but he'd declined. He should go, needed to go, but he'd taken an extra overnight shift so one of the other officers could travel to see family. He'd gotten home, whipped, to find Oliver's bed empty.

He'd texted and called, and finally a blurry Oliver had answered. He claimed he'd driven to the college town up the shore, met some people, gone to a party. He hadn't wanted to drive drunk, so he'd slept in his car. Yes, he'd sobered up and would be home soon, in time for Easter dinner.

Only he wasn't.

"Should we hold up dinner for Oliver?" Cassie asked

him, looking over from the carrots she was chopping for salad.

"No. I don't know when, or if, he'll get here. Sorry for the last-minute change."

"Is he okay?"

"He says he is." Evan rubbed the back of his neck. "He's a little out of control. I need to keep better tabs on him."

"Tough to do when he's legally an adult."

Cassie's mother came back into the kitchen. "Just because your child becomes an adult," she said, "that doesn't mean you stop worrying about them."

"No, it doesn't." Evan exchanged a look with Cassie's mom, probably the first honest connection he'd felt with her since he was a kid visiting her house. "Honestly, I had no idea what to expect when Oliver came to stay with me, but it wasn't this."

"Welcome to parenthood." Mrs. Thomas used a clean spoon to taste the gravy. She shook her head, ground in a little pepper.

Donald was out in the other room watching a basketball game, and Evan intended to join him, knew it was expected. But he found it hard to leave the cozy kitchen.

Watching Cassie and her mom together, cooking and serving, brought back the many days he'd spent at their house, eating grilled cheese sandwiches and tomato soup, at a clean table in a warm kitchen. They'd tasted so good.

In some unformed part of his ten-year-old brain he'd thought: I want this. This warm, safe home. A baby—that had been Cassie—in a bouncy chair, clearly adored by both her mom and her big brother.

It hadn't been perfect. Josh and Cassie's father had been a jerk, and he'd left soon after Cassie had gotten sick, and her mom had slid into the depression and anxiety from which she'd never completely recovered.

No, Evan hadn't really aspired to perfection, even back then, but he'd wanted to live in a home where people loved each other, where their first impulse was to take care of other people rather than following their own desires and addictions.

Of course, Evan had gone on to create exactly the kind of home he'd come from when he'd become a father at seventeen. He hadn't given a thought to what Kelly needed or wanted. He'd spent more time counting how many beers were left in the fridge than counting his blessings. And although he'd changed the occasional diaper and fed the occasional bottle, he'd rarely done it without wishing he were somewhere else, getting something he wanted for himself, feeding his own desires.

Now, he'd welcome the opportunity to help Oliver, care for him, cheer him on. But it was too little, too late.

"The thing is," Cassie said, "you have to let kids make their own mistakes, try things out, live their lives. How else will they learn?"

"Oh, but honey. When mistakes can have such a high price…"

"Exactly," Evan said. "It can be life or death. No way can a parent stand by and watch their child put themselves into danger."

"Sure, but you said Oliver decided not to drive while he was drinking, right? So he's making a responsible choice."

"Your son has been drinking?"

"Without a doubt," Evan said. He looked directly into Mrs. Thomas's eyes. "Runs in the family, you might say."

Donald came into the kitchen. "Dinner about ready? It's halftime."

Mrs. Thomas picked up the big plate of ham and put it into his hands. "Here, carry this to the table. We'll be ready to eat in five minutes, and no, you won't get to see every minute of the second half." She patted his shoulder. "You'll survive."

Donald gave Evan a wry grin as he carried away the ham. Everyone grabbed something, and they were soon eating a very good meal.

Evan sent off a quick text to Oliver with a photo of the table, figuring that if anything drew him, it would be food. But there was no response.

They talked about Josh a little, but it wasn't as sad as Evan would have expected. And although he knew that Cassie worried about her parents, and vice versa, their love for each other was also clear.

It was a sharp contrast to Evan. Both his family of origin, where no holiday dinner would have been peaceful nor alcohol-free, and his nonexistent relationship with his son and failed relationship with his wife and son.

Deliberately, he pushed aside thoughts of the past. The ham was delicious, and the women finally allowed the basketball game to be turned on quietly in the background, and it was almost enjoyable.

Almost. Evan couldn't help but worry about Oliver. Where was he, and what was he doing?

When his phone buzzed he apologized and pulled it out. It wasn't Oliver. It was work. "Sorry," he said, standing, "I have to take this." He walked out into the kitchen. "Hey, Earl, what's up?"

"Sorry to bother you on Easter," his boss said, "but I thought you'd want to know that we brought your son in."

"For what? Is he okay?"

"He's okay," Earl said, "but still drunk. And his car is totaled."

CHAPTER TEN

CASSIE COULD TELL from Evan's face that something was wrong.

"I'll be right down." Evan ended the call and leaned into the dining room. "I have to leave," he said. "I'm sorry, but Oliver is in some kind of trouble."

Cassie stood. "What is it? Can we help?"

He shook his head, his face impassive, closed off. "I need to go."

"Let us know, okay?" Cassie walked him to the door. "I'll be praying for Oliver. And for you."

"Thanks." It was absurd to feel hurt that he wasn't telling her what was going on.

After Evan left and they'd cleaned up, Cassie brought down a doll she was working on and Mom pulled out her embroidery. Donald was still watching basketball, turned low, dozing off and on in the recliner.

"I'm worried about Oliver," Cassie admitted. She shifted around in her chair, trying to get comfortable. Finally, she sat on the floor and laid the pieces of her doll dress out on the coffee table to pin the seams together.

"From Evan's reaction, I expect he's fine, but in trouble with the law." Mom jabbed her needle into the pillow top she was making. Mom had taught Cassie to sew, all those years ago, and they'd spent many evenings doing projects together. "Did you say he just arrived recently to stay with Evan, dear?"

Cassie nodded. "Just about a week ago. Apparently, Evan hadn't seen him for years before that."

"I saw a television show where someone showed up claiming to be the main character's son, but it was an imposter. That's such a pretty fabric, dear."

Cassie held up the dress so Mom could see it better. "No way is Oliver an imposter. He looks exactly how Evan used to look."

"Uh-oh. He'll end up being a ladies' man."

Was Evan a ladies' man? Cassie had to force herself not to ask, even though she really wanted to know, because she didn't want to increase Mom's suspicions about her feelings for Evan.

She herself had been so sheltered, had such limited experience, and he and Josh had been nine years older. By the time she would have understood such a thing as a ladies' man, Evan had moved on into his adult life.

The idea of Evan having lots of conquests struck her wrong. Just another way he was out of her reach.

Cassie pulled up the video of the little girl she was making the doll for on her phone. She held it up so Mom could see.

"Poor little thing," Mom said.

Little Rita *was* a poor little thing, Cassie supposed, just as she herself had been. But in the video, what Cassie saw was restlessness. The child tossed from side to side, face pink and heated-looking, tears drying on her cheeks. She kept pushing herself up to look out the window and then falling back onto the bed.

Cassie could identify with that desire to escape. To love, to be free, to have adventures.

She shouldn't have that desire, feel that restless. She should just want the best for others, Oliver and Evan, Mom and Donald; she shouldn't think about herself. Evan had his hands full trying to connect with his troubled adult son. Mom, who'd sacrificed so much to raise Cassie and Josh alone, was now struggling with depression and anxiety and the loss of her son. Those needs were so much bigger than any desire Cassie had to break out of her cage.

A better person would feel content sitting here sewing with her mother.

But the truth was she was twenty-eight and had the emotions and desires to prove it, despite the occasional limitations of her body.

She should have gone out and had adventures when she was younger, like most kids did, like Josh had. But she hadn't been healthy enough.

Maybe not brave enough.

"I think I'll text Evan, see if he and Oliver can come for dessert." Cassie stood, grabbed her phone and walked quickly into the kitchen.

Mom followed her, and as Cassie scrolled for Evan's name, put a hand on her arm. "Honey."

Cassie looked up. "What?"

"He doesn't want to hear from you right now. You can't bother men when they're coping with something."

Cassie folded her arms. "Is that some kind of a rule?"

"It comes from years of experience with your father and then Donald. Let Evan cope with whatever he's coping with. He'll tell you about it when he's ready, if he ever *is* ready."

"I just want to know if Oliver's okay."

Again, Mom put a hand over hers. "You're having strong feelings for Evan, and it's the first time. You shouldn't follow every one of your own whims about it. Men prefer if you hold back a little."

Slowly, Cassie slid her phone back into her pocket. Was Mom right?

As she heated slices of pie and scooped ice cream, she longed for Josh. He would've been able to tell her how today's relationships really worked.

Mom wasn't right that she'd never had feelings for anyone before. After moving in with Josh, Cassie had started dating one of the men she worked with. They'd both been earning masters degrees and, meanwhile, building up their experience by working in temporary positions as therapeutic support staff. They'd been thrown together a lot, and it had only seemed natural to start dating.

Josh had been great. He'd insisted on meeting the guy, playing the protective big brother, and he'd approved of Derek. He just hadn't liked him. "He's too boring for you," he'd told Cassie. "You need someone with a little more drive."

Someone like Evan, she thought now. What would Josh think about the possibility of the two of them getting together?

But she was being an idiot, she told herself firmly. Whether Mom was right or wrong, Cassie needed to stand on her own two feet, not wring her hands over a guy who was probably inappropriate.

Resolutely, she stuffed her phone in her purse so she wouldn't be tempted to text Evan, and carried plates of pie and ice cream into the living room.

In the doorway, she stopped.

Mom had sat down beside Donald, very close, and he was looking at her with warm adoration in his eyes.

Cassie didn't usually notice that in Donald; he was so practical and so good at caretaking. Now, though, she saw that he and Mom were longing to spend time together. That although Mom was urging caution for Cassie—both of them were, really—the two of them had each other and were headed for adventure.

That didn't mean Cassie could or should do the same, but at a moment like this, she sure wanted to.

AFTER A SHORT conversation with his boss, Earl Green, Evan took Oliver's things and went to the interview room.

Oliver was slumped over at the scarred table, resting his head in his arms.

"Hey." Evan put his hand on Oliver's shoulder. "You okay?"

Oliver jerked as if he'd been sleeping and shrugged away Evan's hand. "Am I free to go?"

"Yeah. I worked it out with Earl. Do you need to go to the hospital? Sounds like it was quite a crash."

"Is my car okay?" Oliver stood and stretched, not even looking stiff, which matched what Earl had said: Oliver seemed to have escaped without a scratch.

"No, your car's not okay." How out of it had Oliver been when they'd brought him in, not to realize the seriousness of the accident? "It's totaled. We'll have someone haul it up the shore, see if we can sell it for parts."

Oliver cursed. "I need my car!"

Evan's eyebrows shot up. "You're lucky to be alive," Evan said, "and you're lucky I was able to work things out with Earl so that there are no charges."

"Thanks." Oliver got to his feet, grabbed his coat and keys from Evan and headed out of the station.

"I'm parked over here." Evan led the way to his truck, and Oliver climbed in. "We need to talk."

"Not now." Oliver leaned his head back against the seat and stared up at the ceiling.

"Yes, now." Evan pulled the truck into the little park beside the bay.

Little kids ran around, dressed in colorful clothes, carrying baskets. It took Evan a minute to realize why: it was Easter.

That brought up thoughts of the Easter dinner they were missing. No way would he take Oliver over to Cassie's place now, not as surly and hungover as he seemed to be. "What happened with the car this morning? Earl said you hit a tree."

"I lost control." Oliver looked out at the kids, and his face brightened. "I remember doing egg hunts."

"Yeah?" Evan didn't know how this parenting thing was supposed to work. Should he stick to Oliver's fairly major infraction, or let him cheer himself up on memory lane?

"Oh, yeah, but you wouldn't know, because you were never there." Oliver's voice was back to surly.

"There were reasons—"

"Like that you were a drunk?"

Evan blew out a breath. He could recognize deflection of blame when he saw it. But maybe the car crash had shaken out Oliver's feelings, and it was best to deal with them before everything went back underground. "When you were little, yes. I was a drunk. That's why your mom gave up on me and moved you guys out of state."

"And then you got sober."

Evan nodded. "Fifteen years last week."

"But you couldn't come visit your son in all that time."

The words stabbed at Evan. "I thought you were better off without me, and so did your mom."

"I probably was." Oliver stared out the window.

Evan had always known he'd hurt his son, failed at the family thing, but the stiff set of his son's back gave him a visceral feeling for what that meant. "I was wrong. I should have pushed past your mom and insisted on being involved in your life."

"Ya think?" Oliver's voice dripped with sarcasm. He opened the truck door. "I'm done with this conversation."

As he slid out, Evan realized that he'd failed again. The talk they'd just had was a small-scale version of his past eighteen years of nonparenting.

He looked back toward the happy families, the daddies helping their kids find eggs, the mommies lifting toddlers into the Easter bunny's lap. Beyond them was the expanse of the bay, idyllic now, dappled in sun.

Evan turned and watched Oliver stalk toward his place, and suddenly he realized he didn't have to do it again. He didn't have to back away. He could push for involvement, connection. And maybe Oliver didn't want that, but Evan was pretty sure he needed it. He started the truck and drove over to pull up beside Oliver. He lowered the window. "Get in."

"No way." Oliver's voice was scornful.

"I mean it. Now."

Oliver's steps slowed, and he looked over at Evan and rolled his eyes.

Just behind the sneering mask, though, Evan saw a world of pain.

He thought about the cop who'd set him straight as a teen. Evan had been younger than Oliver was now, all of eighteen. He'd been drowning his sorrows at a local bar. But he'd also been married, with an angry wife and a col-icky new baby—Oliver—back home in a crappy apartment.

The cop had watched him leave the bar, get into his ancient subcompact and drive a block. Then he'd pulled in front of Evan and forced him off the road. He'd read Evan the riot act, told him he could have killed himself or someone else, driving drunk like that, that he ought to be arrested.

He'd painted such a vivid picture of what all that would look like that Evan had gotten choked up.

And then the cop had told Evan he had two choices—a DUI, or AA and the marines.

The officer had driven Evan home and waited while he talked over the options with Kelly. Since he would have lost his license, which would affect his ability to work—and since they weren't getting along that well, anyway—Kelly had almost immediately green-lighted the marines idea. Evan had quit drinking and attended an AA meeting every day, with that cop calling or stopping by most eve-nings to check on him, and at the end of two weeks Evan had enlisted.

It had worked. Evan had continued attending meetings throughout the years he'd spent in the marines. He'd sent most of his paychecks home to Kelly, and he'd stayed sober. The structure, being told what to do, feeling like he was making something of himself and had a goal, had really fixed up his life.

When he'd gotten out, he'd thought he could make the marriage work, that he could handle drinking again, but he'd been wrong on both counts. Things had gone down-hill with Kelly, and after a few too many nights of coming home drunk, she'd left with Oliver.

At which point he'd hit bottom. Only the structure of the police academy, and a commitment to AA for life, had made him better.

It was too late for him to go back and redo the family life he'd failed at so badly. Probably too late for him to build a decent relationship with his son. But he could maybe pass on the lessons about structure that had pulled him back from the edge.

"Get in here," he ordered Oliver, "or pack up and get out of town."

His heart was pounding because he didn't think he could actually kick out his son. But he kept his drill sergeant face on, didn't let his weakness show.

"How can I leave when I don't have a car?" Oliver kicked at a stone. His voice held a little bit of childlike whining, but Evan figured it was his due: Kelly had dealt with the whining and misbehavior that Oliver, like all kids, must have gone through growing up.

Now it was Evan's turn. Time to be the father he'd never been, or try to be. He lifted one shoulder. "Not my concern. You're only my concern if you get in the truck."

Cursing, Oliver climbed in.

Evan wasn't a really religious man, but he shot up a prayer of thanks. "Let me tell you how it's going to be, from here on out," he began.

CHAPTER ELEVEN

"WELL, THAT WAS UNPRODUCTIVE." Cassie was so frustrated that she had to unclench her fists in order to climb into the passenger seat of Evan's truck. She waved his assistance away. "No, don't. I'm so annoyed with their patronizing attitudes that I'd probably punch you if you helped me into the truck."

Evan backed up, raising his hands. Then waited for her to climb in and closed the door for her. Since it was Evan's day off, they'd taken the afternoon to drive to Minestown to talk to the police in person and see what they could find out about Josh's investigation.

Not much, as it turned out. So now they were going to make another stop.

Evan put the car into gear. "You sure you want to do this?" he asked.

Cassie pushed aside her mixed feelings. "No, but I think it'll help me get closure. And maybe I'll remember something."

"If you're sure, then I agree. It's worth a try."

Twenty minutes later they were parked in front of the row house she'd shared with Josh.

The sun was starting to set, visible through strips of clouds, glowing red-orange. At the same time rain was falling, gentle and light. A strange day.

Cassie stared at the apartment and didn't move, but

her mind worked overtime, playing images. She and Josh laughing on the porch, having a beer together, Cassie's first. Josh helping her carry in a funky dresser from an art show, a token of her independent tastes, different from her mother's. She and Josh playing fetch with Ace in the narrow front yard.

She remembered sitting on the front steps, telling Josh about her dream of working for herself. He'd been the one to encourage her to take her dolls to a professional level. To set up a website, to make what amounted to sales calls to organizations that worked with families of sick kids. Josh had mentored her in business networking, something that hadn't come naturally to her. No one had been happier than Josh when her idea had caught on and the orders had started flowing in.

He'd wanted her to achieve her dreams. Yet, he hadn't had the chance to achieve his.

"I remember this place." Evan pounded a fist on the steering wheel, lightly, and shook his head. "Wish I'd spent more time here."

"I know." This strong, capable man was going through a loss, just as she was. What would have happened if Evan and Josh had stayed close? Or if Josh had consulted Evan, a trained officer of the law, on this last case, rather than trying to deal with it solo?

There was movement on the porch next to their old one, and Cassie's heart filled with poignant warmth. She climbed out of the truck, waving for Evan to stay where he was.

Her old neighbor, Jayla, was coming out her front door.

"Hey, Jay," Cassie called softly, and Jayla turned toward her. The woman's eyes widened and her hand flew to her chest.

"Cassie?"

And then they walked toward each other and hugged for a long time.

"Girl, it is so good to see you," Jayla said as they finally stepped back, clasping each other's hands. "I've been wanting to call you, but...you just never know what to say, you know? I didn't want to make things worse."

"I get it." And she really did. Jayla had been that neighbor who'd turned into a real friend, first to Josh, and then to Josh and Cassie.

She and Josh had been a pair among the neighbors. It must feel wrong for them to be friends with Cassie alone.

Jayla pulled her to the porch where they could stand under the roof, out of the rain. "How *are* you? What have you been doing in the past four months?"

"I spent some time with my mom, healing and helping her out, but now I'm ready to move on. Part of which means, try to figure out who took Josh out and why, what he had going on." She glanced over at the apartment next door, hers and Josh's. "The police have basically given up."

"Big surprise," Jayla said. Everyone knew the Minestown police force was overworked and understaffed.

The lack of progress infuriated Cassie. *Everything* about this situation infuriated her. It wasn't fair that Josh wasn't inside right now, ready to come out with a joke and a smile. Despite the serious nature of his job, he'd been a positive, upbeat person. A person in his prime.

Killing him was like mowing down the spring flowers Jayla had planted along her front walk. They were beautiful, thriving. Not anywhere near the end of their life cycle.

Josh hadn't been, either.

Anger at his murderer wasn't going to help her find the jerk. She needed to stay calm, the way Evan stayed calm.

But Josh had been her brother. Her only brother. She'd looked up to him and loved him since she was a baby. She couldn't help feeling angry, furious, even murderous toward the man who'd stolen his life.

She looked at the less-pretty bushes in front of her old place. And then she gasped and went over and pulled Josh's old football out from where it had been stuck in the thick evergreen branches.

He used to throw a football with kids in the neighborhood, most weekends. The loss of him wasn't just to her, but to a street full of kids who'd looked up to him and, maybe, considered him a role model.

She set down the football in front of the bushes, so it would be visible to the kids Josh had played with. He'd have wanted one of them to have it.

"Who's your helper?" Jayla asked.

Cassie turned back toward the truck and beckoned, and Evan got out.

"Hmm." Jayla's head tilted to one side. "White guys aren't my thing, but if they were…"

"I know, right?" They both watched as he approached, moving in that loose-boned way of his, so at ease in his own skin. "We're not together, though," she said quietly before Evan reached them. "He's Josh's friend."

"Mmm-hmm." Jayla looked sideways at Cassie, then held out her hand and introduced herself to Evan before Cassie could do it. "Why don't y'all come in for a cup of tea? I was headed to Whole Foods, but that can wait."

"You're sure?" Evan asked. "We don't want to derail your plans."

"You have a class tonight, right?" Cassie remembered that Jayla had always taught an evening yoga class on Tuesdays and Thursdays.

"I have extra time. I'll put my errands off until later. Come in. We have to at least catch up for a few minutes."

"Thanks, that would be great," Cassie said, then looked over at Evan. "You don't mind, do you?"

"It's fine," Evan said, and they followed Jayla inside.

Jayla's place was a mirror image of Josh's, but that was where the similarity ended. While Josh's place had been furnished in leather and chrome, Jayla's was all soft colors, fabrics and plants, with yoga cushions and bolsters for the times she taught her private clients at home.

Jayla turned on a teakettle and came to sit with them at an oak table. After they'd exchanged a few pleasantries, Evan said, "It looks like no one is living next door." He nodded toward Josh's place.

"That's right," she said. "There was a tenant for a couple of months, but when she heard in the neighborhood what had happened there, she got scared and moved out." She frowned. "Or at least, I *think* that's why she moved. She wasn't super friendly."

"Any sign of the man who shot Josh returning?" Evan asked, his voice sharp.

Cassie couldn't help going tense at his words. Consciously, she rolled her shoulders and tilted her neck back and forth. Tightening up, physically or mentally, would do her no good.

"Not that I've seen," Jayla said. "It's all quiet." She put a reassuring hand on Cassie's arm.

"So," Cassie said, "the place is empty. Wonder if my key still works."

"Doubtful," Jayla said. "They had everything cleaned and I'm sure they changed the locks. But..." She looked at Cassie, her nose scrunching.

Cassie raised her eyebrows. "Are you thinking what I'm thinking?"

"The porch thing." Jayla got up to turn off the whistling teakettle. She did something with an infuser and then brought three cups to the table, fragrant with peppermint. "But why would you want to go in there? What do you think you'll find?"

Cassie lifted her hands, palms up. "I just wonder if maybe it'll spark an idea," she said. "Help me remember."

"You sure you want to?"

"No," Cassie admitted. "But Evan hasn't seen the place in a long time, and... I don't know. It seems like it's worth a try."

"Then drink your tea and let's go," Jayla said.

They went around back. Cassie climbed onto the railing of their row house's back porch and leaned to the side, with Jayla holding her belt from behind.

"Whoa, whoa, whoa," Evan said. "We can't break and enter."

"It doesn't hurt anything," Jayla told him. "No one lives there now."

"And I *used* to live here." Cassie reached for the kitchen window.

"Geez, Cassie, let me do that," Evan protested from the ground.

"You're too heavy," Jayla informed him. So he went and

stood beneath Cassie, ready to catch her, muttering about illegal activities.

She got ahold of the kitchen window and pushed, and due to a loose board, it came open. She reached through and unlocked the window and then pushed it wider.

"Step two," Jayla said, "and this one you can help with, Officer Evan. We need to hoist her through the window."

"I'm an officer of the law, and this is a crime." But he held out his hands, interlocked, for Cassie to stand on. She climbed and slid and wiggled through.

She was instantly overwhelmed with feelings. *Just keep moving.* She went and opened the back door to let Evan and Jayla in.

"Oh, honey," Jayla said, and that was when Cassie realized that tears were rolling down her cheeks. She wrapped her arms around Cassie. "Worst night of my life, so I know it had to be the worst night of yours."

Cassie found a tissue in her pocket and wiped her eyes.

"You were here?" Evan asked Jayla. "Can you tell me what you remember, exactly as it happened?"

Jayla nodded. "I heard a lot of banging and yelling, and it wasn't like Josh and Cassie. They were quiet neighbors. I was in the process of texting her to find out what was going on when there was a gunshot." Jayla swallowed hard. "I called 911 and grabbed our neighbor on the other side, Darren, who's a hulk, and we went over. The door was open and Josh was…down." She paused a moment and collected herself. "Darren and I ran in just as the cops were pulling up. Darren tried to revive Josh, but it was too late."

Jayla's words brought the night back to Cassie in vivid detail. Mainly, she remembered feeling helpless, like a rabbit, frozen into place and then darting up the stairs. She'd been cowardly, had left the scary thing to Josh. A better person would have insisted on staying downstairs, would have run into the kitchen for a knife, would have grabbed a lamp and hit the intruder over the head.

It had been so loud, the pounding and yelling. And Josh had ordered her upstairs. Cassie had been obeying Josh's orders—everyone's orders—all her life. And she'd recognized his logic: she couldn't fight a gun.

As for Josh, he of course had a permit to carry, but he didn't normally have a weapon on him at home. She didn't even know where he'd kept it. If she had, maybe she'd have grabbed it, fought back.

Except she didn't know how to shoot and it had all happened so fast.

Now she looked around the kitchen where she'd experimented with recipes for Josh, enduring his teasing about her failures and enjoying his praise when she got it right. She'd dreamed that one day she'd need to know how to cook for the husband and children she hoped to have.

Jayla checked her phone. "Look, you guys, I have to go. I have a class over at the studio. But please, please stay in touch. Come back and visit or, if that's too hard, we can meet halfway between."

"You come to Pleasant Shores," Cassie suggested. "It's a beach town, really cute. You'd love it." Being here with Jayla had reminded Cassie of how much she liked the woman. In her grief, she'd lost touch with too many friends.

"I'm there. Text me some weekends that work for you." And with a flurry of hugs, Jayla was out the door.

Once she was gone, Evan looked at Cassie. "Pretty sure this was a bad idea," he said. "This has to be so hard on you, and I don't think—"

"Let's just walk around." She moved slowly through the living room and then headed up the stairs and into Josh's old room, Evan tromping after her. There had to be something here, something to recognize, something that would help them understand what had happened to Josh. There just had to be.

She walked through the upstairs hall and into Josh's now-empty bedroom.

There was a pounding on the door downstairs.

CHAPTER TWELVE

CASSIE'S BREATH CAUGHT. The sound of someone pounding on the door—this particular door—was way too much like the night when Josh had been killed.

Evan walked out of the room and over to the stairs. He squatted and peered down. "Looks like a white guy, bald with a fringe, maybe late 60s? Does that ring a bell?"

Relief washed over her. "I think it's the landlord. He's not dangerous, but…"

"We need to get out of here."

"Right. He's not the understanding type."

"Follow me." Evan sidled down the stairs and she followed, clinging to the railing on the side that wasn't visible from the small window beside the door.

They heard a key turning in the front door's lock and ran through the apartment. Just as they slipped out the back, Cassie looked over her shoulder and saw the front door opening.

"Out, now!" Evan ordered in a low voice.

She exited and he eased the door closed, and then they ran back to the alley and down the block.

Once they were well out of sight of the house, Cassie stopped and bent over, hands on knees, panting. "Oh, man, I am *not* used to running."

"Did you recognize him? Was it the landlord for sure?"

She nodded and caught her breath. "Pretty sure. I only met him once. Josh always dealt with him."

"Someone must have seen us climbing in. But why wouldn't they call 911?"

"It's a weird neighborhood," she said. "Not always cop friendly."

"Must have been someone in the building who called, or a neighbor from across the alley who saw us breaking in." They were walking rapidly around the block now, Evan's head swiveling back and forth. When they got to the spot where they'd be visible to the front of the building, he put out his hand to stop Cassie. "Wait."

He scanned the street. "He must be inside. You wait here, and I'll go get the truck. If he got a report, he's probably looking for two or three people breaking in, not one."

"Be careful." She watched as he strode toward the truck, head held confidently high, shoulders squared. That was partly an act, she knew, because sneaking would be way more obvious. But partly, it was who he was. He wasn't afraid of anything. He'd likely been in all kinds of terrible situations, in his military and police life.

Not only that, but he understood that there were shades of gray in interpreting the law. Yes, they'd been legally wrong to break in, but if it could help them apprehend a killer, that was the greater good.

There was no one she'd rather be in trouble with. And that was about feeling safe, but it was also about more than that. And more than about being attracted, although that was there. He pulled the truck forward and around the corner, and she climbed inside.

He headed the truck out of the neighborhood. "Back to

Pleasant Shores," he asked, "or are there other things we can do here before we go?"

"I'm starving," she said. "There's a little diner where Josh and I used to go, just before you get on the highway. Let's grab dinner there before going back."

"You're sure you're up for more memory lane?" he asked.

She blew out a breath. She'd gotten so agitated by their escape that she'd left her sadness behind. "May as well," she said. "I think about Josh all the time, anyway."

They drove in silence, except for her directions. And now the sadness hit her hard, like a delayed reaction.

He didn't comment on her wiping her eyes and blowing her nose. But once they arrived in the parking lot, he reached over and pulled her in for a hug. "It's understandable," he said. "Going back to the scene where something awful happened. It's hard on anyone."

She nodded against his arm. "I wish I could have done something to save him."

He patted her back, still holding her, which felt so, so good. "I know. That's a common reaction. I have it, too, with Josh. Wish I'd asked him more about what he was working on." Josh had worked out of his home and the police had taken his files and computer. As far as Evan knew, they'd found nothing of interest.

Evan should have asked Josh more questions.

They sat there for a few minutes, just holding each other. Slowly, Cassie grew aware of her surroundings: the rain beating against the truck windshield, the flashes of headlights going by, the sound of Evan's breathing and her own.

The smell of his aftershave, something woodsy and masculine.

She didn't want to move, and he wasn't letting go. She

looked up at him, then reached up and ran a hand along his jawline, feeling the stubble there. "You need to shave."

"Yeah." He took hold of her hand and moved it away from his face. Loosened his arms and eased back from her.

"Is this making you uncomfortable?" She didn't know where this husky, sultry voice was coming from, but it was the only tone she had in her on a rainy evening, in this truck, with these feelings.

He cleared his throat.

Look away. Back away.

Cassie felt skinned of all her restraint and good judgment, her usual calmness. All that was left was something raw and primal.

Something she shouldn't feel. Their focus should be on Josh. Evan wasn't the man for her. She needed to grow her independence so nothing like this would ever happen again, not melt into Evan Stone, Josh's old friend.

But she'd used up all her restraint today, all her good sense, getting through the visit to the police and the apartment, not to mention running away from the place.

She was looking into his eyes, so she saw his gaze flicker down to her lips.

She wet them with her tongue. Heat started low in her belly and radiated out, making her hot and sensitive. Sensitive enough to know what he wanted. What she wanted, too.

"You can kiss me," she said, bold, because life was short and she didn't want to wait and lose her courage.

He studied her. And then his hand crept up and pushed back her hair. He shifted in his seat, leaned closer.

Then he jerked away, climbed out of the truck and stood, the door open, the rain soaking him.

He was still staring at her.

She stared at him, too, because she'd never wanted anything more in her life than for him to kiss her.

That look went on too long.

"I'll get you something to go," he said abruptly. "You can eat in the truck on the way back. We need to leave." He spun and strode toward the diner.

Almost to the door, he turned back. "Shut the door and lock it," he called, and watched while she did so.

Then he disappeared inside, and Cassie sat in the truck, feeling stunned.

What had just happened between them?

Who had called the landlord about their break-in to the old apartment?

And what was she going to do about all of it?

One thing was for sure: she wasn't going to let an awkward moment with Evan derail their attempt to find answers about Josh. No matter how embarrassing, she was going to force Evan to talk with her and continue helping her figure it out.

She sucked in a deep breath. *You're not helpless anymore*, she told herself, and got out of the truck.

EVAN STOOD IN the diner, waiting his turn to order takeout and scanning the environment the way he always did. It was a cop thing. And it might help him regain his cool.

The place was a real old-fashioned diner with chrome-edged tables and turquoise vinyl covering the counter stools and booth benches. At this hour the dinner crowd had mostly cleared out. Three solo diners, all male, hunched over big plates of food. The air was heavy with the smell of fries and coffee. Two of the booths were occupied, one of them with a loud group of women, one with a father and two kids. No threats, at least no obvious ones.

Which left the threat waiting for him out in the truck.

How was he supposed to handle Cassie's telling him he could kiss her? He'd never imagined anything like that, not in his wildest dreams. He'd only expected to deal with his own desires, not hers.

Because it *had* been desire in her husky voice and intense eyes, he was pretty sure of that, and it had thrown him. This was another side of his best friend's little sister, one he hadn't even considered. It would be much better to just have her be off-limits, some kind of pure being you wouldn't dare approach.

Maybe if he just pretended it hadn't happened, gave her the food and turned up the radio on the way home, a hockey game, not romantic music, it would go back to being that.

The door opened behind him and Cassie appeared. Her hair half up and half down, messy and wet, her eyes full of rueful humor and something else he couldn't name, shaking herself like a dog.

If she came on to him again, even a little, he was a goner.

"I told you to wait in the car." His voice came out sounding like a drill sergeant, and the group of women in the nearest booth turned to look.

"I know, but I'd rather eat in here." She raised an eyebrow. "Any problem with that?"

Yes, he wanted to say. Instead, he nodded, raised a hand to get the waitress's attention and pointed to one of the empty booths. "Okay if we sit down?"

"Wherever you like," she said.

So they sat and Evan tried not to look at her, and then he couldn't help it. He was floored by her beauty, her appeal,

her as a grown-up. The fact that they were sitting here together, across from each other in a dive of a diner, was like
a breath, a wish, a charm.

Stop. He couldn't have her. He was an alcoholic who
would definitely like a drink right now. He had a troubled
son back in Pleasant Shores, a son whom he'd failed. And
then there was his promise to Josh.

He couldn't have her. He couldn't.

"Are you done worrying?" Cassie sounded amused as the
waitress held out plastic menus. Cassie took them, handed
one to him and started perusing the other one. "Look, I'm
sorry about that, what happened in the truck. But we need
to talk about next steps."

She sounded so casual, like it hadn't affected her at all.
"You can't do that to me again."

"It was the stress," she said, waving a hand. "I'm sorry.
I'll behave."

He narrowed his eyes at her. "You'd better."

"Okay, okay, I'm sorry!" She glared at him. "But grow
up. We can work together. It was just a moment."

He studied her. "You don't know how you affect men."

"As a matter of fact, I do know that men are easily
aroused, so don't treat me like a ten-year-old." She opened
the menu and scanned it.

Evan's mouth had been open to say more, but at her
words, he closed it. And stared at her. Who *was* she?

"What?" She sounded irritable. "Yes, I've dated, and
yes, I know something about men. So you don't need to
treat me like a child who's playing with matches without
knowing the danger."

He seized on that. "It *is* dangerous."

"Why?" She wasn't taking it the least bit seriously, and

that was a good thing. There was no reason to feel disappointed or let down. He should be glad she hadn't truly been hitting on him.

But he wasn't glad; he was irritated. "It's dangerous," he said, "because I actually *am* attracted to you. I'd like to kiss you and more."

She sucked in a breath and her eyes flicked up to his, then back down to the menu.

"Take your order?" the waitress asked. "Hey, Cassie. Didn't recognize you, it's been forever. Where's Josh?"

Cassie looked up from the menu, then set it down. "You haven't heard," she said.

The waitress tucked her pencil behind her ear. "Heard what, hon?"

"About Josh." Cassie swallowed. "He, um, he passed away."

The woman gasped, audibly. Then she sat down in the booth beside Cassie and pulled her into her arms. "Oh, my word, I'm so sorry. What happened? He wasn't sick, was he?"

Cassie blinked and shook her head. "He was shot," she said, almost whispering.

"Oh, no. You poor dear." She gave Cassie another hug. "You poor, poor dear. I would've come to the funeral if I'd known."

"I know you would have."

Evan knew it, too. Josh had been so well liked by everyone. He grabbed a handful of napkins from the silver holder on the table and handed them to the two women. Both wiped their eyes, and then the waitress got up. "You still have to eat. What can I get you?"

Cassie ordered a grilled chicken salad, Evan a double

cheeseburger. He firmly pushed down the impulse to go over to the other side of the booth, pull her into his arms and hold her.

"Your arteries, Evan, your arteries." Cassie choked out the words as the waitress walked away. "It's the same thing I always told Josh. Sorry about the meltdown."

"You're allowed."

She wiped her eyes again and blew her nose. "Okay. Let's get to work. What's our next step?"

"What do you know about the last cases he was working on?"

She frowned, waited while the waitress served them both sodas and squeezed Cassie's shoulder, then walked away.

"He was in a little bit of a slump," she said. "I know he had to take some cases of the kind he didn't really like. Cheating spouses, that kind of thing."

Evan nodded. It was a downside of being a private detective, and was enough to keep Evan from even contemplating that line of work. "Did he talk about any of it? Didn't you sometimes help him with the business?"

"Yeah." She sipped soda, then dabbed at the condensation ring with her napkin. "I helped some, but he tried to keep me away from the sleazier cases. The latest one was a guy trying to find out what his girlfriend was doing, and Josh was thinking about returning his retainer and dropping the case."

Evan felt a prickle of concern. "Did he drop it? Do you know why?"

"I think he might have dropped it the day, or the day before, he was killed." She frowned. "He said it was an older guy who was jealous about his girlfriend and wanted her followed. When Josh saw how young the girl was, he said…" She trailed off.

"He said what?"

"He said she reminded him of me, and he didn't want to help the guy. He needed the money and they had a contract and everything, but he didn't feel right about it."

"Do you think that could have had anything to do with the shooting?"

"Not really. The guy was a professional, a teacher or something. It wasn't like he was a gang member or drug dealer. When I told the police about it, they didn't seem to take it very seriously."

Evan knew that a person's appearance or place of employment didn't make him incapable of murder. "We need to know more, about that case and any other recent ones."

Their food came, and despite the emotions of the day, they both ate with a hearty appetite, Cassie stealing fries from his plate just as she had when she was a kid. They finished quickly and Evan insisted on paying the check, and they were soon on their way back to Pleasant Shores.

"Take a nap, why don't you? You've had quite a day."

"I will." She yawned hugely. "You're a lot like Josh, you know? All protective and stuff." She leaned back, rested her head against the window and pulled her coat around her like a blanket.

Evan turned on some quiet music and drove, thinking.

He was flattered that Cassie thought he was like Josh, but it wasn't true. He wasn't nearly as good as Josh was.

He thought of Josh, back when they were in their early twenties, rounding up the guys for a game of pickup basketball. Calling Evan to join them, even though Evan had been deep into drinking and unequipped to do sports. Josh had been the only person in his life who'd cared enough to sit him down and talk to him about his drinking and what he could do about it, providing the location of the nearest AA meetings.

Josh had been the only person who'd consistently asked about his son.

And now Josh was gone, and no, Evan wasn't anywhere near as good, but he had to honor Josh's legacy. Had to remember his promises.

And that meant he needed to avoid being alone with Cassie as much as he could…while trying to work with her on a murder investigation. Right, then. He'd do that.

AVERY WAS GLAD to get called into work on Thursday night. Her savings account was growing, but slowly, and she could use the boost. Glad, at least, until she walked into the Gull and saw Darcy's sour face.

Oliver was standing beside her, looking glum. What was *he* doing here?

"New project for you tonight," Darcy said. "You're training him."

Avery looked from one to the other. Weird how she was constantly getting thrown together with this kid. "Training him for what?"

"His dad wants him to get a job." Darcy sounded disgusted. "And since I don't want to tick off the local cops, I'm giving him one."

That was strange, that Evan was encouraging Oliver to work at a place where he'd gotten drunk in the past. Maybe, like what had happened to her, there were no other jobs available in town.

Or maybe Evan expected Avery to babysit him on the job, too.

"He's not taking my job away, is he?" she asked Darcy.

Darcy waved a hand. "Who knows. We'll start him off busing tables and see how it goes. Show him where everything is, will you?" She stomped off into the kitchen.

That left Avery to look at Oliver and realize that he hadn't said one word. "What do you think about all this?" she asked. "What happened?"

He blew out a breath and sat down on a bar stool, obviously not realizing that sitting around wasn't the way to win Darcy's heart. "My dad gave me an ultimatum, or rather, a series of them. Because I wrecked my car."

Her eyebrows shot up. "That cute little SUV?"

He nodded, his expression glum. "Yeah, so I've been dealing with the insurance company. That's part of my punishment."

Avery tilted her head to one side. "That's part of what happens when you have a wreck. You're lucky you have insurance." And she bet he didn't pay for it himself.

"Yeah, but it's real complicated. My dad won't help. He says it's my responsibility. And my mom's too mad to help, so…" He spread his hands. "I'm on my own with it."

"So you're feeling like you have it rough, handling your own insurance claim?"

He stared down at the floor. "And having to get a job. And even if I get cash from the insurance company, I'm not allowed to buy another car. Dad says I can't drive for a while."

She studied him. "That stinks, but…you're of age, right? If you don't like your dad's rules, you can just leave."

"And go where?" The words burst out of him. "I dropped out of college. My mom hates me. And I'm broke."

"Any training going on out there," Darcy hollered from the kitchen, "or is it all just one big gabfest?"

Oliver's brows drew together. "We're just—"

Avery clapped a hand over Oliver's mouth before he could say anything whiny or incriminating. She took his arm and tugged him to where a bunch of aprons were hanging. "Getting started," she called to Darcy. "Sorry." She noticed Oliver's sneer and pointed a finger at him. "That's lesson one. You kiss up to the boss, instead of answering her back and arguing with her. She's right. We were gabbing on the clock." It was annoying that touching him made her feel something. Just an emotional hangover from her baby's jerky father, an Oliver lookalike. Act-alike, too; he'd been whiny. Men.

"Here are the cleanup bins for clearing tables," she said, showing him. "Your first job is to make sure you get everything off the tables, then clean and sanitize them before another customer sits down. Here's the clean rags and disinfectant spray."

He sighed, heavy and dramatic. "I've been to a restaurant."

"I'm sure you have, but right now you're not a customer. You're the help. So cut the attitude." She scanned the restaurant. There were a couple of tables that hadn't been cleared yet. "Come on, I'll show you how now, while it's not busy."

She led the way to the table. Oliver followed behind, but slowly, carrying the bin.

"Okay, clear off everything," she said, then stood back to let him do it.

He put the bin down and started haphazardly loading the dishes into it.

"Uh-huh. Now try to carry it."

He picked up the bin and staggered, because it was so much heavier on one side than the other. She steadied him. "So next time, stack them evenly. Come on. You have to hustle."

"Geez, slow down!"

"No, you speed up." She walked faster. "Your waiter will need you to fill water and sometimes help serve food," she said. "If you do a good job you get some tips shared with you, but don't expect that at first."

"Really? Why not?"

"Because to be honest, it looks like you're going to be bad at the job." She showed him where to put the dirty dishes and, since Darcy was making no move to do it, introduced him to the chef.

As the evening went on, she realized she hadn't been wrong: he had a lot to learn. Like when he bumped against a table and made water glasses fly to the floor.

She helped him clean up when she saw he had no idea how. "Who knew you were such a klutz?" she teased when she saw he was really upset.

"My mom cleaned up after me," he admitted.

"Then this is gonna be good for your love life," she said. "Women don't like a helpless baby or a man who won't get his hands dirty."

"How about you?" he asked. "What do you like?"

"I like serving my tables. Go get ice water for sixteen."

She was spinning back toward the kitchen when she felt a hand on her butt.

She spun. "Hey!"

The hand was gone. It was some creepy older guy. "What?" he asked, his face all innocent.

"Hands off," she warned.

"I didn't touch you." He called her a name under his breath.

Oliver came to her side and shoved the guy.

The man stumbled back and his face went ugly.

"Hey, cool it!" Darcy came out and stepped in between them. "What happened?"

"That twerp shoved me." The stranger pointed at Oliver.

"Because he put his hand on my butt," Avery explained. "And called me a name."

"Fine. Sir, we'll bring your food to go. Oliver, Avery, in the back with me." As soon as they were there, she snapped at them. "One more action like that and you're both fired. It's a bar. You handle things. Doesn't mean you have to put up with someone touching you, but be quiet about it, tactful. Don't start a fight if you can help it."

"Sure," Avery said.

Oliver opened his mouth, looking like he was going to protest, but at a glare from her, he snapped it shut.

Oliver was going to be a handicap in the job, but still, she couldn't dislike him for coming to her rescue.

BERTIE ENJOYED GETTING *into character, had enjoyed it ever since he'd been small. Now, as he walked toward the shooting range, he made his walk mimic the wide-legged stance of the muscular louts who patronized the place.*

Had full camo gear been overboard? But no; he saw that several other men lined up to shoot were dressed similarly.

He went through the preliminaries, making sure to match his grammar—or lack of it—to that of the other patrons.

Even with his augmented stage muscles, he was slighter of build than most of them, and he wasn't a regular. He felt their eyes on him. Just as all eyes were on him onstage.

As soon as he started to shoot, though, the comments ceased. The silence was respectful.

That was all he was after: respect.

No, that wasn't all; the truth was he liked to shoot. Liked the power of it. Deep down he'd liked killing that arrogant detective.

But it had been wrong, a sin. Mother had been so angry.

Every week or so he punished himself by returning to the scene of the crime.

The last time he'd been rewarded; the witness had come to the apartment. A good coincidence, or maybe it was a reward for his self-punishment.

But she'd had a man with her, a man who handled himself like a cop. She wasn't letting it go.

He'd hoped the landlord would handle it, arrest them for trespassing, scare them. He didn't want to get his hands dirty, not again.

With the cop's help, she'd escaped before the landlord saw them. He hadn't even been able to follow her, but he had gotten a license plate from the vehicle they'd used. That was all he needed to find her.

He sighted, braced, fired. Fired again. Felt the power of it, and it calmed him.

As he sighted the target his mind played a trick, turning the image into his brother, Charles. And then into his mother... His focus wavered, his hands sweating, and for the first time today, he missed the target.

He refocused, pushed away the mental glitch. He'd never hurt a family member.

As the paper figure accumulated bullet holes, he planned his next move.

CHAPTER THIRTEEN

CASSIE RUBBED HER palms down the sides of her pants as she and Evan arrived at the parking lot of the local amphitheater, adjoining the park and always busy in the summer, but empty in the off-season. It was Saturday, and Evan's first day off since the trip to Minestown on Tuesday.

"Nervous?" he asked her.

"No! I mean, not about the driving." She laughed a little. She was nervous about being with Evan, which was ridiculous.

She'd made a mistake on Tuesday, flirting with him, as much as forcing him to admit he was attracted to her. That reality had shimmered and shone before her for a couple of days, during which she'd managed to avoid him. She couldn't trust herself right at first.

Every time she thought about that moment in the truck, butterflies had danced in her chest. What would it be like to kiss him?

What did it mean that he'd admitted he wanted to kiss her, too?

But that kind of speculation would only make her miserable when it couldn't amount to anything. So she'd kept busy getting the teen program organized and meeting with some of the kids to get them started on doll projects. When she wasn't doing that, she'd thrown herself into her doll making, completing two projects and working to improve her website. To her surprise, she'd already gotten a couple of new orders.

The days had gone on with friendly waves and safe distance between her and Evan, and slowly, her emotions about him had settled back down to normal. They both knew getting together wouldn't work. They were better off as friends. "Thanks for doing this," she said to him now, and to solidify what she understood their relationship to be, added, "I'm glad we're friends."

He met her eyes for a second too long. "Right. Friends."

That extra-long gaze was enough to remind her that her relationship with Evan felt less and less like simple friendship and more and more like something else. But maybe that was natural given the circumstances. She'd known they shared grief about losing Josh, but that had become so vivid on the day in Minestown. And then the emotional impact of being back in the place where it had all happened, and the adrenaline of escaping out the back door of the apartment…it made sense that they'd bonded.

"Okay," he said, "so how much do you know about driving a stick?"

She wrinkled her nose. "Sadly, nothing. Except that you use two feet."

He laughed and rolled his eyes a little. "It's a start. Look down here." He moved his feet and showed her the pedals. "This left hand one is the clutch. It has to be pushed in when you shift gears."

"Which you do with this." She put a hand on the gearshift in between them. "See, I know a little."

"Right. So I'm going to push in the clutch—still with my foot on the brake. It can roll otherwise—and you try moving the gearshift around."

She did, but nothing clicked into place.

"Here, watch." He nudged her hand off the gearshift and took hold of it. "Reverse, you push it in and back. First, to get started, is directly forward. Once you're moving, pull it back into second and then over into third. Fourth is for going faster, and we won't even deal with fifth today."

She tried, and with his help she got the hang of it.

His hand was all capable and manly over hers, working the gears. Could she help it that her heart beat faster? Any woman would have that reaction to Evan Stone.

He took his hand away—drat—and made her do the rotation over and over until she had a sense of it. "Now, what do you think I've been doing with the pedals all this time?"

"Um, I have no idea?"

He blew out a little chuckle and looked up through the sunroof. "I've had one foot on the clutch pedal, pushing it all the way in, and the other on the brake, so we don't roll. He took a foot off the brake, and the car started to roll backward. He braked to stop it. "And if you let go of the clutch, it'll jerk and stall." He demonstrated. "Either way, the most important thing you can know is how to brake."

He had her get into the driver's seat then, and laughed at how far she had to move it up. And then he patiently walked her through the motions, again and again, until she could let out the clutch and shift gears relatively smoothly. "You're doing fine," he encouraged her when she stalled out the car yet again. "Everyone does that at first. It's why we're starting in an empty parking lot. Pull into that space over there, and we'll take a break."

She pulled in, jerking, and braked, and he talked her through turning off the ignition with the car in Neutral, and setting the brake. Then they climbed out, and she stretched her back. "I feel like I've been taking a calculus exam," she said. "That's hard."

"You did fine. It'll take a few practice sessions before it's natural to you. And then you'll be able to drive wherever you like."

"I can't really imagine doing it alone," she admitted. "But don't worry, I'll get there." She was saying it as much to convince herself as to convince him.

Without discussing it, they turned to head toward the water. It was a warm day, the ground rich with the smell of springtime, the gulls cawing, the breeze soft against her sweaty skin. Out on the bay a couple of fishing boats and a couple of pleasure boats dotted the horizon. "Such a beautiful place," she said. "Do you think you'll stay here in Pleasant Shores?"

"I would like to," he said. "I do better with a slower pace and some time to relax."

She tilted her head to look at him. "Doesn't seem like you take a lot of time off."

"True. But the work is community focused. More school safety lessons than homicides." He frowned. "Speaking of which, we should try some other angles on Josh's assailant. Don't want to let the case, or our energy, get too cold."

"Good point." She appreciated that he was sharing it all with her, not trying to limit her involvement or block her out.

A little kid, following his dad on a bike, swerved and almost hit him. "Whoa, little fellow," Evan said, catching the small bike before it tipped. "Keep looking forward. It'll help you keep your balance." He steadied the bike while the child got started again. The father, up ahead, turned around and waved.

"You're good with kids. Do you want to have any?" Then she clapped a hand over her mouth. "I'm sorry. I keep forgetting you already have a child."

"A man-child," Evan said. "And it's not like I had a hand in raising him, not really."

"How's he doing with the new job?" Evan had told her about his ultimatums to his son, and how Oliver had gotten a job at the Gusty Gull.

Evan lifted his hands, palms up. "Okay, I guess. He doesn't say much, but his crush on Avery helps make working more palatable."

"Oh, that's sweet."

"Kind of. Brings up a whole new set of worries. At least…"

"He can't get her pregnant," she finished, and they both laughed a little.

"Is that wrong, to be glad about that?" Evan asked.

They strolled down to the water and leaned on the boardwalk's wall, looking out into the bay. "It's not wrong, but let me ask you this. What if he falls in love with her and they get together? Is he up for becoming a dad at his age?"

"No," Evan said bluntly. "Of course, neither was I."

"Oh. Yeah, I bet." Maybe Mom was right, and she just wasn't equipped to deal with a man as complicated as Evan. "I'm sorry, I seem to be bringing up painful subjects."

"Not a problem, but let's talk about something else." He looked over at her. "Let's figure out how to move forward with Josh's case. I keep thinking about how he wanted to give back that retainer and quit his last client."

"Me, too," she said. "I wish I could remember exactly what he said."

"Do you think the guy was dangerous? Violent?"

She frowned. "Josh didn't seem worried, exactly," she said. "More disgusted with the guy. He didn't want to take on a case involving a young girl and an older man. He even mentioned something about reporting him to the cops."

"Can't blame him, if she was underage, or if he was harassing her."

"She was over eighteen, I think, because she was a student at the college."

"After he finished a case, did he destroy the records?"

"He shredded any paperwork," she said. "In fact, that's one of the things I did for him—oh, Evan!" She gripped his arm. "He used a phone service. I forgot all about it until just now."

"The police would have culled through those records, or they should have."

She shook her head. "Not necessarily, because it wasn't a big official service. It was a friend of his who was just getting started, someone local, and he wanted to give her the business. I'm trying to remember her name." She thought. "Bliss… Gartshore, I think it was?"

"First name of Bliss isn't that common," he said. "We can try to find her."

"Because maybe she remembers some of his calls, or something." They turned back toward the car. "Let's go get on my computer and see what we can find."

BACK AT HER PLACE, they located a likely number, and Cassie placed a call, then put her phone on speaker. "Bliss? This is Cassie Thomas, Josh Thomas's sister. He was one of your former clients?"

She heard a sharp intake of breath. "Oh, my goodness,

I heard about Josh. I'm so sorry. I couldn't get away for the services."

"It's okay. Thanks." She was learning to push past her sadness enough to stay on track. "Hey, listen, I wondered if I could talk to you about what kind of calls Josh was getting right before he passed away."

"Um, hmm." Bliss didn't say anything for a moment. Then, "I'm not really sure what privacy requirements there are in a case like this."

Evan leaned forward. "Bliss, this is Evan Stone. I'm a friend of Josh and Cassie, and a police officer in another jurisdiction. We can get your local police involved, or just chat informally. Whichever works better for you."

Again, Bliss paused.

"We're just trying to get a window into what was going on in his life right before the shooting," Cassie explained. "The police haven't found out anything, and they're overworked. They've basically given up. Could you at least tell us if anything unusual was going on?"

Bliss breathed in and out, audibly. "I can," she said. "It would be better if we could meet. That way I can make sure you really are who you say you are."

Cassie looked over at Evan.

"I'm off in the morning Sunday and Monday. Would either day work for you, Bliss?"

"Sunday morning." She gave them her address and ended the call.

Cassie set down her phone and looked over at Evan. "She sound weird to you?"

He nodded. "A little. You said she was Josh's old friend. What kind of friend?"

"I don't know, but I had the feeling she was a romantic interest at one time."

"That would explain the tone." He leaned back in his chair. "I should go. Leave you to your Saturday."

But she didn't want him to. "Stay," she said impulsively. "I'll fix us lunch. It's only fair, since you put up with being jerked around by a bad stick-shift driver."

"Hey, you did well. I didn't mind." He smiled. "But I also wouldn't mind lunch."

She fixed them grilled cheese sandwiches and heated up some potato soup she'd made the day before. "Carb heavy," she said, handing him his plate and bowl to take outside, "but tasty."

"I'm in favor of carbs." He carried out his dish, then returned to grab the pitcher of iced tea she'd set out. In minutes they were enjoying lunch on Victory Cottage's little deck. "Can't beat this," he said, nodding toward the bay, the boats, the sunshine.

And for a few minutes they just enjoyed the breeze and the bay, together.

"This *is* nice. About as far from Minestown as you can get." Cassie set down the crust of her sandwich. "Truth is I wouldn't mind living in a place like this."

"It's a lot busier in the summer," he warned. "But there are art festivals and the like. You could sell your wares."

She snorted. "Makes me sound like a pots-and-pans salesman. My dolls aren't for everyone. Although I'm optimistic about internet sales."

He shrugged. "The dolls seemed like a hit with the kids the other day."

"Yes, and when I met with the girls, they were still super

enthusiastic. Josh always said I needed to be more confident, that I had more potential than I realized."

"I think he was right." He smiled at her. "You're very talented, Cassie."

Her face heated. "Um, thanks. So, uh, how long do you think Oliver will stay?"

"Nice change of subject. He's good for a few more weeks, because he's broke and has no car."

She tilted her head to one side. "Do you think you'll, you know, stay in touch after this?"

"I don't know." He looked unseeingly out to the bay. "I made him mad, forcing him to get a job, but I'm hoping he'll see the merit of it at some point." He shook his head. "I learned very little about parenting and family life from my folks. At any rate, very little I'd want to emulate."

"Most of us would probably make some changes to the way our parents did things, although for sure, your parents were…difficult."

He looked over at her. "Your mom was great. Right?"

"Oh, she was, but she had her struggles. She loved Dad, but he wasn't cut out for family life." Especially when it involved a sick kid.

"Yeah. That's an alcoholic for you." He stared at his hands and then looked over at her with a forced smile. "I have faith that you'll pull it together and be a great parent someday. Me, not so much. I had my chance, and I blew it."

She shoved aside his comment about her being a great parent and put a hand over his. "I'm sorry you feel that way. I don't agree."

He shrugged. "I'm not looking for pity. I'm just being accountable for myself, for what went wrong. I wasn't a good father, nor a good husband."

She raised an eyebrow. "At seventeen, how many people would be?"

"How many people make that dumb of a mistake and mess up their lives at seventeen?"

A protective kind of irritation grew in her. "If you're determined to blame yourself, I can't help you. But if you could open your mind..." She shook her head.

"What?"

"If you could get over seeing yourself as a loser, you'd probably be a better parent to Oliver." *And you wouldn't be so opposed to seeing me as an actual woman.*

Which was a thought she shouldn't be having. *She* needed to be opposed to being with him, because of his alcoholism that mirrored what she'd grown up with. Because he was too complicated of a man for her. Because being with him would lead to heartache on both sides.

"Why are you trying to talk me into liking myself?" He sounded genuinely puzzled. "What's it to you?"

Her drive to help him was stronger than her sense of caution and self-protection. She moved her chair closer to his, looked into his eyes. "You're a good man, Evan," she said. "I just hate to see you beating yourself up. You're way underestimating yourself."

He blew out a breath and looked away. "Oh, the things you don't know."

"Like what?" She studied him. "Try me. Tell me one of your awful secrets."

He laughed a little, shook his head. "You don't want to know."

Maybe he was right. Maybe she didn't want to know. Because right now she wanted nothing to soften the magnetic pull she felt toward him: so strong that even the effort to pull away caused a physical ache in her heart.

She wanted to be closer to him, wanted it more than her doubts and her mother's warnings and her own prickly independence. She wanted to soften, to take him in. To soothe the hurt she'd just glimpsed, and to touch the fire that burned in him. Keeping her gaze locked with his, she moved over to perch on the arm of his chair, reached toward his face and ran a finger along his strong jawline, feeling the bristly stubble there.

The fire in his eyes gave her courage. "Kiss me," she said in a husky voice she barely recognized.

He opened his mouth like he was going to protest, so she put a finger over his lips. Then she leaned in and pressed her lips to his.

The minute their lips touched, a spark ignited. He pulled her closer, and with a hand on either side of her face, took control and kissed her, a kiss that went deep into her soul.

The bird singing from a fence post, the waves lapping against the shore, the breeze that lifted her hair, cooling her neck—all of it became dim background as her whole self, breath and life and history, centered on the connection between them.

Then he pulled away from her, put his hands on her shoulders and eased her away from him. "There. See? I'm a bad bet."

Cassie could barely catch her breath. "That was bad?"

He narrowed his eyes at her. "For someone who promised your big brother he would keep his distance, yes. Yes, that was very bad."

"Then I want to do more bad things," she dared to say, and moved close again.

CHAPTER FOURTEEN

KISSING CASSIE WAS everything he'd dreamed of and nothing he'd imagined, all at the same time.

He'd known her lips would be soft, but he'd never guessed that she'd be so responsive. That she'd suck in little gasps of air, like she was surprised, and in a good way.

He buried his fingers in her hair—soft and silky—and tugged her closer until she was perched on his lap. She was so small and yet so sturdy. He'd always thought of Cassie as fragile, but muscle curved her arms and shoulders, and her back was straight and strong.

Heat rose between them, seeming to burn wherever their skin made contact. His heart drummed in his chest as his hands moved, exploring her face, her neck, her slender waist. He wanted to take it further: one part of him wanted to, but he wouldn't. This was enough, that he could hold her. This was more than enough.

When he looked into her eyes, he saw that they were dark with what had to be passion. He put a hand on the back of her head and guided her closer, kissed her more deeply, drowning in a sea of feelings and sensations.

The desire was different from what he'd felt with other women. It was physical, but it was more: a longing for closeness of the heart, for connection, for family.

That thought made him pull back, pull her against him and wrap his arms around her, but loosely, trying to quell the heat and desire and replace them with the caring he'd always felt for Cassie.

Another squeeze, and then he eased her off his lap. They stood together, looking at each other, and Evan knew there'd be the devil to pay and that it couldn't happen again.

Maybe it was that that made him pull her close, their whole bodies pressed against each other, and hold her next to him for what had to be the last time.

HE WOKE UP the next morning ashamed of what he'd done. He'd lost control, and he'd touched her, held her, kissed her. What would Josh have said?

He'd broken a promise that had been made for very good reasons. And the worst of it was he had to spend the morning with Cassie today. There was no chance to get distance on his feelings; they'd be driving to Minestown to meet the message service owner, Bliss, and learn what she knew about Josh's death.

When Cassie met him at his truck, her face held some of the same mixed feelings that roiled in him. But there was enough hope and vulnerability in her eyes that he felt like even more of a cad.

The first minutes of the drive were occupied with GPS and making impersonal plans about what they'd do today, what Bliss had said. Then, a few minutes of awkward silence had Evan's fingers twitching with the desire to turn on the radio, loud.

But that would be cowardly. He had to confront the issue between them. "Look, Cassie, I apologize for what happened yesterday."

"No need to apologize," she said quickly. "I started things."

That was what had made it so great. And so awful. "There can't be any more of that," he said firmly.

"You sound like a dad." She was trying to joke, but underneath the humor, he heard a thread of hurt that nearly shattered him.

Better a little hurt now, though, than the bigger hurt that would be caused by her getting involved with him. Josh would have said the same.

"I'm serious," he said. "I don't want to get involved that way. It was a mistake." He hoped she'd believe the lie.

"It seemed pretty mutual."

"It shouldn't have been. I should have stopped you." He steered the car onto the highway. "You don't know what you're doing." It was a deliberate putdown, and he hated doing it, but he had to cauterize the opening between them.

"I don't know what I'm...oh, man." She made a disgusted sound. "Way to patronize me."

"I'm older than you are and more experienced. You don't know what—"

"How do you know you're more experienced? It's not as if you're my first kiss."

Of course he wasn't, but her words still jabbed at him.

"I've been with men. I know what you felt, what you wanted to do, because I wanted it, too."

He gripped the steering wheel as anger rose in him. "Are you telling the truth?"

"About what?"

"About being with men."

She threw up her hands. "Good heavens, it's not your business. You're not my—"

She broke off, and he instantly knew what she'd been going to say. *You're not my brother.*

No, her brother was looking down from heaven and completely disgusted with his so-called friend who'd broken a promise. "Look, Cass, it was a mistake," he said as his heart twisted inside him.

He couldn't look at her, at the hurt he was causing. If he did, he'd pull her close and tell her how much he wished it could be different.

But yesterday she'd pushed aside his objections as irrelevant. She'd likely do that again, and if she did, he was pretty sure he wouldn't have the strength of character to pull away from her a second time. "It was a mistake," he repeated. "We can be friends, but that's all. Just friends." And then he turned up the radio and kept his eyes on the road.

CASSIE MARCHED AHEAD of Evan to Bliss Gartshore's door and knocked, hard.

She wasn't even going to look at Evan. He'd called their kiss, the sweetest kiss of her life, a mistake. He'd apologized for it like he was the upper-crust gentleman in some Victorian novel, who'd behaved in a less-than-chivalrous way with a housemaid and was sorry for it. He wanted to brush it aside and move on. To be *friends*.

Fine. If he could brush it aside that easily, she could, too.

The woman who opened the door was nothing like she expected. She was pretty sure Bliss was a woman with whom Josh had had a fling, and she'd expected Bliss to be like several other of Josh's ex-girlfriends she'd known. Skinny and blond and peppy.

But Bliss was several years older, with dark hair and substantial curves. "Come in, come in," she said, ushering them in and looking around before she closed the door behind them. "We can talk in my office. My kids are still asleep. Teenagers," she clarified.

In the office, after introductions had been made, they sat around a small table. Evan opened his mouth, no doubt to take charge because of his vast experience, but Bliss laid a hand on Cassie's. "I'm so sorry for your loss," she said, her voice a little choked. "Josh was one of the good ones."

Her kind words made Cassie swallow hard. "He was. Thank you."

"What was your relationship with Josh?" Evan's question was rude enough that Cassie's eyes widened, but his tone was neutral, not harsh, and Bliss didn't seem to take offense. "We were…close, occasionally," she said. "I didn't want anything serious, and he was looking for love, so our goals were too different for us to be a couple. But we cared for each other, so when he was between girlfriends—more appropriate girlfriends—we'd usually spend some time together." She tilted her head, looking at Cassie. "I'm sorry. I don't suppose he told you about me."

"He just said you were a friend starting a business, and he wanted to help you out." Cassie looked thoughtfully at Bliss. "I… I could tell from the way he spoke of you that there was something more there than friendship."

"Did you talk with Josh in the days before his death?" Evan asked.

"I did." She looked down, then from Evan to Cassie. "There was a man who was calling him frequently, to the point of harassment. I contacted Josh to ask what I should do about the calls."

Cassie's heart jumped. If Bliss had information that would lead them to Josh's killer, put him behind bars…

"What did Josh say?" Evan asked.

"He said he'd take care of it, that I should block his number." She frowned. "So I did."

"What kinds of things did the harassing guy say, when he called?" Cassie leaned forward. Maybe it was because she had no other leads, but she felt that Bliss had some information that could help them.

Bliss lifted both hands, palms up. "He wanted me to track Josh down. Got very annoyed when I explained that I was just an answering service."

"What was he like, on the phone?" Cassie asked.

"Any accents, a style of speech you recognized?" Evan added.

The woman frowned. "He sounded…very articulate. Almost pretentious." Her desk phone buzzed but she ignored it.

"Is it possible to trace where the calls came from?"

She shook her head. "With cell phone numbers being all over the map, no, not precisely. But…" She paused and bit her lip. "This is a police investigation, right?"

"Yes." Cassie glanced at Evan. There was a police investigation going on, and Evan was a cop. They didn't need to remind Bliss of the fact that the two were unconnected.

"Okay. Because I have paperwork, a contract, and part of it is that whatever's said in people's messages is confidential. It's a normal part of the business. But if there's an active police investigation, then that goes out the window."

Cassie tried to stifle her impatience as the woman worked it all out in her head. "So…you were saying you couldn't identify where the calls came from, precisely. But did you get an idea?"

Bliss nodded, slowly. "He said he had classes and important research, how he didn't have time to track Josh down and it was an emergency to get in touch with him."

"Classes and research?" Evan glanced at Cassie, and she figured he was thinking the same thing she was: they'd been right, the perp was a professional person, some kind of teacher. "No information about where he was working?"

Bliss shook her head. "I did get the feeling he was local." Her phone was buzzing continually now, and she glanced at it, then up at them. "Is there anything else? I really can't stay off the message service for long."

"Can you give us the phone number you blocked?"

"No." Bliss shook her head immediately. "No, those records are deleted." She hesitated. "Also, can you keep me out of the investigation? I'm afraid of this dude. I don't want to be in his path. I feel like he's smart and he'd find out where you guys got the number. I'm a single mom. I need to stay safe for my kids."

As they walked out, Cassie thought about what they'd learned. Josh had had a customer who wanted to get in touch with him and was highly articulate and threatening. Probably someone local.

Evan opened the door for her and helped her up into the truck.

The touch of his hand burned like fire.

She flushed. "It's not much to go on," she said. That was what she *had* to do: stick to the matter at hand. The case. For Josh's sake.

He nodded as if he wasn't even listening. "It's not much to go on," he said slowly, "but it's something. A guy who's very articulate, local, with classes and research."

She frowned. "Local. I wonder if he teaches, or taught,

at Price?" Price was a medium-sized private university just outside Minestown.

"Tell me again what you remember about him." Evan started to drive through town toward the highway. "We could have something. Does it ring true, the idea that he could be a professor?"

Cassie thought about the guy. "He definitely didn't seem like a drug dealer or gang member," she said. "For one thing, I don't think he was real young. Also, he wasn't that strong-looking. He was tall, but not a linebacker by any means."

"Would you recognize him? I mean, you thought you saw him on the bay path…"

"That's true." She frowned. "I might. I'm not sure. But Price is a big school. We can't exactly go sit on the quad and hope he happens to walk across."

"No," he said, "but I know a couple of people in security there. I could talk with them, see if there's anything going on with any of the faculty."

That sparked an idea. "You know, I went to Price," she said. "There's someone who works there that I could talk to. She'd know the gossip, if anyone would." Her heart picked up its pace. Maybe they'd actually accomplished something today. "Are you going to be up for visiting the campus on your next day off? Tuesday, right?"

"Wednesday. I had to trade."

"Do you think it would be worth it to—"

"Worth a try," he interrupted. "We'll have to leave by eight." And then he turned up the radio, clearly uninterested in any more talk.

Cassie stewed for a few minutes about his attitude. And then she decided she wasn't going to stew. "I'll go," she said, "but only if we can settle this business between us. I want to be friends, too, like you said. So I promise not to make any more moves on you."

He looked sideways at her. "You do, huh?"

"I do. I don't want to hurt our friendship." She was telling the truth about that, too. Having Evan in her life mattered, even if there would be no more delicious kissing. "It's important to me, Evan, and…and I think it would be important to Josh, too. In fact," she added as the brainstorm hit her, "we should do something fun together. As friends."

"What kind of something?" He sounded skeptical.

"I don't know, like, a book discussion, or a festival, or a wine tasting." She felt desperate not to lose him, not to close the door to spending time together. She'd explore the reasons for that desperation later. Maybe.

"Those activities sound pretty date-like."

"It's all in how you approach them, right?"

He glanced over. "I guess so."

"So if I find something like that for us to do…as sort of practice for being just friends…will you do it?" She didn't add "for Josh," because that would be manipulative. But she really hoped he'd say yes.

She didn't want to examine exactly why she hoped that with her whole heart.

He let out a sigh. "Sure, Cass. We can do something as friends. In fact… How about helping me talk to a bunch of preschoolers this week?"

"*You're* talking to preschoolers?"

He grinned, the first genuine smile he'd had on his face all day. "We both are. Since we're *friends*. Be ready, Tuesday at 9 a.m."

CHAPTER FIFTEEN

CASSIE WAS GLAD she'd already planned to meet Mary for milkshakes on Sunday night. It would give her a chance to get out of her head and to stop thinking about Evan. Mary was happily single, from what she and everyone said, and that was what Cassie needed to get back to. Thinking about herself, her life, as a happy single woman, not some man's—Evan's—girlfriend or wife. Cassie had known she wasn't likely to have a family of her own since forever. But her attraction to Evan had made her forget.

No more. Mary would be a good role model for Cassie.

They'd agreed to bring their dogs, so they ordered from Goody, the no-nonsense owner of the ice cream shop, and took their chocolate shakes to a table on the patio. "You sit where you can see the sun setting over the bay, dear," Mary insisted. "I get to see it all the time, but you're a visitor." As she sank into her seat, she added, "unless you think you might stay in Pleasant Shores?"

Cassie sat down, and Ace sniffed Mary's dog and then settled at Cassie's feet. She thought about what to say. Of course she wanted to be positive about Mary's hometown, and that wasn't hard. Pleasant Shores was a great place, and being away from the scene of all her pain—being away from her mother's pain, too—all of it was helping her start to heal.

Being around Evan, though, spending all this time with

him, was making her ache for things she couldn't have. So his presence here might be a deal breaker.

Not that she could tell Mary that. "I love it here," she said, "and I'd consider moving here, but…you met my mom. She's up in Minestown and may need my support going forward."

"Hmm. She's enjoying the Ireland trip?"

"A lot, from the texts. We're supposed to do a video call soon and I'll know more."

"You worry about her." Mary sipped her shake and smiled. "Delicious. Goody is the master of chocolate shakes."

Cassie took a sip, and the chocolate intensity exploded in her mouth. She closed her eyes. "Fantastic."

After they'd both enjoyed the shakes for another moment, Mary shifted forward. "So you love Pleasant Shores, and I must say you fit right in. And yet you're planning to leave at the end of your three-month stint in Victory Cottage because of a sense of duty?"

"I mean…yeah. She's my mom."

"She's your mom, and I'm guessing she wants the best for you. In fact, I know she does. That's what she said when I met her."

"Of course." Why was Mary pushing her on this, making her question herself? "She would never ask me to stay home with her, but I want to help her. The way she helped me all the years I was sick." *That's what families do*, she wanted to add, only she didn't want to act like she knew more about families than Mary did. Mary was kind, a good person, generous in the community. If she didn't understand Cassie's compulsion to help her mother, well, not everyone would.

Not everyone had lost a brother, leaving them in charge of a struggling parent's peace of mind.

Only Mary wouldn't drop the subject. "Do you think you'll need to stay close to her for the rest of her life?"

Cassie sipped more milkshake and told herself not to get defensive. "In the same town, probably. She's doing better now that Donald's in her life, and I suspect he'll propose on this trip, so…maybe that'll change things. But for now I feel responsible, more than ever since my brother's gone."

Mary nodded. "You're a good daughter. But what about your own dreams? Don't you want to focus on the business you're building? And eventually, don't you want a family of your own, a home, kids?"

Where did this woman get off being so nosy? "Look, there are some issues." She opened her mouth to tell Mary she was pretty sure she couldn't have kids—that awkward admission would make Mary uncomfortable, which would serve her right—and then closed it again.

"Health-wise? Emotionally?"

Cassie let out an exasperated breath. "You're really asking me that."

Mary sipped more milkshake, reached out and squeezed Cassie's hand. "It's the prerogative of elders, dear. Plus, even though the Victory Cottage program offers counseling, you declined it. I know you're trying to find your brother's killer—"

"You know that?" Cassie stared at her, amazed. Was there anything Mary *didn't* know?

"I know that." Mary didn't elaborate on exactly *how* she knew it. "I also know, since I've lost a family member to violence myself, that it's possible to channel all your energy into investigating and forget about the emotional healing that needs to take place."

If Mary could be blunt and intrusive, so could Cassie. "Did you lose a brother or sister?" The tone came out challenging, but Cassie was annoyed. She just bet that Mary had lost, at most, a distant relative.

Mary gazed at her for a good thirty seconds, blue eyes piercing. "No," she said finally. "My five-year-old daughter was killed by her own father."

Cassie gasped and automatically reached out for Mary's hand as everything she thought she knew about the woman shifted, settling like a kaleidoscope image into a different pattern. "I'm so sorry. How awful."

"Yes, it was." Mary looked to the side, then bent to pick up a straw wrapper someone had dropped. "It wasn't on purpose. He was trying to kill me. So you see, I know a lot about coping with loss. I tried most of the unhealthy methods before I really opened up to other people and started working through the feelings."

"Wow." Cassie studied the older woman and realized, for the first time, that those sharp eyes held depth and wisdom and pain, not just curiosity. "I guess you do know a lot about loss."

"For a long time," Mary said, "I cut myself off from moving forward into the future. Are you doing something similar?"

Neat, that, how she'd turned the conversation back to Cassie and her problems. But it felt different now. "I'm trying to move into the future," she said slowly, "but I have health issues that would make it hard for me to have a family. Emotional ones, too, since my dad, our dad, was an alcoholic. Josh never settled down with anyone to start a family, either."

Mary nodded. "Are the health issues related to getting pregnant, or related to actually having a husband and kids?"

"Both. The chemo I had may have affected my fertility. But also, I have to pace myself. I tend to get fatigued, and stress doesn't help. I wouldn't want to be the kind of wife and mother who was always lying down." As she heard herself say it aloud, she realized what she meant.

She didn't want to be the kind of mother her own mother had been.

Mary nodded matter-of-factly. "At my age, I have to pace myself, too," she said. "But keeping active, seeing people, working on causes I love, all of those keep me going." She reached down and petted Coco's head. "Plus this sweet girl. She keeps me on my toes, too, makes sure I do a lot of walking."

Goody, the owner of the ice cream shop, came out and started lowering the umbrellas attached to each table. She looked over at Ace. "Is that dog neutered?"

Cassie blinked. The bluntness of this town's elders took some getting used to. "Yes."

"Good. I don't want any dogs running wild around here when Cupcake is coming into heat." She dipped a rag into a bucket and started cleaning off tables. "We had a disaster with that, a couple of years ago."

Mary leaned down and patted her dog's side until she rolled over for a belly rub. "You can't call the creation of this masterpiece a disaster, my friend." She looked over at Cassie. "A local goldendoodle got loose and, shall we say, fell in love with Goody's poodle. My Coco is the result, or one of them."

"Beautiful dog." It felt like the only tactful thing Cassie could say.

"Why don't you bring Cupcake out? She'd love to see her daughter."

Goody puffed out a breath, looked down at Coco, who was still lolling on her back, and bent to give her a quick chest rub. "Maybe I will."

"Ladies." The familiar deep voice seemed to massage Cassie's nerves, and she looked toward the street to see Evan walking past the shop. In uniform. He waved but didn't stop.

Cassie watched him. She couldn't, actually, take her eyes away.

When he was nearly out of sight, she looked back to see both older women watching her. "He's a good man," Mary said.

Cassie cleared her throat. "He is." But not for her. She had to remember, he was not for her.

And that was fine. She was an independent woman, like these two happy, independent women. She didn't need a man. She needed to reach for her own dreams, like Mary and Goody had, rather than moping after Evan.

Mary's phone buzzed and she picked it up, studied the face and shook her head, her cheeks going pink. "He has to text me every night. I've told him and told him it's not necessary, but he thinks it is."

Cassie lifted an eyebrow. "Boyfriend?"

Goody had gone back to wiping tables, and now she wrung out her rag. "She's a little old for a *boy* friend."

Mary laughed. "I call him my gentleman friend," she said. The corners of her mouth turned up, and she looked softer, happy. "I've had a lot of issues in the past," she said, "and it's taken me a long time to get to the point of letting a man in. I *think* Kirk James might be that man, but I'm not sure where I want to go with it."

"Has he come up with a ring yet?" Goody asked, propping her hip on a table.

"I haven't let him. But... I wouldn't be surprised if he's carrying one around in his pocket," she said, laughing, looking rueful but happy, too. "He's nothing if not prepared."

"A woman without a man is like a fish without a bicycle," Goody said, pushing off the table and turning toward the shop. "You remember that, Mary Rhoades. And I'm getting ready to close, so finish up."

Maybe Pleasant Shores nosiness was contagious, like a disease. She found herself wondering about Mary's boyfriend, the guy whose text was making a dignified older woman blush like a teenager.

She stifled her curiosity, though. It wasn't her business, and if she was smart, she'd step entirely away from the topic of love and romance.

How could she do that, though, when the sight of Evan walking by in his police uniform made her go warm all over?

Cassie carried Mary's empty cup and her own to the trash can, then untied Ace's leash. "You two are good examples of independence," she said to Mary. Because the truth was although Mary had a man interested in her, she was very much her own woman.

Mary untied her own dog, then stood. "Independence is a good thing," she said slowly. "But so is connection. I waited too long to see that."

Cassie studied her. "You seem happy."

"I am happy. But I waited too long." She put a hand on Cassie's shoulder. "Don't wait too long, dear. And I've just thought of something, some people I'd like for you to meet."

"Uh-oh." Cassie let Ace sniff the trash can, but pulled him away from a piece of ice cream cone that had fallen to the ground. Was Mary going to start matchmaking?

Mary laughed. "You're going to regret not just doing the counseling with a professional," she said. "But I'd like for you to meet two sisters, Erica and Amber Rowe. Well, they both have different last names now. They're both married. But they've struggled through health problems and infertility, too."

Gee, that sounds fun. Not.

"They've both worked through it all so well. I'm going to arrange for you to meet them."

"Um, okay." There was no real point in arguing with this woman, since she seemed to know something about everything, and didn't appear to understand the word *no*.

As they strolled down the darkening street, Cassie glanced back in the direction Evan had gone. *He* wasn't carrying a ring around in his pocket, no way. She didn't want him to. She wanted to be strong and independent. *Was* strong and independent.

But Mary's words had struck a chord, because Cassie knew for sure that life was short, and that waiting too long meant that some beloved dreams wouldn't, couldn't, come true.

She just didn't know whether her daydreams of Evan and her together were foolish fantasies, or possibilities she'd regret not pursuing.

At least they'd be friends. He'd agreed to that.

You could never have too many friends.

EVAN WASN'T SO sure this was a great idea.

Getting together to show their commitment to be *just friends* was counterproductive when seeing Cassie made him want to pull her into his arms. It would've worked better for them to stay completely apart. Like, on different continents.

But he had to admit he didn't want to do that. Didn't want Cassie to completely exit his world. So when she'd suggested they do something friend-like together, he'd agreed.

As he parked his cruiser and waited to be let into the preschool, he realized that maybe this friend-type activity would be perfect. The noise level was high, the lights and colors bright. The place was sparkling clean, but there was a faint odor of sour milk and sweaty kids and disinfectant.

Totally unromantic.

"Hey, sorry to be running late!" Cassie came hurrying up behind him, and he turned to see that her hair was half out of her ponytail, her cheeks pink. "I was up early working on a doll, and I lost track of time."

She was carrying a big box, and he held the door for her and caught a whiff of something sweet from it, and something flowery from her hair.

He scrubbed his hand over his chin. The environment was unromantic, yeah, but she smelled so good.

Her eyes skimmed him. "Very official."

He glanced down at his uniform. "Gotta look the part."

"You definitely do!" Meg Harris, the director of the school, walked toward them, holding out a hand and shaking Evan's. "Thank you for coming in. We love having members of the community talk with the students. Who's your helper?"

"I'm Cassie Thomas," she said before Evan could introduce her, shaking Meg's hand. "I'm staying in Victory Cottage and I'm a doll maker by trade. I'm here to help Evan, but it'll be great to see what kids are playing with these days. Helps me stay up-to-date."

"Very good. Their toy interests do change quickly."

"Hey, Evan!" The school janitor walked up and gave him a huge hug, which he returned. Sylvie was relatively new in town and had gone through some tough times connected with an ex-boyfriend, but was now settled into the community, dating the minister and from what he could tell, ridiculously happy. He introduced Cassie, and she was just as warm in her greeting as Sylvie was.

As they left the other women behind and climbed the stairs to the classroom he was scheduled to visit, Cassie smiled over at him. "I love how friendly everyone is here," she said. "They all seem to know and like you."

"That's why I enjoy small-town police work." This was going to go okay, this friend thing. He'd get used to being around Cassie in all her moods and outfits and all times of day. He'd stop feeling that increased heart rate around her.

They walked into the classroom to applause and cheers. "Nothing like kids, little ones, to boost your ego," he joked to Cassie. And then he greeted Kayla, the teacher. She introduced him and Cassie to the kids, and he sat on a little chair and talked to the group about how police were there to help the community. That was important; some of the kids were afraid of cops or had already had bad experiences with them.

Cassie helped him pass around toy badges and held the other end of the crime scene tape as he showed it to the kids, but otherwise, she faded into the background.

Kayla, always the teacher, held up a big cardboard letter "P" for policeman and had the kids sound it out.

"He's a cop, that's K!" a little boy yelled, so they had to get into a discussion of C versus K.

That got a little girl thinking. "My dad calls you the Po-Po," she said. "That's a 'P,' too."

Kayla lifted her hands, palms out toward the kids. "Let's let our guest do some of the talking," she said.

"How many of you have met a police officer before?" Evan asked, and then realized his mistake when little Bennie Miller raised his hand. "When my mom and dad have parties, sometimes the police come," he said.

Cassie raised her hand, and he called on her gratefully.

"A policeman helped me when I was having a bad time," she said to the students.

No, not that.

But of course, Cassie knew better than to talk about her brother's murder with kids. "I have a big dog," she said, "and one day we couldn't find him anywhere. He's old and doesn't hear well, and we were so worried about what had happened to him. We looked everywhere, and when we got back home, we were really sad. But there was a police car in the driveway with Ace in the back. They'd found him running through a parking lot and brought him home."

She showed a picture of Ace on her phone, and the kids crowded around to look.

After a little more talk it was time for a break, and Cassie opened her box. "Your teacher said it's okay for everyone to have one cupcake," she said. "No nuts, no gluten."

Evan looked inside and was amazed to see cupcakes decorated to match the occasion: some crossed with police tape, some with the number 911 and some with badges. The frosting job was just crooked enough that he could tell she'd made and decorated them herself.

As the kids dug in, accompanied by quiet music, Kayla beckoned Evan and Cassie to the back of the classroom. "That was wonderful. Thank you both for coming in," she said. "Amazing cupcakes, Cassie. Where'd you get the idea?"

"Pinterest," Cassie said. "I did decide not to make the ones with guns and handcuffs on them."

Evan almost snorted his bottled water. "Good idea," he said. "And by the way, thanks for moving the discussion off the topic of which families see the police most often. My bad, asking about that."

"Yeah, not your best move," she said, laughing at him. "Although after my story about Ace, you could end up getting a lot of lost dog calls."

It was nice, standing here with Cassie, talking over what had just happened. "I'd rather have them comfortable enough to call."

"That's why you're a good cop," Kayla said. "And I'm sorry about the *Po-Po* comment. I hope it wasn't disrespectful. She doesn't know." She wiped sweat from her forehead and leaned against the counter. "Sorry, I'm tired. I'm pregnant."

"Congratulations!" It was news to Evan, and he felt a surprising stab of envy. "Bet Tony's thrilled."

"He is."

As Cassie asked the kind of questions women tended to ask in this situation, Evan watched them talk, and watched the kids and thought about things.

Cassie turned out to be great with kids. He hadn't really expected that, not with little ones. In fact, Cassie was outpacing his expectations in a lot of areas. Working with teens, helping with the investigation and now charming preschool kids.

Kayla clapped her hands as the kids started getting restless, having finished or scattered their snacks. "Let's say goodbye to Officer Stone and Ms. Thomas."

The kids ran up and hugged them both, their faces and hands sticky. Cassie knelt right down and was a part of it, clearly loved it.

He got an image of her then, with kids. *His* kids.

He'd now seen another side of her that he liked even better than all the sides he'd seen before. A side that made him think about picket fences and bedrooms with bunk beds, painted pink and blue.

Except he knew, for sure, he was a bad bet for that.

This friend activity had backfired.

CASSIE CHOSE TO stroll home from the preschool rather than accept a ride with Evan. She needed to think. But when her phone rang, and she saw her mom's number, she took the call. "Hey, Mom, how's the trip?"

"We're having a lovely time." Mom's voice sounded brighter than it had in a long time. "We visited the most beautiful castle yesterday, and we're seeing a cathedral today. How are you, dear? What have you been doing?"

"Just now, visiting a preschool class with Evan."

The silence at the other end told her she shouldn't have blurted that out.

"It was a community service activity," she quickly explained. "He does a lot of that, visiting schools, getting kids started early at viewing police as helpful, not hostile."

"Mmm."

"So tell me more about your trip. How's the weather?"

Mom ignored the question. "I'm worried about you, Cassie. I realize you and Evan are friends, but you need to be cautious. We talked about this."

A prickle climbed up and down Cassie's spine, because she'd been thinking the same thing. But for her to think it was one thing; for her mother to think it was just annoying. "I remember what you told me about his history, Mom. I'm aware."

You're aware that you like kissing him, too.

"It's more than that," Mom said. "Evan's a police officer. His life will always be dangerous. What if you lose him, the way we lost Josh?"

"I mean…" Cassie passed a mother pushing a baby carriage and turned the corner toward Victory Cottage. "Yes, there are risks, but he works in a small town, not New York City."

"And what if he goes off on one of his alcoholic binges?" Mom's voice rose a little. "You're strong now. I know that. Very strong. But you don't know what it's like to have the man you love go off on a bender, risking his life and who knows what else, using up savings, getting into accidents… oh, honey, I don't want you to…"

There was a murmur in the background. Good. Donald was there. He'd help Mom calm down.

Meanwhile, inside Cassie, annoyance fought with love and very real fear. "Are you okay?" she asked.

"Yes, yes, I'm just worried."

"Mom, no need for warnings. Evan and I are friends." Then she stopped, uncomfortable with the half-truth.

Mom's points were actually pretty valid. Evan was a cop, and while Pleasant Shores was safe, she'd heard a few stories of out-of-towners thinking they could set up in the area to avoid the law. Evan had been deeply involved in breaking up a dangerous dog-fighting ring, according to Bisky.

And he was good on the alcohol, but not perfect. She'd seen, and he'd said, that there were still challenges.

But oh, the feeling of being in his arms…

Based on how she'd felt watching him interact with the kids today, she was pretty sure she and Evan were kidding themselves about being just friends. Or at least, she was kidding herself.

But she needed to remember her goals. Gain independence; get justice for Josh.

Mom cleared her throat. "Any news about Josh's case?"

"Actually…" How much to tell Mom? she wondered. "We paid a visit to Minestown. Trying to track down some leads."

"More time with Evan?"

Cassie's cheeks heated. "Yes, but it's fine. Like I said, we're friends."

"I'm concerned."

"We're just looking into a few things, but don't hold your breath. You have fun with Donald, and don't give a thought to things back here."

"All right, as long as you'll let me know the minute you find anything out."

"Of course." She ended the call and headed home on a thoughtful feeling. Mom was right in some ways, but could Cassie's own feelings also be right?

CHAPTER SIXTEEN

ON MONDAY MORNING Avery opened all the windows of her dad's ancient El Dorado and beckoned for Oliver to get in. "Come on, road trip!" she crowed.

Oliver threw his backpack on the passenger-side floor and climbed in. "Cool car," he said.

Avery laughed and peeled out, headed for the highway that led up the shore.

Warm air blew in the windows, and sunlight sparkled on the bay. She had an entire day off for the first time since she'd started her new jobs, and there was a cute boy beside her. She felt like a kid again.

Oliver leaned his head back against the seat. "Thanks for springing me," he said. "I feel so trapped since I can't drive."

Avery tamped down the "your own fault" and "you're lucky you didn't get a DUI" comments that sprang immediately to mind. She was being paid to babysit Oliver, not to lecture him.

Evan didn't require her to keep tabs on Oliver when they were off work, but Avery had always been one to try to excel at everything she did. She was headed up the shore to look around at Bayshore University, and on impulse, she'd called Oliver to see if he wanted to come along. She'd keep tabs on him, maybe even nudge him back in the college direction.

And she couldn't pretend it was all altruistic or professional. Oliver was cute and could be a lot of fun. Plus, he'd stood up for her the other night when that creep had put his hands on her. She liked him and was glad to have his company.

In fact, since they were developing a sort of friendship, she felt a little guilty about taking money from his dad. She needed it, but she didn't like lying or misleading anyone.

She'd keep accepting the money for maybe one more week, and then tell Evan she was through with the baby-sitting gig.

There was a clanking sound, and she looked over to see Oliver pulling something out of his backpack.

A bottle. Then he pulled out a second one. "Want a beer?"

She rolled her eyes. No wonder he needed a babysitter. "It's 11 a.m. and you're drinking? We have a local AA meeting, you know."

"So I hear." He twisted the cap off and guzzled, then wiped his mouth with the back of his hand. "My dad goes."

"He *does*?" She'd never have pegged a police officer, especially a cool one like Evan, to have a drinking problem.

"Forget I said that." Oliver sounded uncomfortable. "It's supposed to be confidential."

"I won't say anything. I respect him for taking care of a problem." She knew about AA and alcoholism from the yearly health-class lectures, but she'd never known anyone who actually attended.

He held out the second bottle to her again. "Want one?"

"No way! And get rid of yours, too. We have open-container laws and the last thing I need is to get arrested."

Rather than dumping his beer, he tipped his head back

and guzzled the rest down, then tossed the empty in the backseat. "Problem solved. But if we weren't in a car and you weren't driving, would you drink? Do you ever?"

"I *did*." Avery slowed for a light and put on the turn signal. "In case you haven't noticed, I'm pregnant."

"You *are*?" Oliver sounded stunned.

His reaction made her feel a little embarrassed, especially since she thought Oliver was a little hot. A goof-off, maybe, but hot. Still, this was her life. She lifted her chin. "Yes. That's why I dropped out of Price, and why I'm looking at attending a local college part-time."

"Who's the dad?"

She glanced over at him. "Rude."

"What? I'm just curious. I haven't seen you with anyone."

"I'm not with him."

She drove on for a few minutes in silence. As they approached the university, Oliver spoke again. "I just can't imagine becoming a father at my age. How are you going to manage becoming a mom?"

"If you have to, you do it," she said. Then she looked at him. "Actually, I'm terrified."

"I bet." He sank down in the seat and pulled his knees up to his chest. "My mom still talks about how terrible childbirth pain is."

She waved a hand at him as she turned into the parking lot of the biggest building. She was unfamiliar with the campus, but there was a big sign that looked like a map of the place. "I'm not afraid of the pain. I'm afraid I'll have a baby and be a waitress at the Gusty Gull all my life." She turned off the car and rewound what she'd just said.

That was the first time she'd admitted it to herself. It was her mother's fear, based on what had happened in her own life when she'd become pregnant with twins. Her dream of going to college and becoming a teacher had been dashed. This was all news to Avery; she'd never realized Mom was the least bit unhappy with her choices until the past few weeks.

They climbed out and walked over to study the sign. "Ugh, this gives me bad flashbacks," Oliver said. "I hated college, other than the partying."

"Really? I loved my classes, at least the ones that didn't have weird, creepy professors. Most of them were great. Can't wait to get back to it, part-time at least."

He shook his head. "My classes were boring. I couldn't make myself wake up for them."

"What did you study?" She asked it absentmindedly as she glanced around and got her bearings. "Come on, let's walk toward the science buildings."

"Undecided." He grinned.

She rolled her eyes, something she seemed to do almost constantly around Oliver. "Well, I had a focus. I studied biology, so I could do something in medicine."

"Lots of labs?"

She nodded.

"Sounds hard." He reached for his backpack and pulled out another beer, this one in a can, then fumbled around for a can cooler.

"Stop." She grabbed the beer out of his hand and dropped it in a nearby trash can.

"Hey!"

"I'm sure you're not allowed to walk around campus with a beer."

"That's what this is for," he said, waving the can cooler at her.

"Well, I don't want to hang around with a drunk. Ruin my day."

"You're worse than my dad."

"No, I care about you. Just like your dad does."

"You do?" He moved closer and slung an arm around her.

She elbowed him in the side, hard.

"Ow!" He stepped away.

"Don't be like that," she scolded, and then turned her attention to the campus.

The science building—all the buildings, really—was older than the ones they'd had at Price, which after all was an elite school. When they walked inside and strolled down the hall, she could see that the classes were bigger, the equipment more out-of-date.

Still, the familiar smells made her smile. She couldn't wait to get back to her studies. She'd panicked when she'd found out she was pregnant, but she should have just kept going to school for the rest of the semester.

Except…yeah. It was better to change schools.

"Come on," she said, and led the way out of the science building and across the quad.

"What are we even doing?" he asked, his voice holding a little whine.

"We're going to walk around and get a feel for the place, and then we're going to the admissions office to see what it takes to apply. So for Pete's sake, chew some gum. You smell like a brewery." She fumbled in her purse, pulled out a pack and handed it to him.

"You're such a mom already, you know?" He took a piece of gum and handed the pack back to her.

As they walked across the quad, Avery soaked it all in: the students sitting on the grass, talking or paging through textbooks; the trees starting to come into bloom, their fragrance wafting through the air; a professor lecturing as her students sat in a circle around her.

"I love this so much," she said, wrapping her arms around herself.

She hadn't admitted it to herself before, how much she'd missed this environment. She'd been to this campus a few times before, for a couple of summer programs and a Women in Science day, and she'd always liked it. Then she'd gotten the scholarship and decided to go to Price, and that was that. Those were the only two campuses she'd ever seen, and sure, Price had the better reputation, but there was good stuff going on here, too; she could feel it.

Beside her, Oliver shrugged. "I just don't get it."

"That's because you take it for granted. You probably always knew you'd go to college."

He nodded. "Yeah, most kids in my high school did."

"And you had your tuition paid for by your parents, right?"

"My dad," he admitted.

"So you're lucky and you don't even know it." She studied him. "How old are you?"

"Twenty-one," he said.

"How old's your dad?"

He shrugged. "I don't know, thirty-eight? Thirty-nine?"

"He's way younger than my parents. He was young to be a father." She added it up in her head. "Like seventeen or eighteen? Wow." She patted her belly. "I think I'm young, but he was younger."

They'd reached a fountain where students were clustered, and by unspoken agreement they stopped and leaned on the railing, looking at the water. "My dad was never around," Oliver said. "Truth is Mom hated him."

"Hard on you," she said automatically. "Did he pay child support? In addition to paying for your college?"

"Yeah, he did."

"Interesting." She was thinking of her baby. Could she get child support from Mike while keeping him away from the baby?

Oliver frowned, looking moody. "I don't know what I'm gonna do, how long I can stay here. I'm basically not welcome with my mom and her husband. They're mad at me."

"And your dad? Is he okay with your staying?"

"Not sure."

They turned and walked toward the administration building. "Your dad's a good guy," she said. "I doubt he'd kick you out. Unless you're a complete jerk to him." She shoulder-bumped him to show that she was kidding.

He didn't laugh. "I kind of have been," he admitted. "But you're right. He hasn't said anything about how I should get on the road."

"Do you like the area?" she asked.

He looked around. "Well, yeah. I mean, it's pretty. People are nice."

"Then why don't you think about staying?"

Half an hour later they were emerging from the building with colorful brochures and vouchers that would allow them to apply to the college for free.

"Your dad would be a lot happier if you had a goal," she said. "Why don't you apply?"

"We could go to college together," he said in a fake-sappy voice.

"Exactly!" She laughed.

Truth to tell, the thought was pleasant. She imagined sharing rides up the coast and studying with a friend. Not to mention joining some of the clubs that she'd seen advertised in the science building.

But you're pregnant. You're going to have a baby.

She had to remember that college wasn't going to be what it had been. She wasn't going to be the carefree kid who threw a Frisbee across the lawn, like some of the kids she saw now in front of her.

Still, though, she felt hopeful.

"Well," Oliver said. "Maybe. Look, I'm sorry I've been a drunk jerk around you. I'm just confused."

"It's okay," she said. "Everyone gets confused sometimes."

"I appreciate that you actually think I could get into college and do something."

She looked at him sideways. "Of course you can. What do you want to major in, though? No more of this undecided baloney."

He laughed. "Baloney. I haven't heard that since my grandma passed."

"Well, what do you like?"

He shook his head. "I like doing things hands-on. The truth is I'm not much on reading or studying."

"Hmm, that is a problem when you're a college student," she said. "What about, say, engineering? Are you good at math?"

"I'm not bad." He shrugged. "I honestly just don't want to be in college."

"There goes my dream of having a study buddy." She put on a disappointed expression that was only half joking.

"Look, if you don't want to go, you shouldn't go. There are all kinds of things you can train to do at the community college. Or you can just get a job." She studied him. "I can't see you picking crabs, but people always need extra crews during the height of oyster or crab season."

"You mean like work on a boat?"

She laughed. "Don't sound so horrified. It's a job where you're outside all day, on the water. No need to go to the gym after work, because you've been doing physical stuff all day. And some jobs like that pay pretty well."

He looked thoughtful, maybe for the first time since she'd met him. "Thanks," he said, and took her hand. "You're really smart, you know that? Not just book smart. Real smart."

As they walked back across the quad toward the car, he didn't let go. Avery lifted her face to the breeze and relished the feeling of having a man doing something simple, holding her hand.

She didn't want to be involved with anyone; at least she was pretty sure about that. Between working three jobs—and here, she thought about the job of babysitting Oliver, which she definitely needed to reconsider—going to school and having a baby, there wasn't time for a relationship.

But Oliver's hand felt nice.

It was nice, too, that he knew she was pregnant and still liked her.

She saw a woman about her age, maybe a little older, studying on a blanket on the lawn. A baby lay beside her, cooing, reaching for the sky.

That could be me.

The sight filled her with hope.

She was starting to see her life fall into place. If that

woman could do it, she could do it. In fact, she couldn't wait to get started.

"Thanks for coming with me today." She squeezed Oliver's hand and then leaned over and kissed his cheek.

He turned and looked at her, eyes speculative. Their gaze held a little too long.

Wow. Okay. She backed away and tossed him the keys. "Feel like driving back? It's balky."

"Balky I can deal with." He opened the passenger door with a flourish. "Milady?"

She climbed in and wondered what this extra-warm feeling in her chest could be called.

CASSIE APPROACHED A big, rambling beach house on Tuesday night, carrying a bowl of fruit salad.

Music and voices came from the back of the place, so she walked around the side and was greeted by a loud, deep woof. A large bloodhound ambled toward her and she stood still, letting him sniff her.

"Sorry, sorry, that's Sarge," said a red-haired woman, hurrying over and taking the bowl out of her hands. She nudged the dog aside with one leg. "And I'm Amber. You must be Cassie. You're as pretty as Mary said you were. Come meet everyone. Not that it's a huge party, just a few friends and family."

"Thanks for inviting me," Cassie said. She nodded toward the bowl. "I went healthy. Hope it fits with what you're having."

"It looks delicious! Thank you for bringing it." Amber led her toward the small group of chattering adults and kids.

Cassie scanned the crowd. Was Evan here?

As soon as she realized what she was doing, Cassie

kicked herself mentally. It didn't matter. It would be better if he wasn't here, since they were spending time together tomorrow and had already seen each other earlier today. She needed to kick her obsession with him, anyway.

"Here's the most important person for you to meet," Amber said as an earnest-looking boy approached them. He looked to be around six. "My son, Davey. Say hi to Miss Cassie."

"Hi, pleased to meetcha." He rubbed a hand on his jeans and held it out.

"I'm pleased to meet you, too," Cassie said, shaking his hand.

"It's a school night," he explained. "So you can't stay late."

"Davey! Miss Cassie can stay as long as she wants. It's *you* who can't stay up late." She rubbed a hand over his head, ruffling his hair.

"Mom! Don't!" He spotted a boy kicking a soccer ball and ran off toward him.

Stark envy rose in Cassie's chest. She wanted a child to complain to her, wanted to be someone's mom. Back in Minestown, most of her friends had been single, but Pleasant Shores appeared to be more family-centered. She hadn't met many people who weren't married with kids.

"I still get a thrill every time he calls me mom," Amber said as she put the fruit salad on a long table alongside big bowls of potato and macaroni salad.

"He's not yours?"

"He is," Amber said, "but not by birth. He's my husband, Paul's, son, but I've adopted him and I'm his mom in every way that matters."

Realization hit. "Did Mary tell you to tell me about that?"

"Yes, she did. You may as well come meet my sister. She has a similar story. Hey, Erica, c'mere." She beckoned, and a petite, darker-haired woman detached herself from the cluster around the grill and came over, wiping her hands on a paper towel.

Amber introduced them and tugged them both toward a set of lawn chairs. "Cassie's the one Mary was talking about," she explained to her sister.

Cassie's face warmed. "I made the mistake of confiding to Mary that I don't think I can have kids and that my health isn't the greatest for having a family, anyway. I think she thought you guys would be an inspiration. Sorry about the forced togetherness."

Amber glanced at Erica. "What kind of health problems?"

Erica elbowed her sister. "If you feel comfortable sharing."

Cassie looked out over the bay, then back at the sisters. Behind them, the men around the grill broke out laughing, a deep, happy sound. "It's no secret. I had cancer when I was a kid, and I have fatigue, muscle pain, stuff like that. Nothing I can't manage, but my doctors are pretty sure I won't..." Her throat tightened a little, but she pushed the rest of it out. "That I won't be able to have kids."

Amber patted her arm. "That stinks. I got pregnant young, before I had my cancer. So I was lucky enough to have one child before..." She gestured at her torso. "Before everything."

"So you're a survivor." This was starting to make more sense.

"Two times. I struggle with fatigue, too. Mary was right. We should definitely be friends."

"Definitely!" Cassie didn't know many other survivors. "Are you able to work, in addition to taking care of a family?"

"At home. I'm a writer."

"We're very proud of her," Erica said. "What about you, Cassie? What's your line of work?"

"I make dolls." She waited for the laugh that often followed, but it didn't come. Instead, both women looked intrigued. "So I work at home as well. Mostly, they're lookalike dolls for kids with cancer and other serious illnesses."

"That is so cool. I'd love to see them sometime." Amber leaned forward and slid her chair closer. "I'm so glad you came to Pleasant Shores. I'm sure it's not under the best of circumstances, since you're in Victory Cottage, but you seem like you'll fit right in."

"Mama." A little boy came over, rubbing teary eyes, and buried his face in Erica's lap. "Davey and Jax won't play with me."

Amber's lips flattened and she glared out over the crowd. She gave a piercing whistle, pointed at Davey and another boy and beckoned them over.

"It's okay, they can work it out," Erica said.

"They'd better." Amber reached out a hand to each of the two approaching boys. "Hunter says you won't play with him."

"We'll play," Davey said immediately. "You can be the dog."

The smaller boy, Hunter, turned his head to one side, tears gone. "I wanna be the dog trainer," he said.

"You can't…" Davey looked at Amber. "Okay. We can all take turns being dogs and trainers."

"Okay!" Hunter shouted. All three boys ran over to the other side of the yard, where Sarge and a big St. Bernard rolled in the grass.

"Little negotiator." Erica chuckled, looking after him. Then she looked back at Cassie. "He's not mine biologically, either. Long story, but I can't have kids myself. Hunter's adopted, and I love him to pieces."

A tall man came over, tapped Amber's shoulder and whispered in her ear, sneaking in a kiss immediately after. Amber laughed and stood. "Hostess duty calls," she said, and walked toward the house as the man slid an arm around her.

"Her husband?" Cassie couldn't take her eyes off the pair; they seemed so happy together.

"Yes, that's Paul. I'm sorry I didn't think to introduce you. See, you fit right in. I forgot you were new."

"Thanks. And thanks for telling me your story and inviting me to your family gathering."

"You're welcome. You'll have to come over for dinner at my house next. Trey and I love having company. We're kind of rattling around in our house right now. Hoping to adopt more kids, but it hasn't happened yet."

"Kids, plural?"

Erica nodded. "Maybe a sibling group in the foster care system. So I'd better get used to cooking for a crowd. Maybe I'll invite Evan, too."

Cassie raised an eyebrow. Were she and Evan paired up in people's minds?

"Trey used to be a cop," she explained. "He and Evan

are friends, and I know Evan's involved with the Victory Cottage program. You two know each other, right?"

"Yes, we do," she said faintly.

"Come on, I'll introduce you to everyone else," Erica said, and Cassie was swept into the friendly crowd.

Inside, though, she was thinking.

Erica and Amber had both had their share of problems. But they were both managing. They were lucky to have each other, and to have this supportive community.

Could Cassie maybe, possibly, hope for the same?

CHAPTER SEVENTEEN

EVAN HAD MIXED feelings about taking Cassie along to visit Price University. They got even more mixed when she climbed into his truck on Wednesday morning wearing tight, ripped jeans and a sweater that showed a sliver of her flat stomach.

Evan managed not to stare, but any man would notice how good she looked. In fact, he thought about going all paternal on her and sending her inside to change.

She looked at him, an eyebrow raised. "Is something wrong?"

"No. We should get going. I have to be back to work at one." He turned up the radio and tried to focus on the news during the hour-long drive to the campus.

When they got there, he parked near the campus police office and then looked over at her. "I don't want you by yourself at the university," he said. "You'll need to come in with me."

Her eyes widened. "You want me to sit in on your talk with your cop friend?"

"Yes, and then I'll come with you to talk to your friend. We'll stick together."

She shook her head and opened the truck door, swung her legs around and slid out, nimble and girlish. She could easily be mistaken for a college student. "That won't work."

She slammed the door behind her, leaving Evan to scramble around to her side lest she walk away and leave him.

"It's not negotiable." He fell into step beside her as she headed away from the police office. "And it's not about you. We're talking about a crime here. Safety comes first."

"Look, Wendy won't talk openly to me if you're there."

He had to admit that he hadn't paid a lot of attention to who this Wendy was, that she wanted to speak with. He tried bluffing. "So your friend's afraid of cops?"

She stopped and turned to face him. "No," she said patiently, "she's a female secretary at an institution that favors men with advanced degrees. She needs the job, so she has to watch her back a little bit."

It was coming back to him now: Cassie had worked for the art department as a student, and she'd gotten to be friends with the department secretary. And sure, what Cassie said made sense: secretaries were some of the most in-the-know people in any organization. But keeping Cassie safe had to take priority. "We're at a place where a suspected killer works. The man who knows you witnessed him shooting Josh. If we're right, if he *is* here, you're a walking target."

She swallowed hard, then crossed her arms and studied him. "Price has more than ten thousand students and a lot more people who work here. And our man, if he really *is* our man, has no idea we're here. The odds are strong in my favor that he won't see me, but if you're that worried…" She dug through her big shoulder bag and pulled out a ball cap and big sunglasses. "There. I'm in disguise."

"Not a bad idea," he admitted.

"Thanks. I try." She patted his arm like she was consoling him. "Your contact will be more open if I'm not there, anyway."

"I...hadn't envisioned that you'd actually sit in on the interview."

Her hands moved to her hips. "Help me understand this. You want me to sit in some outer office while you do all the serious work, and then *if* we have time, which we probably won't, we can go see my friend, where you'll loom over us like Big Brother?"

"Like I said, it's not about you. Any police officer would take the same approach with a witness in the vicinity of a possible perp."

"I want to catch him, Evan." Her voice shook, just a little. "We may have to take some chances. So far we've come up with zilch."

"I'm doing the best I can."

"Good," she said. "Go do it." She gave him a little shove in the direction from which they'd come. "I'll meet you back at the truck in an hour."

"Cassie!"

She looked over her shoulder, her steps barely slowing. "I'm a grown-up, Evan. You don't get to decide what I do with my time. See you in an hour."

She was right, he thought as he stared after her, his fists balling in frustration. He didn't like it, not even a little, but he had no right to force her to play a subordinate role.

He just hated more than anything that she might be at risk.

CASSIE KNOCKED ON the half-closed door of Wendy's office. "Hey, can you photocopy me eighty-five double-sided pages by eleven?"

Wendy turned, mouth open, forehead wrinkled in a frown, and then her face cleared and she stood and hurried to the door, arms wide for a hug. "You stinker! Trying to raise my blood pressure!"

They hugged for a long time. Cassie had been the department's work-study assistant throughout her college years, which meant that Wendy was her supervisor, but it had turned into so much more.

Wendy had mother-henned her while also encouraging her to spread her wings. The older woman had shown her, by direct instruction and example, how to manage the world of work with dignity and grace. They'd shared many laughs about the absentminded professors and demanding administrators who made their work a challenge, but also kept things interesting.

Wendy was the only person from Price who'd come to Josh's funeral; not because she'd known Josh, but because she wanted to support Cassie.

"How's your mom?" she asked now, stepping back but keeping her hands planted on Cassie's shoulders. "Is she doing okay?"

Wendy had known of Cassie's mother's struggles and the way they had impacted Cassie's studies and ability to work. She'd been understanding on days Cassie didn't dare leave Mom alone, and they'd figured out ways for Cassie to do her work remotely. Wendy was the real deal, a genuine good person with a huge heart, and just seeing her lifted Cassie's spirits. "She's doing pretty well, actually," she said. "The Ireland trip seems to be working out, so far."

"That's good. And how are you? How's the doll business? Any men in the picture?"

Cassie waved off the questions, laughing at first, and

then not. "Can we talk about something kind of serious?" she asked.

Wendy grabbed her jacket off a hook. "Let's go outside. Otherwise, it'll be nothing but interruptions. Somebody *will* want me to photocopy eighty-five pages in five minutes." She flipped the sign on her door to "back in 30 minutes," and they headed down the stairs and out onto the quad.

Cassie tried to calm herself for the discussion to come by focusing on the fresh smell of new-mown grass and the beds of colorful tulips in front of the library. How could she phrase what she wanted to know without making Wendy think she was crazy? Let alone do it in thirty minutes, so that Wendy could get back to work and Cassie could meet Evan in time to prevent him from going into a full police panic.

Once they were strolling along a lightly trafficked sidewalk lined with redbuds in full bloom, Cassie sucked in a breath and then spoke up. "So tell me the latest gossip, and yes, I'm fishing for something. Is there anyone on staff who's been causing trouble lately, misbehaving?"

Wendy gave her a sideways glance. "Misbehaving how?" she asked, her voice a little guarded.

"Messing with the students, getting in trouble with the administration."

"You mean like one of the janitors or cafeteria workers, maybe a part-timer? Because I don't know all of the new hires."

Cassie shook her head. "No, probably a department head or professor. Messing with girls, say. Getting obsessed with someone."

Wendy stopped and stared at her. "Why are you asking? You don't work here anymore."

"No, but I have reasons." She needed to explain, at least a little. "I figured you were the person to ask, because you know everyone here." Wendy had started working at the university right out of high school more than forty years ago. She'd been an administrative assistant in various departments and also moonlighted in food services when her family needed extra funds. "It's important. Really important."

Wendy puffed out a breath. "Well… Let me think." She frowned. "There's Bowman, he gets handsy with the kids in the biology lab, or so I've heard. One of the adjuncts in English was just let go because he offered a girl an A for a…you know."

"Ugh." Cassie knew that the majority of workers here, from professors to groundsmen, were good people. It stunk that Wendy could think of examples of the bad seeds right away. "Do you think either one of them could be violent?"

Wendy's eyes widened. "Is this about Josh?"

"Possibly. It's a long shot, but we're at the long-shot stage now."

"I guess it's possible. Bowman's harmless, but the English guy, I think his name was Ketchum, seemed a little angry." Wendy frowned, looking at the ground, obviously thinking. Students called to one another at a distance, a couple of guys throwing a football, girls wearing too-skimpy tank tops, shivering in the cool wind. Cassie remembered her days here with fondness. If only she'd known to appreciate what she had then, back before Josh had been killed and the world had gone dark.

She had to make things right, as right as they could be. "Okay, Bowman, Ketchum," she said into her phone, recording the names.

"One other guy," Wendy said finally. "Professor Halofax. Do you remember him?"

Cassie shook her head. "What department?"

"Theater," she said. "He's good-looking, and he had a few student girlfriends in the past."

"That's against the rules, isn't it?"

"Yes, and nowadays they actually enforce it. Plus, girls aren't like they used to be, and he's not as young and good-looking as he used to be. I hear some girl wouldn't play his game, and he threatened the girl's new boyfriend, something like that."

"Threatened with violence?"

Wendy nodded. "It's all gossip, but where there's smoke…"

"Right."

They walked on, and Wendy ticked off a couple more candidates, someone in IT who had a reputation for looking up questionable stuff on work computers, one of the campus police who was reputed to offer drunk girls more than rides home. Cassie audio-recorded their names on her phone as they turned and headed back toward the building. "I'm sure I can find out something about some of these guys online." And at least she had a starting point, a grain of hope.

They were passing the spot where the truck was parked, and Cassie spotted Evan striding toward them. "There's my ride," she said. "Thank you so much."

Wendy looked at Evan, then at Cassie and raised an eyebrow. "Your ride, huh?"

"Yes. My ride," Cassie said firmly. Then she hugged the woman. "It was so good to see you. Call me and we'll get together soon. I've missed you."

She let go and watched as her friend walked away, wondering what Evan would say to her new information.

CASSIE WAS STILL pondering what she'd learned when she walked into the fabric store up the coast, Avery at her side. "Thanks for keeping me company today," she said. Avery's friendly chatter had kept Cassie from being annoyed with how Evan had handled her news.

Not that he was wrong in what he'd done. He'd had her send him the names and was no doubt using his police resources to find out what he could about each potential problem. He'd also taken over communicating the information to the Minestown Police.

The trouble was, he'd kicked her off the case.

Cassie's job, at least according to Evan, was to go back to doll making and leave the sleuthing alone.

"No problem! I was glad to come along." Avery studied a bolt of blue calico. "Plus, I'll be better than Evan about picking out doll supplies."

"That's for sure," Cassie said. And it was. Evan would be lost in a fabric store. Plus, being with Evan would distract her from her work. Stupid of her, since he'd let her know he had no interest in pursuing anything with her.

They spent almost an hour choosing fabric for dolls: various skin tones, and yarn for hair and most fun of all, fabric for clothing. They picked out enough materials for ten dolls. Cassie would separate the supplies into packets that each interested teen could work on.

"I was looking at your website," Avery said as they finished paying. "I could help you to update it."

"That's tactful. I know it's way primitive." She chuckled a little, remembering how Josh had pushed her to create a website; then, when he'd seen it, he'd laughed and urged her to get a professional designer. "But I can't ask you to do that. You're so busy."

"How about if I show a couple of the teenagers who don't like sewing how to do it? They could get the word out about the nonprofit dolls and build up their skills, too."

Cassie gave Avery a quick, spontaneous hug. "I've been wondering how to engage the kids who don't really want to make dolls. This will take care of at least a couple of them. You're brilliant!"

Avery laughed. "Tell that to everyone who's on my case for dropping out of college."

Cassie thought Avery sounded a little bitter. "That's really tough. What happened?"

"Had a full ride, but then this happened." Avery patted her belly, now protruding just a little.

"Do you think you'll go back?"

"Already planning it. But not to Price. I'll have to live in Pleasant Shores and commute up to Bayshore, part-time."

Cassie had been loading their materials onto the cash register belt, but then she perceived what Avery had said. "Price? You went to Price?"

"Yeah, for a year and a half. Why?"

They paid for their purchases and headed out of the store, Cassie debating with herself about how much to tell Avery. She couldn't help thinking about the girl as a kid, but the reality was she was about to become a mother. And at age twenty, she was only eight years younger than Cassie.

"If I show you the names of some people who work at Price, will you tell me what you know about them?" She doubted Avery knew as much as Wendy had, but on the other hand, Avery had been in a different network than Wendy. Students had their own sources of information.

They piled their packages into the backseat of the car. "Show me the list," Avery said. "I'll look while you drive."

In the car Cassie checked her messages, only to find three texts and two calls from Evan. Her heart jumped and brightened, but she tamped down that brief moment of happiness. She swiped the messages away and held out the phone to Avery, showing her the notes page where she'd listed the men Wendy had named.

She let out the clutch slowly, and the car jolted forward.

She wasn't going to call Evan back. He'd kicked her off the case and he hadn't wanted to talk to her for the past couple of days, so no way.

"Bowman, yeah, heard he's too friendly. Ketchum… don't know him." Avery paused. "Halofax. Professor Halofax, in the theater department."

There was something in her voice. "You know him?"

"A little. Stay away from that guy. He's a weirdo."

"How do you know?" She shifted, wincing as the gears made a grinding sound.

"He thinks he's super attractive. And I guess he is, for an older guy. But I was unlucky enough to get extra attention from him."

"Really?" Cassie stared at the younger woman. "Tell me more."

"It's a long and stupid story."

"We have time. Half an hour, anyway. And we need something to distract us from the bumpy ride." Cassie was getting better with the stick shift, but she was no expert. "So tell me about Professor Halofax. Why'd you say he was weird?"

Avery tore open a candy bar and offered a piece to Cassie. After they'd both crunched down a bite, she spoke. "He thought he was in love with me. Thought I was in love with him, too, because I went to office hours for help once."

She made a disgusted sound. "I was glad to get away from him. He was psycho."

Cassie was instantly concerned. "Did he, like, single you out from other students, or did he act that way with a lot of them?"

"Not sure." Avery spoke around a mouthful, then crumpled up the wrapper and dropped it into her purse. "He seemed to focus on me, but a couple of the girls said he'd been in trouble before for hassling female students."

"Wow." Cassie swallowed. That fit in with what she'd learned from Wendy, and Bliss and Josh. Except how did a guy go from hassling girls to shooting a man?

Thinking about what Avery was saying, Cassie forgot to push in the clutch as she shifted gears, and the vehicle balked and jerked. Flustered, she steered onto the berm as the car jolted to a halt.

"Sorry, I'll be fine, it's just the whole stick-shift thing," she explained in response to Avery's questioning expression. "So…you weren't real worried about this professor?"

Avery shrugged. "He was an older jerk. I've been around them before. No big deal."

Cassie rolled down the car window, thinking. Her surroundings came back into her awareness: the brackish scent of water from the swamp beside them, the chirp of birds, the rush of wind as cars sped by.

"Hey, your phone is blowing up," Avery said.

Cassie turned away from the window, took the phone from Avery's hand and studied the additional messages. She just needed to call Evan, get it over with, so she did. She hated that she was anticipating talking to him with any kind of pleasure. She wanted to be mad at him, but she kept getting sidetracked by her heart. "What's going on?" she asked, hearing the brusqueness in her own voice.

"Why haven't you been answering? Where are you?" He said something to someone in the background.

"Shopping for doll supplies," she said warily, and glancing over at Avery, switched the phone to speaker. "With Avery. Why, what's up? You're on speaker, by the way."

"I didn't know where you were. Don't do that to me!"

What did it mean, this urgent, repeated calling? Was it loving care and concern, like a romantic partner might feel?

Or, what was more likely, was it him being a cop?

Oliver spoke in the background, his voice distinctly slurred. "He's been freaking out. You witnessed a crime, you're at risk, yada, yada, yada."

"Oliver, geez!" Avery spoke up, sounding disgusted. "Of course your dad is worried about her. It only makes sense, if she witnessed a crime. Have a heart."

"I do have a heart. I gave him beer." Oliver laughed at his own joke. "Come on and party with us. Both of you."

"I don't know about that," Cassie said, "but we're on our way back to Pleasant Shores." She ended the call and glanced over at Avery. "They sound out of control."

"They do. And not in a good way." Avery frowned. "It's three o'clock. I'm pretty sure Oliver works tonight at five."

"And I'm pretty sure Evan shouldn't be drinking. Let's go." Carefully, she steered the car out onto the road and headed toward Pleasant Shores. "And on the way, you can tell me exactly what happened with creepy Professor Halofax."

CHAPTER EIGHTEEN

EVAN SAT WITH his son on the back deck of his cottage. Drinking beer, which wasn't good, but they were bonding for the first time since Oliver had arrived in town.

The air was soft with salty, beachy humidity, and a breeze rustled through the long-needled pines. A lonely seagull flew overhead. Out on the bay, two fishing boats were barely visible, but the sound of their motors came clearly across the water.

Evan had only had two beers, nothing to a guy of his size. He was enjoying his son's company, another first, and it was because of his old friend, alcohol.

Dimly, he recognized it as the kind of stinkin' thinkin' derided in AA meetings. Knew that his excuses—being upset about Cassie not returning his calls, being angry that the Minestown Police weren't doing more with the professor tip—wouldn't hold water.

On some level he recognized that he was thumbing his nose at his duties and responsibilities. He felt entitled to drink, and that was bad, a slippery slope he'd fallen down before.

He could lose everything. And now everything included not only his job, and Oliver, but also Cassie.

Cassie. The fear that she'd gone missing had pounded a big, rusty stake through the middle of his chest.

When he'd come out onto the deck and seen Oliver with

the cooler of beer beside him, he should have immediately called his sponsor. Given his emotional state, he should have left the scene or poured every one of those beers out.

But Oliver had held out a can to him, and beneath his son's cocky grin, Evan had seen the little boy Oliver had been. He'd seen the insecurity, the *do you love me, Dad?*

In that moment, given where Oliver was in life, given what kind of father Evan had been, or *hadn't* been, there had been no choice to make. He'd taken the beer, cracked it open.

They'd drunk beer and looked at their phones and talked a little. Finally reached Cassie and Avery and talked to them. Drank some more. That was all, but it was a start at connecting.

Next door Cassie pulled up and jolted to a halt in Josh's car. She and Avery climbed out, carrying shopping bags. Avery waved; Cassie didn't.

Fitted, frayed jeans and sneakers made her look like a kid. The white sweater that was falling off her shoulder, revealing a tantalizing glimpse of skin, reminded him that she was all woman.

He shouldn't be thinking about either thing, really. He glanced over at Oliver, who was grabbing another beer.

Father-worry pushed at him, mingling with shame. What was he doing? Why had he thought that drinking with Oliver was a good thing to do? If Cassie had been here, she'd have set him straight. In her presence he wanted to be better than he was.

Cassie and Avery disappeared into Victory Cottage and then, minutes later, came out the back door.

"Over here," Oliver called. "Come have a drink."

Avery marched over, hands on hips. "You have to work in two hours," she said to Oliver.

Evan winced. He should be the one doing the scolding, not Avery. Instead, he'd encouraged the drinking.

Which was right on par for him. He was a bad father. He was an alcoholic. He didn't deserve to have either Cassie or Oliver in his life.

Cassie frowned at Evan. "I didn't think you drank."

"Made an exception for my son," he said, cracking open another one. He shouldn't, but this was his last chance before going back on the wagon. Just one more.

More stinkin' thinkin', and he knew it. Before he could get deeper into it, he stood and dumped the contents of the can off the edge of the deck, regret burning in his throat.

"Come on," Avery said to Oliver. "I'll make you some coffee at my place."

Evan watched as Avery led Oliver off.

Cassie leaned back against the railing. "You okay?"

He tossed the empty can into the trash, where it clanked against others. Too many others. "I shouldn't have been drinking, but it was a good chance to connect with Oliver."

Her eyebrows drew together as she studied him, and more shame washed over him. Cassie knew. She'd had an alcoholic father. "I know what you're thinking. I need to go to a meeting tonight. Get back on track."

"I hope you do," she said, and her tense expression softened. "Hey, I need to talk to you about something."

His heart leaped, against his own will. Did she want to talk about them, their relationship, her feelings toward him? Which he shouldn't want, but he did.

"Did you know Avery went to Price?" she asked.

It took him a minute to shift gears. "No, I didn't," he said slowly.

"And she knew Professor Halofax."

"What?" He stared at her, trying to understand. "Avery knew him? Did she have any insight into what he's like?"

"Yeah." Cassie pushed off from the railing and paced the deck. "She did. In fact, she said he bothered her. Stalked her, even. Evan, I'm wondering if she's the young woman Josh didn't want to look for, the reason he decided to back off from the case."

Evan felt dead sober now. "That would be insane. What are the odds that you'd move in, and the girl who was involved in Josh's case would move in right next door? In Pleasant Shores, which has no connection whatsoever with Price University."

"Right, it doesn't make any sense. Except that a lot of people from this region go to Price. I did. Avery did. And a lot of people from other parts of the state vacation here." She paced. "Evan, she recognized his name right away. She had him for a theater class, to meet her arts requirement, and she went to see him during his office hours, once, to get help with a paper. After that, she said, he wouldn't leave her alone."

He pressed his fingers to his temples, his mind working on the puzzle, trying to figure out all the connections.

"If it's true, if the professor *is* Josh's client and he was looking for Avery, I'm worried about her safety," she said. "And…and mine, to be honest. If this guy got so outraged that he was willing to shoot and kill Josh…" Her voice broke.

He slid an arm around her shoulder, tugged her toward him. He wasn't worth much, but he could share his strength, comfort and protect her. "Does Halofax know where Avery is?"

"She doesn't think so. She broke off all communication with him."

"But if he's a faculty member, wouldn't he have access to her home address? Or else a way to get it? If he knew someone in the registrar's office, say." He shook his head. "I don't like it. I don't like it one bit."

"I don't, either." She stepped away from him and looked out over the bay. Her lips trembled a little, and his heart nearly broke. She was afraid and trying not to show it. His hands itched to comfort her, but he squeezed them into fists instead.

The best comfort would be a solution to the problem. Getting this jerk behind bars. His chest burned to think of a man who would harass a young college student, who would shoot an unarmed man in his home, in front of his sister.

"I'm giving one more call to Minestown and another to the Price campus police," he said. "I'll share this information and see what they say."

"Good."

And he didn't add: if there was no result, he was going after the guy himself. What he wasn't going to do was inform Cassie, because he couldn't put her at risk.

"I'll take care of it," he said, standing, his resolve strengthening as he looked at Cassie, so brave and yet so vulnerable. There was no way he would allow her to be hurt. Somehow, someway, he'd get the evidence that would put this loser behind bars. So he couldn't hurt anyone else.

And as for himself, he needed to keep his distance, because look what he'd just been doing: drinking in the middle of the afternoon. Which dialed his days of sobriety back to zero.

He was a bad bet for any woman, and he needed to remember that. But especially for Cassie, who'd known too much pain, part of it stemming from her alcoholic father, and part from the loss of her brother.

Even though what he really wanted to do was to pull her into his arms.

On Saturday morning Avery walked down toward the bike path that ran along the bay, her pace slowing with every step.

She really, really didn't want to meet up with her baby's father. Didn't want him involved in her life at all.

But when he'd texted, asking her to meet, she'd paused in the act of saying no. Talking to Oliver about his father, realizing that Evan had supported his son from a distance, she'd started to wonder: Could she get some child support out of Mike?

Of course, that would mean she had to tell him she was pregnant. How would he react to that? Would he even believe her, or believe that he was the father?

Telling Mike the truth could create a big mess she wasn't sure she was ready to deal with.

She saw his subcompact pull into the parking area where they'd agreed to meet, and her stomach lurched. She'd once been drawn to him, and then she'd been angry. Now she was curious to see what he wanted. She'd figured he'd moved on to the next girl, hoped he had. Really hoped this wasn't something like "let's get back together."

He got out of the car, slammed the door and looked around.

Seeing him, she felt the same way she'd felt when she'd visited her primary school, right before she'd left for college, when she'd seen the colorful hallways and heard the excited yells of kids on the playground. It was a warm, slightly sad remembrance of a good time when life was a lot less complicated.

Simple fun. She and Mike had had that together. Even though it hadn't lasted, he'd been her first real boyfriend. Her first time, too.

But she needed to focus on now, be practical, sensible, impersonal. Ignore the mushy emotions she'd felt for Mike during their brief time together.

"Hey," she called.

He walked toward her, and they met on the path. Would he hug her? Would she allow it?

She was disappointed in herself that she kind of wanted him to hug her. But after all, they'd shared the most intense thing a man and woman could share. It had meant something to her, even if it hadn't meant the same thing to him.

It made sense that she'd have all the feelings. He was the father of the child growing inside her. Whatever his flaws, they'd made something together, *someone*, who was going to be amazing.

And, she scolded herself, her feelings for Mike couldn't have been all that serious, since she was having feelings for Oliver now. Boy, did she know how to pick them.

She stuck out a hand to shake his and preclude the hug she still wanted a little. "How have you been?" she asked before registering the frown on his face.

"Not good." He gave her a limp-fish handshake. "Can you call off your new boyfriend, let him know we're not together?"

She tilted her head to one side, trying to process how he might have learned about Oliver. "I don't have a new boyfriend."

"The professor," he said impatiently. "Halofax? He's been hassling me to tell him where you're living, saying you and he just had a little disagreement. He's weird and he scares me."

"Me, too." She frowned, turned and started walking along the path, gesturing for Mike to join her. "And he's not my new boyfriend. What has he been saying?"

"He's stopped short of threatening me, but just. He's weird. He's come to my house, and my mom actually told me to come talk to you."

"Please don't tell him where I am. He kinda stalked me."

"Oh, geez." Mike rolled his eyes. "I wish we never... Look, Avery, I'm sorry about what happened, but I didn't know it was going to turn into all this."

A couple of bikes whizzed past them. A family of three knelt beside the water, the baby staring at a bucket of bay water the dad had brought over. She shouted and splashed it, making both parents laugh.

The scene shot a small, painful arrow into Avery's heart. *That* father liked his baby and his wife, from the looks of things. *That* couple was happy together. *That* baby would grow up with both parents.

She put a hand protectively over her belly. Mike was a coward, insensitive, and the baby would be better off without him.

Someday she'd have to tell him, though; the baby would

need to know he or she had a father. That was something Avery's mom had made clear, and Avery knew it was true. "Look," she said, "I'm not asking you for anything, but..." She looked out toward the bay. How to say it?

She looked back toward Mike, and a movement caught her eye. A white sedan, moving slowly along where they were walking. The man behind the wheel was... "It's him!" Without thinking, she pulled Mike off the boardwalk and into the sand that led to the bay.

"Who?"

"Halofax! At least, I think it is."

"Where?"

She pointed, but the car sped up and drove away.

Shoving aside the strange fear that seeing her creepy former professor created in her, Avery stepped away from Mike and faced him, hands on hips. "Did Halofax follow you here?"

Mike shrugged. "I don't know. I don't even remember what kind of car he has."

She blew out a breath. "If he's been bugging you about where I am, wouldn't it make sense that you'd look in your rearview mirror every now and then to make sure he wasn't following you?" Which wasn't fair, and she knew it.

"Like I said, I didn't know sleeping with you was going to make such a mess. I would never have done it if I'd known."

"Thanks a lot." What a dodo. The baby would for sure be better off without him. "Look, I don't want Halofax in my life, or you, either, for that matter. If he's bothering you, call the police."

She'd report this possible sighting herself, maybe, or at least tell Evan about it. Between the sighting and what Mike had said, and Cassie's having him on a list of questionable guys from the university, she was getting uneasy about her former professor and what he might do.

CHAPTER NINETEEN

SATURDAY EVAN HAD worked the early shift. On his way home, midafternoon, he stopped by the hardware store where Cassie and the teenagers were scheduled to do a work session in the back room.

She'd told him she didn't need him to come, but on top of what had happened yesterday, taking his first drink in fifteen years—and his last, he told himself firmly—he felt like a loser. He could at least fulfill his responsibilities to help out with the at-risk teens, the way he'd told Bisky and William he was going to.

Only when he got there, he realized his important male influence wasn't that important at all.

Isaac Roberts, who ran the hardware store, was back there, talking with a group of about eight teenagers. A bald man whom Evan belatedly recognized as Kirk James, Mary Rhoades's sometimes boyfriend, was kneeling beside a small stack of wood, discussing it with one of the teen boys.

Cassie had her laptop open, and she and a couple of the kids were studying it and laughing.

Cassie was like a flower, gathering all the honeybees around her. Even Ace leaned against her, accepting treats and pats from the kids.

Evan felt a primitive urge to wade in there and claim her, let everyone know *he* was the guy who'd brought her here, who'd known her since she was a kid. Let them know she was his.

Talk about primitive and stereotypical and macho.

He pushed the door open and went in, and the room quieted. Of course. For a minute he'd forgotten he was still in uniform.

And although he and the other cops in Pleasant Shores worked to build positive relationships with the community, some of these kids had bad experiences with police, ones that were hard to overcome.

"Look what the cat dragged in." Isaac walked over and gave him a light punch on the arm. "You here to pretend you're doing your share?"

He let out a laugh. Good. Let the kids see someone joking with an officer, unafraid of consequences. "Don't get your expectations up. My dad wasn't exactly the handyman type. I'll be learning right along with the rest of you."

"Shoulda figured." Isaac clapped him on the shoulder. "Come on, then, let me show you how to saw a board."

"He could sew," one of the girls said slyly.

Cassie smiled and looked up at him, one eyebrow arched. "We can teach you."

He opened his mouth to say something cute and then shut it again. For one thing, they had an audience. For another, he wasn't getting involved with Cassie, no way, so he didn't need to play at it.

Instead, he shrugged and looked from the wood workstation to the sewing supplies. "Wherever you need me."

"The truth is," Kirk said, "most of these kids know more about fixing things than you or I will ever know."

"What do you think?" Cassie asked, looking around at

the teens. "Do we need more help with the sewing or the woodworking?"

"Sewing," one of the girls, Emerald, said, and then blushed. She was a shy, quiet girl, and a couple of the others exchanged glances and smirked.

Emerald's shoulders hunched and she leaned over the fabric she was working with.

Evan smiled in her direction. "I'm fine with sewing. Put me to work."

Cassie had watched the interchange. "How about cutting out the pieces after Emerald pins pattern pieces on the fabric? No offense, but that'll be hard to mess up."

"Sure." He took a seat beside Emerald. A quick eye-lock with Cassie, and he could tell they were both on the same page: stop bullying before it started, model being kind to the student who struggled a little.

The work session went well after that, and Evan was glad he'd come. Especially when one of the boys held up a little fishing boat made of wood, and a girl gasped excitedly and took a boy doll over to sit in it.

It was cute, and when the boys showed how they'd made a moving sail for the boat, they all clapped. "Some kid's going to be happy," Evan commented.

"My little brother," Emerald said quietly.

A lightbulb went off. Evan hadn't realized they were making this for a particular kid from right around here. He also got a window into why Emerald didn't seem really happy.

From the surprised looks on the other kids' faces, they hadn't realized it, either.

"I'll get the boat painted tomorrow," one of the boys said. "What's your brother's favorite color?"

Emerald glanced up and then back down. "Red," she said, her voice so low it was hard to hear.

"And then we can do some kind of delivery," Cassie added. "Emerald, you'll be involved, for sure, but it depends on how much social interaction your brother is up for."

"He's pretty sick," Emerald said in a barely audible whisper.

"If we can't all be there, take pictures," another girl urged. "We all want to see."

"We will. And if we get permission, we'll post them on social media," Cassie said. "You all can share, and it'll help get the word out on what we're doing. We wouldn't mind attracting some donors."

As THEY USHERED everyone out at the end, Evan volunteered to stay and help Cassie clean up.

Once again Isaac clapped him on the shoulder. "I'm gonna let you lock up, man. I trust you." He lowered his voice. "Make good use of the time, brother."

Now, why had Isaac had to say that?

Of course, the truth was that Evan had been thinking of being alone with Cassie when he'd volunteered. So he could talk to her more about what she'd revealed yesterday. But he had to be honest with himself. That wasn't the only reason.

There was a broom standing in the back of the storeroom, and Evan started sweeping up the fabric scraps and sawdust. Cassie folded and packed away fabric, along with two partially made dolls.

"I appreciate your stopping in tonight," she said as she closed the last box. "It wasn't necessary, but I think it was good for the boys to see a cop's softer side."

"I enjoyed it," he said.

She started to pick up a box, but Evan lifted it out of her hands. "Let me do the heavy lifting," he said. When she started to protest, he added, "I have to regain my manliness after spending an hour cutting out doll clothes."

She snickered and pointed at two more boxes. "Those need to come, too. I'm parked just outside."

They walked through the deserted hardware store. The smell of sawdust mingled with faint aromas of oil and paint. "It's so quiet in here," she said, shivering.

"Scared?" He nudged her. "Chicken."

"Shouldn't be, but..." She gave a funny little shrug.

And he felt like a heel. "Sorry. Every now and then I forget you have reason to be scared."

He loaded the boxes into her car.

"Want a ride home?" she asked.

"Nah. I've got the cruiser."

Their eyes met and held. They were standing close enough that he could feel the warmth of her body, smell the floral fragrance of her hair.

He didn't want to leave her. He wanted to stay in this deserted twilight place and taste the sweetness he'd liked so much the first time.

He glanced down at her lips and saw them part a little, saw her breathing quicken.

His whole body reacted instantly, fueled by a heart that pounded like a drum.

She tucked a strand of hair behind her ear, nervously. "I guess I'll be going."

He wanted to kiss her, wanted it in the worst way. And he had the feeling that she wanted the same thing. She even half reached for him.

His chest pulsed with complicated emotions for the petite, pretty woman in front of him. She'd suffered so much as a kid, and later caring for her mom; she was practically a battle survivor. He was right to admire her. A better man would leave it at that, admiration.

But he was Evan Stone, jerk extraordinaire. Of course, he was going to kiss her, anyway.

He reached for her wrist and felt her pulse racing. Racing, and that meant she was attracted, too, but she was also afraid. And so she should be. She should run as fast as she could from him.

"Later," he said, dropping her hand. And then he forced himself to turn around and walk away.

BERTIE WAS GROWING concerned. Had he chosen poorly?

His innocent love wasn't as innocent as she had first appeared.

Had she reconnected with her idiot boyfriend? Why else would he have come to visit her?

Ah, well, he was no real threat. He was stupid; stupid enough to lead Bertie directly to his love.

As for Avery, after all, she was just a student. She had to be taught. Perhaps punished.

He had bigger, thornier problems to work out. The tenure committee had met to assess his file, and afterward, none of them had been able to meet his eyes.

Mother was proud of his status as a professor, if not of his field. If he lost his position... His heart raced as he imagined her reaction.

All the more reason he needed to cement his marriage plans, get started producing the grandchildren she wanted.

As he pictured her face, though, sudden doubts assailed him. Would she be pleased? As a child, he'd tried and *failed to please her on so many occasions, made so many mistakes.*

Sometimes he just wished he could be alone. Away from Mother, Charles, even his love. Safe and alone.

He took deep breaths, shook out his hands, stage techniques he used automatically to focus on the role at hand. It was a role that was about to change. He had a plan, and he'd stick to it and it would work.

He'd found them an apartment just down the street from Mother's. Had decimated his savings to pay the first and last month's rent and get his car trip-ready, clean inside and out, beautiful, as befitted his lovely lady.

Soon, these troubles would be behind them and they would go forward, into their life together.

He just needed to make sure the witness didn't squeal. He had a plan for that, too.

ON SUNDAY AFTER CHURCH Cassie met up with Emerald and gave her a ride home, to where her family lived in a small, ancient trailer on the docks.

She greeted the father when Emerald introduced her. She'd learned on the way over that her mom wasn't in the picture. "Okay if I talk to your son a bit?" she asked.

"Go ahead. Cheer him up."

She pulled out a sterile mask and put it on, and Emerald did the same and led her into the trailer.

Inside, the living room was set up like a hospital room, and Cassie sucked in a breath as memories took her.

Part of her wanted to turn around, run and forget. But she had a responsibility, a calling, even. "Hi," she said quietly to the little boy in the bed.

His eyes flickered open. "Hi," he said, his voice weak.

"I'm Cassie," she said, pulling up a chair to the edge of the bed while Emerald perched on the end of it. "We made you something."

He tried to sit up and then sank back against the bed.

"He just had a treatment two days ago," Emerald explained quietly. "They wipe him out."

"I get it." She smiled at the little boy. "I had cancer when I was a kid, too. I remember being tired a lot."

His eyes widened. "You're healthy now."

"I am," she said. She didn't want to make promises that he'd heal completely, too, because she didn't know any details about his condition. She remembered the people who had made hearty claims about how she'd be all better soon. She'd learned to detect the insincerity and ignorance instantly. This child was young, but she had the feeling he could already do the same.

At least she could be an example, a kind of visual aid, showing that people did get well after childhood cancer. And she didn't need to tell him that her recovery wasn't perfect, that there were aftereffects from the chemo. Treatments affected everyone differently, and he didn't need more to worry about right now.

So she told him a little more about her own treatments, how she'd felt, being honest about the struggle but emphasizing the good results. Then they showed the little boy the boat and doll, and he loved them, loved that the doll was a fisherman like his dad was. Emerald caught it all on video, and made her dad and brother pose for pictures with the boat and the doll. She promised to send all of it to the rest of the kids as well as to Cassie, so it could be posted on her website and social media.

Soon Cassie recognized signs that the boy was getting

more tired—wow, did that ever take her back, that sense of bone-deep exhaustion—and took her leave. She chatted a little with the boy's father and then headed out into a dark, rainy afternoon. It was a good thing she'd come in the car rather than walking.

She drove home through the rainstorm, feeling pretty confident about driving the stick shift now. Feeling good about the work she was doing, too. In all likelihood that family would never have found out about the dolls, that sweet child would never have had his day brightened, if she hadn't come to Victory Cottage. Being here was a good thing.

She climbed out and bent back into the car for her purse.

There was a popping sound. Shock and terror propelled her back into the car.

A year ago she'd have had no idea of what that sound meant, but she knew now. Even before her brain fully registered what was going on, her body knew to duck down.

Time seemed to stop. Rain drenched her feet, still outside the car, and she pulled them in. Had she imagined the gunshot sound? Could it be firecrackers, or a vehicle backfiring?

She should reach behind her, shut the door. The car was low-slung, though. If she lifted her head—

There was another pop, and the windshield shattered.

Panic seized her. Her whole body trembled and her breath rasped loud. The innocence that had started to re-bloom inside her, the hope that all would be well, shattered just as the windshield had.

Pleasant Shores, this safe, friendly, happy place, had been invaded by evil.

Of course it's not a safe haven. Those don't exist. Only children think they do.

Heart pounding, body flooded with adrenaline, she pulled the door shut behind her and fumbled for the keys. She dropped them twice before she managed to start the car back up, click down the door locks.

She tried to pull out while staying ducked down. Stalled.

Why had it stalled? She pushed in the clutch, sinking as low as she could in the seat, started the car again.

What had Evan said? Let it out slowly, push the gas pedal, slow, give it gas… *You can remember; you have to remember; your life depends on it.*

Mom can't lose another child.

She squealed out of the parking place and floored it down the road, headed for the police station.

CHAPTER TWENTY

EVAN OFTEN SPENT Sunday afternoons at the station, even though he wasn't officially on duty. Especially on a cold, rainy day like this, it was a good time to get paperwork done.

He finished one week's reports and started on the next.

Rain tapped against the windows and rolled down, making trails, casting the world into a silvery haze. He could see the street in front of the station, but it was mostly empty. Everyone was staying inside, it seemed.

He had to admit to himself that half his motivation for being here was to keep Cassie out of his mind.

That was getting harder and harder to do.

He was coming to admire her, a weird sensation. Prior to her arrival here in Pleasant Shores, he'd thought of her as young, innocent, naive. Vulnerable, because of how sick she'd been as a kid. Though technically she'd become an adult, he'd dismissed that.

Now, seeing the work she did, the way she handled the teenagers, the courage with which she faced what had happened to Josh and the threats to her own safety, he realized that the difficulties of her childhood had forged in her a steely strength that couldn't be damaged by outside factors. Her coming to Pleasant Shores hadn't been so much about her needing support in her victim status, but rather, it was a way for her to ensure that her mother gained the worry-free respite she needed. She knew how to reach out for help when necessary, but she knew how to stand on her own as well.

He walked over to a file cabinet where some old records were stored and started flipping through, trying to find an earlier address for one of the petty thieves who had lived in the area all his life, dating back to pre-internet times.

His new awareness of Cassie's strength was complicating his feelings about her. He'd started out by getting physically attracted to her, that visceral thing that Josh had noticed before Evan had noticed it himself. That was still there; in fact, it burned hotter every time he was close to her. But aside from the physical, he was realizing he actually liked her, would want to know her even if there was no romantic spark between them, would be honored to have her as a friend.

She was the kind of woman he'd have liked to marry, if he were fool enough—cruel enough—to try for marriage a second time.

He opened the window to get a little air and was turning away when a car squealed into the otherwise empty parking lot.

Cassie's car. She jerked to a halt, jumped out and rushed toward the station door.

He jogged to open it, ushered her in. "What's wrong?"

"He's there. He's at my house."

"The man who killed Josh?"

She nodded, pressing her fists to the sides of her head.

"Inside?"

"No, he shot at me. Would've hit me if I hadn't ducked back into the car to grab my purse." She was breathing hard. "I had to get out of there so rather than calling 911, I came here. Come on, let's go try to find him."

"Take a minute to breathe." He grabbed a roll of paper towels and handed her a couple. "You're soaked."

"Doesn't matter. We're losing time."

Yes, she was courageous, but she'd also been deeply affected by being in the house when Josh was shot. It made her nervous, unsteady, quick to see an enemy when there wasn't one. "Come sit down, and I'll get you a cup of coffee."

"You've got to be kidding me. Come out. Look at my car."

"I can see it out the window." He really didn't want her out in the cold rain again.

"Can you see the spider crack where the bullet went through the windshield?"

"What?" He spun. "Stay here," he ordered and then strode out to the parking lot.

The bull's-eye hole in the middle of her car's windshield set him straight, nearly gutted him because of how easily it could have hit her. They'd dig the bullet out from wherever it had landed, analyze it, but not now. He ran back in, holstered up and grabbed his jacket. "You said this happened in front of Victory Cottage? From what direction?"

"I'll tell you on the way." She pushed out the door ahead of him.

He didn't want her to come, would rather she stayed safe, but he needed to know the story and the cruiser was bulletproof. "Okay, if you stay in the cruiser."

They climbed in and he zipped through town, didn't hit the lights because he didn't want to alert the shooter. "Tell me what, where, when," he ordered, and she complied with only a little shake in her voice.

"I'm worried about Ace," she finished. "I didn't hear him barking. I should have gone in and gotten him."

"You'd do him no good if you got shot. I'll check on him." Evan berated himself for not staying home this afternoon. Maybe he'd have noticed something.

When they pulled up, there was a white sedan—nondescript, looked like a rental—parked in front of the next house down. As they approached, it pulled away.

Cassie was leaning forward. "Got the license," she said.

"Good. We can't know if that was him, but maybe. I'll look around." He pulled up close to her back door to provide himself with maximum cover. "Stay low. These windows are bulletproof, but I don't want to test it."

He got out, checked all around her house, his, the one on the other side. Now Ace was barking. A relief.

He saw footprints dissolving in the sandy mud, behind a clump of bushes at the far side of her yard. He took a couple of photos, eyeballed the trajectory from there to where she'd said her car had been and walked it out. He got lucky and found a slug in the post that held up her mailbox. Another bit of evidence. He checked the area one more time, checked the inside of the cottage thoroughly, with Ace trotting excitedly after him, and then escorted her inside.

He watched her joyous reunion with Ace while guilty thoughts churned inside him. If he hadn't been so busy trying to restrain himself from making a move on her, maybe he could have talked to her seriously about the interconnections in the case, figured it out and stopped this from happening.

He *had* to stop anything more from happening. He

needed to sit down and discuss it all with her, interview Avery, figure it all out.

About to suggest that they spend time doing that, he looked at her as she leaned back, letting Ace lick her face, and realized how pale and exhausted she looked. Now wasn't the time.

"You need to get some rest," he announced. "Maybe food first." He opened her refrigerator, found a container with leftover pizza and held it up. "I'll microwave this for you, okay?"

"I'm not hungry, but…" She checked the time on her phone. "I haven't eaten since breakfast, so yeah. You can help me finish it."

"I will, and then you can make it an early night."

She frowned. "Don't patronize me, Evan. It's not even dark out."

"I'm staying here," he said. "I'll grab my toothbrush and come back and sleep on your couch. You're in danger. I'm going to run that plate and get our forensics guy, such as he is, to take a look at your car and the slug I found in your mailbox." He put the pizza into the microwave. "This guy, whoever he is, tried to kill you. We need to stop him."

His words made her snap her jaws together and go pale. "What about Avery?" she asked. "If it's the professor, then he's a danger to her as well. I'm going to call her, make sure she's okay."

"Tell her we'll see about getting her some protection, too. Maybe even have her move into one of the bedrooms upstairs for a bit. Easier to protect you both here, and you can look out for each other."

"That's a good idea." The microwave pinged, and she stood.

"Sit down. I'm serving." He managed a smile. "This is the best you'll get from me."

She ate a piece of pizza and he ate three. Then he went next door to grab a change of clothes and a toothbrush. When he got back she was pressed close to Ace, sitting down on the floor. Away from the windows. She looked shaky and she didn't stand, and his heart went out to her. He knew what it was like to be shot at, to narrowly escape a bullet. Even for a trained professional, the aftereffects were significant.

He walked over and sat down beside her, leaning against the couch, on the other side from where Ace leaned against her. "Tough day, kid," he said, putting an arm around her.

"Yeah." She leaned against him. "Thanks, Evan."

"For what?"

"For being there. Staying with me. Helping me try to find this murderer."

"It's the least I can do." He squeezed her shoulders, brushed a stray strand of hair out of her eyes. "We'll figure it out, Cass. We'll work on it tomorrow. For now your job is to get some rest."

He didn't think she'd listen, but to his surprise, she nodded and let him walk her upstairs. He waited outside her bedroom while she changed into flannel pants and a T-shirt.

She sat down on her bed, then crawled in and pulled up the covers.

"Want me to lie with you until you fall asleep?" he asked.

Her brows drew together and she sucked in a breath, opened her mouth.

He spoke first. "Nothing's going to happen. Say no if you don't want me to. I just thought it might make you feel safer."

She looked into his eyes and then nodded. "Okay." She scooted over and turned her back to him, and he lay down behind her and spooned her, the covers in between them. Ace jumped up onto the foot of the bed and settled at her feet.

"He's not usually allowed to," she said, her voice a little sleepy, "but it's a special night." She reached down and rubbed the big dog's head, and Ace inched up and stretched out on her other side.

"I'm not usually allowed to, either," he said.

She glanced back over her shoulder. "That's right, and this doesn't change anything."

"I know. Shh. Go to sleep."

So he lay there with her in his arms. He was gladder than glad that she trusted him enough to drop off almost immediately.

It left him to take in the flowery fragrance of her hair and to feel the wiry strength of her body, even relaxed in sleep.

This wasn't easy, but it was heaven. He wished it could go on and on.

But it couldn't. Once she was breathing regularly, Ace snoring beside her, he eased out of the bed, dropped a kiss on her cheek and walked downstairs.

He felt a momentary gladness that he'd kept it platonic, just creature comfort. But that didn't last long.

So he was managing the part of his promise to Josh where he didn't seduce Cassie. But he was failing utterly at his promise to protect her.

A failure that wasn't unexpected, but was devastating all the same.

Cassie's refrigerator was like a magnet, because when he'd found her the pizza, he'd seen what else was inside.

A box of wine.

He walked over there, opened the door. Lifted the box and realized that it was nearly full.

He pulled it out and reached into the cupboard for a glass. He bypassed the wineglasses for a bigger water glass. It would hold more, and if anyone saw him, they wouldn't immediately know what he was drinking.

He put the box on the counter. Held the glass under the spigot.

Don't do it.

The voice of his AA sponsor echoed in his head. *We're all a drink away from the gutter.*

But Evan had never been in the gutter, not exactly. He'd always held some kind of a job, had never lived on the street.

You ruined your marriage and your chance to be a father.

But now he was bonding with Oliver. They'd bonded over beers two days ago, and he hadn't even been tempted to overdo it.

This day had been tough. This situation, staying with Cassie, dealing with his feelings for her, his worries about keeping her safe—his worries about Oliver, too, for that matter, and now for Avery—all of it was stress of a different kind than he was used to. It was interpersonal stress, relationship stress.

He'd faced down criminals on his job, risked his life. Had served active duty in the Middle East and been known for his steady head in a crisis. Things didn't scare him the way they scared other people.

Whereas this stress, much less on the surface, was different. This chipped past the ice around his heart, made him vulnerable in a different way, not physical, but emotional.

The interpersonal stuff was exactly what he didn't know how to handle. What he'd never seen his parents handle well. In the family where he'd grown up, emotions had gone from zero to throwing bottles and ashtrays in a matter of seconds.

And yeah, he'd escaped to Josh and Cassie's house, where he'd found a far more stable adult in their mother. But even that had been different from what he was facing now. After Josh and Cassie's dad had left, Cassie's mom had withdrawn rather than getting involved with a man, until she'd had a whole lot of time and therapy.

His glass still in his hand, he walked away from the wine box and sat down at the kitchen table.

Here was yet another reason he couldn't dream of making something out of his feelings for the woman sleeping upstairs: he didn't know how. Didn't know how to do the softer things a woman required.

Didn't know how to handle conflict when it came up, other than through a bottle. That was what had led to the end of his marriage.

He'd never thought to feel anything strong for another woman. He'd thought his basic urges could be satisfied through the willing women he occasionally dated, who didn't expect anything and didn't give anything beyond the physical. There were plenty of those around, and he'd gotten this far without hurting anyone, that he knew of, since his ex-wife.

But it had paled. The women willing to take that route weren't that interesting to him anymore.

Yet, a woman like Cassie wouldn't be willing to go for a quick bed and done. She had heart, and depth and she could love. That was what he wanted now, he realized.

That was what he couldn't have, because he didn't know how and because he destroyed any heart he touched. He was damaged, damaged by genetics and upbringing.

He stood again, walked over to the wine box, brought it to the table. Held his glass under the spigot and filled it to the top. Stood to put the box back in the fridge—it was still pretty full, good—and then decided it probably wasn't worth it. He'd just go for more once this glass was done.

Save himself some steps.

He sat back down, lifted the glass of wine and sniffed it. White Zin wasn't his drink of choice, but it would go down easy and do the job.

Do the job. The job of sending him right back onto the path he'd been on.

Because yeah, he'd never hit rock bottom, but he couldn't do police work if he was drinking. Once he started, he wouldn't be able to make it eight hours without a drink, not to mention the aftereffects of a binge. A small-town officer couldn't call in sick; not often, anyway.

Still, what was his job compared to the pleasures of a good drunk?

There was a sound upstairs, a loud thump. He shoved the glass and box aside, spilling some, and ran up, gun out.

Ace paused in the act of turning in circles, looking up at him, head tilted. When Evan didn't say anything or move closer, the big dog turned twice more and settled onto the floor with an audible sigh. And a thump.

So that had been what he'd heard: Ace jumping off the bed.

Cassie was still sleeping. She'd shifted to lie on her back. Her hair was a tangle and the T-shirt she wore had ridden up, showing a few inches of pale, slender belly.

He swallowed against a sudden dryness in his throat, then shoved his gun into his waistband.

Even though he could never have her, this woman meant the world to him. If he took a drink, he'd take another, and more and he'd be even more useless than he already was as a protector.

He pulled the sheet up to cover her.

Then he walked downstairs and emptied the glass, and then the entire box of wine, into the sink.

CHAPTER TWENTY-ONE

WEDNESDAY AFTERNOON AVERY was at Lighthouse Lit, shelving a box of new fantasy novels. Taking her time, thinking about whether she could afford a couple with her employee discount. She and Aiden had devoured fantasy novels throughout childhood, and he was still big on them. Sometime during high school, Avery had gotten away from that kind of book, going for more suspenseful, real-world thrillers.

Now, though, she felt the need to escape from the everyday world. Especially when it contained not only a lot of responsibilities, but also a creepy professor who seemed to be stalking her again. One who'd shot at poor Cassie right in front of their houses.

She'd talked to Evan, shared what she knew about Halofax, and he'd taken down all her information and told her the police had their eye out for him, too. Evan had suggested that she move into Victory Cottage with him and Cassie, but no way. For one thing, she'd just gotten out on her own, and she wasn't about to give up her freedom.

For another, she could tell there was something going on between Evan and Cassie. So even though he'd explained that his own move into Victory Cottage was about protecting Cassie, who'd witnessed a crime, Avery didn't want to be the third wheel.

She was a strong woman. She'd be fine on her own.

Oliver walked into Lighthouse Lit, and just looking at him lifted her spirits. What was *that* all about?

She didn't need to be so happy to see him. But ever since their visit to Bayshore last week, she'd felt warm toward him. Warmer. Not just in a physical spark kind of way, although that was there. Now that he'd let down his cocky, arrogant mask, she actually liked him as a person.

He went to the counter and spoke to Mary, and Avery abandoned all pretense of working and just watched him. She really needed to get off his dad's payroll, because the babysitting Evan had asked her to do didn't seem right, now that Oliver was a friend. No one needed to pay her to be with him; she wanted to be.

She'd kind of hoped he was here to see her, but Mary led him over to the nonfiction shelves and they stood there, talking, Mary showing him several books. Then Mary gestured toward Avery, so she had to smile and wave and pretend she hadn't already been staring at them.

Oliver actually looked a little embarrassed, which made her curious. She shelved the books in her hands and then walked over. "Shopping?" she asked him. "Mary knows every book in the store. She'll help you find whatever you need." It wasn't just flattery, either; the older woman was amazing, seeming to have a photographic memory for books.

Mary patted Oliver's back. "Let me know if you have questions or need more recommendations. Like Avery said, I'm full of them." She smiled at Avery and headed toward another customer.

"So what're you reading?" she asked just to make conversation.

He sighed and held up the two books in his hands. "*Careers in the Trades* and *If College Isn't for You*."

"Really? That's awesome."

He shook his head. "I'm just thinking about stuff. Never really thought about not going to college until lately."

"Now's a good time to figure out careers. Most people our age are still working on it."

"People will think I'm dumb."

"Who?"

"You? My mom?"

"Not me," she said. "Anyone who does an honest day's work gets my respect. That's how I grew up." She tilted her head to one side. "You need to come hang out on the docks with me sometime."

"How about now?" he said with a little of the old cockiness in his voice. "I'll buy you an ice cream cone on the way." He lifted his eyebrows up and down, teasing her.

"Well…" She pretended to hesitate, knowing she was going to say yes. "I get off in half an hour."

"It's a date. I'll run over to the bank machine and be right back."

"I have money," she said.

His mouth twisted to one side as he shook his head at her. "No way. I'm the guy. I'm paying."

She rolled her eyes a little, but secretly, she liked that. Mike had let her pay her own way, on the few occasions when they'd gone out.

By four o'clock they were strolling toward the docks, drinking Goody's chocolate milkshakes. She'd explained to Oliver that you had to start there, with a shake. That was Goody's specialty, and as soon as he'd tasted it, he'd agreed.

The day was warm enough that Avery tied her hoodie

around her shoulders, the sun hitting her face like she might actually get some color. There was always a breeze off the bay, but today it was soft, not sharp.

She wondered what he thought of this part of Pleasant Shores. Houses of various types, from big, sprawling two-stories to trailers, were across the street from the water, most matched up with docks and fishing shacks by the bay.

Where the road curved in, there were a few trailers on the water side, including Avery's family home. They'd survived there for years because their place sat on a little raised bluff, which gave some protection from storm waves.

Of course, Oliver had seen the place before, when he'd helped her move, but he hadn't paid attention. He'd been so hungover that she was sure he hadn't taken notice of much except how rotten he was feeling.

She felt funny about showing her family's home to Oliver. It was clear from his car and his clothes that he'd grown up richer. "Did you ever see the inside of a trailer?" she asked him.

"Honestly? No." He shrugged. "I wouldn't be opposed, though."

"Your dad's been to our place. How are you guys getting along, anyway?"

"Better, since he's staying over at Victory Cottage. Says it's to protect Cassie, but I think they've got a thing."

"Protect her from what? I mean, I heard about her brother, but why did things get more serious now?" Avery was pretty sure Cassie wasn't the type to get jittery over nothing. "I hope she's okay."

"Hey, college gal!" Old Rooker Smits yelled from his boat. He climbed out and tied her up, his movements slow with age and arthritis.

She wasn't exactly a college gal, but there was no explaining that to Rooker, who'd known her all her life and been so proud when she'd headed off to college. She went toward him to say hey, and when Oliver didn't follow, she turned and beckoned to him. "Come meet Mr. Smits. He's a fixture." She continued down to the old man's dock. "Want me to bring your crab buckets in?"

"I'd appreciate the help," he said, and sat down heavily on the bench in front of his shack. "Who's this young man?"

She beckoned again to Oliver, who'd hung back on land, and he came out and shook Rooker's hand. "This is Oliver. Evan Stone's son."

"New police officer?" Rooker thought of anyone who'd been in town less than five years as brand-new. He looked Oliver up and down. "You resemble him."

"Come give me a hand," Avery said. Oliver did, and she had to admit he hauled the bulky wire contraptions with more ease than she did.

When they'd brought in the buckets, she sat down on the edge of the dock and gestured for Oliver to join her. She talked with Rooker about his haul, an idea growing in her mind. "You know," she said to him, "if you need a hand this spring and summer, Oliver, here, might be looking for work."

"Know anything about crabbing, boy?"

Oliver spread his hands. "Not a thing," he said. "I probably wouldn't be much help."

"My seven-year-old great-grandson helps," Rooker said, his blue eyes bright on Oliver. "Suppose you're as smart as he is, and a sight stronger."

"I work hard," Oliver said, then glanced over at Avery. "Or, well, I can."

"Being a busboy isn't your dream job," she said, trying to be tactful, "but you do okay at it."

Oliver and Rooker agreed to stay in touch and exchanged phone numbers, which led to a conversation about the latest iPhone. Rooker loved technology and was in the market for a new one, even though his own was only a year old.

Finally, she got Oliver away from the old man and led him down toward her parents' place.

Her folks weren't home, which made it easier to take him inside and show him around. She tried to look at the home she'd lived in all her life with an outsider's eyes. The flowered wallpaper, the old-fashioned green table with aluminum around the edges, surrounded by four matching chairs. One of them had a crack in the vinyl that covered the seat, and a line of white stuffing was coming out. When she and Aiden were both home, it was kind of a game to see who could get to the table first and avoid it.

Why hadn't they ever gotten it fixed? They should get it fixed. Or pitch it and buy a new one, although when she thought about it, nobody probably sold this type of chair anymore.

Maybe she'd ask around, see who did that kind of repair work, and surprise Mom and Dad with it. She was old enough now to know that things cost money, and that she shouldn't just complain about household problems, but should help to fix them.

The front window looked out to the street, while the big open one to the back gave the view of the bay she'd loved all her life without knowing how spectacular and special it was. Black-and-white tile on the kitchen floor, and appliances so old they were back in style.

"Seriously vintage," Oliver said, looking around. "Nice view."

So he wasn't going to make fun. Of course not; he was nicer than that. "Come on back," she said, and led him to the bedrooms. Hers in the back, Aiden's in the front, connected by a tiny half bath. She looked at the dark wood paneling; the twin bed and dresser topped by a small bookshelf that held her childhood favorite novels, mostly fantasy; the poster of RBG on the wall. "My castle," she joked, opening the venetian blinds to check on what the next-door neighbors were doing.

"Um...cozy?" He grinned. "I can't see fitting in here, literally." He stretched out on the bed and had to bend his knees.

She laughed and led him through the bathroom to Aiden's room. "He got the bigger room so we could fit in an extra-long twin bed," she said. She looked around at Aiden's marine biology posters, his fishing supplies neatly organized on the wall, and a wave of missing him hit her hard.

Would it ever feel the same, just her and her brother, now that she was adding a baby to the mix?

It struck her now, too, that Mom might want to use these bedrooms for something else once she and Aiden had grown up and moved on. She'd always talked about building on a room for her crafting supplies, but she and Dad had never gotten around to it.

They'd kept her bedroom and Aiden's exactly as they'd left them, since the place she'd moved into was furnished, and she'd taken it for granted that she could come home anytime she wanted to. Now, though, she realized that had been a sacrifice. It wasn't as if they had room to spare in the trailer.

Was she getting more empathy for her mother now that

she was going to become a mother herself? Avery didn't know, but she resolved to make the suggestion to Mom that if she wanted, she could redo Avery's room as a craft room.

She led the way out the back, and if the inside of the trailer had been small, the expansiveness of the bay more than made up for it. "Wow," Oliver said. "It's an even better view from out here."

"Come sit on the dock," Avery suggested, and led the way, hanging her purse on a hook by the shed before leading him out to the end.

They sat and dangled their feet over the edge—not in the water yet, it was too cold for that—and he asked her more about her childhood, and fishing, and her family, what it was like to be a twin.

"How come you're being so nice?" she asked.

He shrugged. "You've done a lot for me. I came into town knowing nobody, and you've been a big help. Welcomed me in, been a friend."

Uneasiness tugged at her. He shouldn't give her credit for being so great when she'd done it for pay. She definitely had to remedy that.

"I like you a lot." He reached over and pushed back her hair.

And then he leaned closer and kissed her.

It was sweet and tender, which she wouldn't have expected. Not like Mike, who'd been all rough and tough, trying to act cool.

Oliver acted like he cared whether she liked it or not.

She *did* like it. She reached up and tangled a hand in his hair, ran her thumb over his cheek bristles.

He smiled against her mouth.

"What?" she asked.

"Kissing on the dock of the bay. Who'd have thought?"

"Kissing at my house, where my mom and dad might come home any minute." But she felt a strange sense of possibility.

She tried to squash it. "Look, you haven't forgotten I'm pregnant, right? Isn't that weird?"

He sat back, shrugged, his smile easy. "No. It's not weird, as long as you're done with the guy."

"I'm done with the guy," she said. "But seriously, my parents will be home from work soon, and I don't want you to make a bad impression."

"I don't, either." He sprang to his feet and reached out a hand to help her up. Which was getting ever so slightly harder than it used to be. She wasn't huge, not yet, but she was definitely a little thicker than before.

They walked back down the dock, hand in hand. She was seriously getting excited, her heart all fluttery and everything. The sun shone and the breeze was cool, and she was here, in her favorite place in the world, with a boy who really seemed to like her.

"Hey, don't forget this." He grabbed her purse off the hook where she'd hung it, but he caught it off center and a bunch of stuff spilled out.

"Oh, man, I'm sorry!" They ran around picking up lipsticks and keys and her wallet as everything blew around in the bay breeze. He handed her a container of gum and a receipt from the grocery store. "Geez, you keep everything in there, don't you?"

He grabbed another envelope just as it was about to fall off the dock. "Here," he said, and she saw what it was. Her hand moved toward his in slow motion. *Don't look, don't look.*

"Hey," he said, pulling his hand back, "that's my dad's writing. What's this?"

"Nothing." She reached out to take the envelope from him. If she could just stuff it back in her purse, she could think up some excuse.

But the envelope's flap was only tucked, not sealed. "There's money in here," he said. "Cash. Why's my dad giving you cash?"

"Umm…" She couldn't think of a lie, had never been good at that.

He held out the money, his eyes never leaving hers, his smile fading. "Care to explain?"

No. No, she didn't. But she had to. "He's been paying me to kind of…watch out for you," she admitted.

"Watch *out* for me? What do you mean?"

"Like, try to keep you from getting into trouble, let him know if you screw up, that kind of thing."

"Babysit me? Seriously?" His face got red. "You mean all along I thought you wanted to be my friend, and you were just doing it for *pay*?"

"No, no. I mean, yeah, at first. But pretty soon it was because I liked you and we got along. I was going to tell him to stop the arrangement."

He nodded, looking off to the side. "Sure you were."

She reached out for his arm, but he flung her hand away. "Don't fake me out anymore. Don't you touch me." He spun and strode rapidly toward the road.

"Wait, Oliver, where are you going?" She ran after him.

"Why? Gonna report me to my dad if I go drink a case of beer?" He didn't stop, just glared at her.

Finally, she stopped trying to keep up with him. She just

watched until he got out of sight, his steps fast and angry. Then she sank down onto the big rock beside the driveway.

She'd just ruined something that might have been really good. Through her greed and carelessness, her desire for just a little more money, she'd hurt someone she cared about, badly.

Not only that, but she was pretty sure he was headed off to make trouble. And if anything happened to him, it was on her.

CHAPTER TWENTY-TWO

CASSIE SAT AT her laptop and tried to concentrate, but it was hard to do. She was so annoyed with Evan.

Ever since he'd moved into Victory Cottage after the shooting, he'd treated her more like a bodyguard's client than an adult woman he was interested in. She was back to living in a protective cocoon.

Even after she'd gotten a text from Wendy and told him about it—Halofax left the state, some new job out west, department in an uproar—he hadn't let up on the protective behavior. Said he wanted to check for himself before believing that Halofax was truly gone.

She scanned her emails and was happy to find several people asking about the possibility of having a doll made: for a child's birthday, a niece who was sick in the hospital, even a doll in a graduation gown for a granddaughter who collected dolls.

Good. The improved website was doing its job.

She was about to close her computer when a little popup ad caught her eye, for an artsy-looking B&B on Teaberry Island.

That was nearby. She clicked and scrolled through, trying to find out more.

Apparently, the island was becoming a vacation spot and artists' colony. It looked cute, and there were several places where you could stay besides the B&B she'd initially seen in the ad.

She'd like to go. Maybe Mary or Avery would join her. But no, they were both working. Unlike her, their work couldn't be transported to a new location.

She'd have *liked* to go with Evan, if their relationship progressed along a normal pathway, but that wasn't going to happen.

She studied the pictures longingly. And then it hit her: she could go alone.

She didn't have to stay in a protective swaddling. She was an adult. She could just decide to go, and go. There was no law against a twenty-eight-year-old woman going on a few days' trip by herself. People went to Europe, to Africa, to Antarctica. She could go to a nearby island.

Evan would be angry, of course. He wanted her to stay isolated in her home, as if she were still a sick little girl. As if she were a victim.

And she was, in a sense; that was why she was here in Victory Cottage.

But if Halofax had truly left the region, she didn't need a safe sanctuary anymore.

She would go. Prove to Evan and to herself that she could. She booked a room at the B&B, then called the twice-daily charter service, found that there were seats available and gave them her credit card number.

Before she could lose courage, she packed a bag with her personal needs and another with her doll-making supplies. She carried them downstairs, feeling like a teenager sneaking out of the house when her parents were away.

Which was really wrong. She shouldn't feel like that

about doing something any other woman would do as a matter of course.

Well, any other woman who was the independent type and hadn't recently been shot at.

But, she reminded herself, Halofax was gone. Most likely. Even if Evan happened to be right, and Wendy wrong, Halofax wouldn't know to look for her at a place she'd only just noticed online, a place she'd never been before.

Ace trotted alongside her, panting, his tongue hanging out in a doggy smile.

"Oh, Ace. You can't go along. It's a boat and little hotel." She thought, then texted Avery. Got an almost immediate response: Sure, he can stay at my place, I'll give him lots of TLC and walkies. I'll pick him up after work.

So that was good. She texted Avery the location of her hidden outdoor key and then sat down to write a note to Evan. She definitely couldn't just disappear without having him panic, given how overprotective he'd become. She *felt* like a defiant teenager, but she would act like a responsible adult and let him know where she was going.

But she'd make it a pen-and-paper note, rather than a text, so he wouldn't receive it until she was long gone.

Headed away for a few days R&R. No need for you to stay with Ace—Avery's going to take him to her place. She paused. What else to say? Should she tell him her planned location?

She should. What if someone needed to contact her? On the other hand, she didn't want him going all overprotective and following her.

I'm headed to Heidi's HomeAway on Teaberry Island,

but I'd rather you didn't try to contact me. I'm fine, just need a little me-time to work on dolls.

There. That would have to do. She left it open on the table, setting a saltshaker on top of it to keep it from blowing away.

And then she grabbed her bags, threw them into the trunk of the car and headed down to the docks, excited and nervous about her first-ever trip alone.

ON HIS WAY out of the church, Evan stopped to talk with Pastor Steve, who was becoming a friend. "Extra AA meeting," he volunteered. Steve was tactful and knew the ways of twelve-step programs, and he wouldn't have inquired about why Evan was in the church on a Wednesday evening. And there had been a time when Evan wouldn't have admitted the problem, would have wanted to hide, but together with his sponsor he'd decided he needed to be up front about the whole thing.

"Everything okay?" the pastor asked.

"Yeah. A few stresses, but it'll all work out. I'm headed for dinner with William and Bisky."

"Ah, very good. Nothing like a meal with friends, and Bisky's a great cook. And no," he added, forestalling Evan's next question, "I don't want you to wrangle me an invitation. Sylvie's cooking *pasta e fagioli* tonight."

"Special occasion?"

"An anniversary that's only important to the two of us." His smile said that it was important indeed, and that he was a happy man.

Evan was glad for him and clapped him on the shoulder. "Enjoy."

"I will."

Evan strolled down the bay path toward Bisky and William's place. He'd been right to go to the meeting. It had calmed him down after his panicky anger upon receiving Cassie's note.

Because really, what was she thinking, going off by herself so soon after she'd nearly taken a bullet?

After the anger had come the desire to drink, but this time he'd hustled to a meeting, fortunately scheduled for today. There he'd gotten the soothing, uplifting reminder to Let Go and Let God. Had remembered that he was only responsible for himself, that he couldn't care for and manage the world.

You couldn't get much more secluded than Teaberry Island, anyway. Surely, she'd be safe there, although as a cop, Evan knew better than to take that for granted. "It's what you know for sure that comes back to bite you," was one of the few bits of wisdom imparted from his father. For better or worse, he'd always remembered it.

The sun warmed his back, and the gulls cawed out an accompaniment to his steps. The bay's waves lapped against the pilings, and the fresh, salty air cleared his head so that by the time he arrived at his friends' place, he felt like he could be decent company.

William met him outside, offering him a bottle of cold water and gesturing toward a cluster of chairs. "Bisky says we'd just be in the way inside. Let's stay out and enjoy the only peace and quiet we'll get tonight."

They both sat down and propped their feet on the picnic table bench. Evan sipped water, had a second of wishing it were a cold beer, and blew out a sigh. He'd definitely set himself back, drinking with his son.

"Everything going okay?" William asked.

Instead of answering, Evan responded with a question. "What do you know about Teaberry Island?"

"Nice place. Isolated. You thinking of going there?"

Evan shook his head. "No, but Cassie went for a few days."

"Must be staying at the new bed-and-breakfast. I heard an older couple there is opening their farm as one."

"Think it's a safe place?"

William frowned. "Yes, very safe. It's only accessible by boat, so you're not getting outsiders there. Sunny goes over fairly often, alone, and we feel fine about it even though she's young, a college student. Another woman we know, an artist, actually lives there."

"That's good, then."

"So why'd she go?" William asked. It was one of the things Evan liked about the big man: he was blunt.

"Maybe because I was overbearing in trying to protect her? I don't know. When someone you..." His words stuttered to a halt. He'd been about to say "someone you love," but that couldn't be right, could it? "When someone you care about gets shot at, you tend to go caveman on them."

Then he realized what he'd said and dropped his head into his hand for a second, then looked at William. "Hey, man, I'm sorry."

"Don't be. I think about Jenna every day. And if I could have known, I'd have gone caveman on her, too."

"Yeah."

Evan didn't want to say more, didn't want to bring the man pain by continuing the discussion, but William pushed on himself. "You asked if Cassie would be in danger there. You're worried the shooter is still targeting her?"

"I am. That's why I offered—insisted, really—that I

stay at Victory Cottage with her. But if it pushed her away, it backfired."

"She's an adult who can make her own choices."

"Not if she's…" He cut off the sentence before he could say the word *dead*. For William's sake, but also for his own, because he couldn't bear the thought of a world without Cassie in it.

"Daddy!" William's toddler came running out and flung herself at William, who lifted her into his lap and then bounced her on his knee. Cute kid, and her chatter cut off any more serious talk they might have done.

Bisky came out a few minutes later and sat on the arm of William's chair. "Dinner's ready when you are."

As they went inside, Evan watched the loving, affectionate family and tamped down his envy. Seeing Bisky and William and their daughter clarified what he wanted, deep inside: love and a family. Not just with anyone, but with Cassie.

But he wasn't going to get it. Not when he'd pushed her away. Not when he still struggled with drinking. Not when the only way he could think of to bond with his son was to drink with him, contributing to Oliver's problems.

So the next best thing was for him to go to Minestown and hunt down Josh's killer. If he couldn't have Cassie, he could at least keep her safe and solve her problems.

It wasn't until the next morning that he discovered the glitch in his plans.

HE WAS ALMOST READY.

He'd had to juggle some things. Create a story at the university and perform the role of the disgruntled employee to perfection.

Since it was partially true, it had been easy to do. He was disgruntled about the tenure decision, and he was planning to move across the country. He'd be setting up a new life close to Mother, and he'd halt the increasingly disturbing inquiries from the witness and the cop.

Only two more tasks remained: making sure the witness had stopped looking for him, and collecting his love for the cross-country trip.

It was disgustingly easy to break into the witness's house.

He'd looked at a few videos, picked up some tools and now here he was, inside.

She wasn't there, but she'd be easy to find. She'd written down her plans and left them for her cop-boyfriend.

She didn't know it, but she'd just given him a road map.

He had several costumes in his luggage, and knowing she was staying at a bed-and-breakfast, he decided instantly what one would work best.

The thought of playing a role, of actually talking to her, filled him with excitement. It would be the biggest, most important performance of his career.

CHAPTER TWENTY-THREE

ON THURSDAY MORNING Avery climbed into Evan's cruiser and tried to distract herself from the sinking, unhappy feeling in her stomach by looking around. She'd never been in a police vehicle. "Won't this freak Oliver out, the cop car?" she asked Evan.

"Since he stole my truck, I don't have much of a choice." Evan's voice was grim. "And he'll also be mad when he sees us together—if we find him, that is—but I think we have a better chance of hunting him down this way."

"You're right." It was the day after Oliver had made his discovery about the babysitting arrangement, and she hadn't been able to reach him since. She wasn't really worried, and neither was Evan as far as she could see. Most likely, Oliver was just off sulking somewhere. "Like I said, I'm really sorry I let him find out you were paying me to watch over him."

"I'm sorry I suggested it. It's my fault." Evan's jaw was all squared off. Avery could see why Cassie liked Evan: he was good-looking for a dad-aged guy. Even when he was angry, like now. And he didn't blame other people when things went wrong, but took responsibility.

Cassie wasn't around—she'd gone off somewhere and left Ace in Avery's care. And Avery hadn't wanted to leave the big dog home with just the other dogs for company, not when it happened often enough due to her work schedule, so she'd brought him along. She reached into the back and rubbed his fur.

"Did you put it out over, like, the police radio, that Oliver's missing?" she asked. She felt better if she kept asking factual questions. It kept her from thinking about how she'd ruined everything.

"Informally. I don't want to get him arrested, although if we don't find him within an hour or two, I will." He pressed his lips together, then drew in a breath like he was trying to calm himself down. "I've got a few ideas of where he might have gone, but what do you think?"

She frowned. "I don't think he'd head far away. He doesn't know too many people in the area. And he likes the bay. I'm thinking he would have found a spot along the shoreline."

"I think so, too," Evan said. "I'll take some of the smaller roads closer to the bay, then."

"Maybe the Nature Reserve. I heard him talking to our boss about it."

"Good idea."

They drove along in silence. The cloud cover was heavy in spots, but variable, like most days at this time of year. They caught glimpses of the bay here and there through the trees, as gray and choppy as Avery felt inside.

They passed the seafood processing plant, smelled it before they saw it. It was surrounded by cars. Never a day off in that business, and Avery said a prayer of thanks that she'd pieced together enough part-time jobs to avoid working there.

Of course, part of that piecing together had been the income from her sort of babysitting job. Maybe she should've bitten the bullet and worked as a picker, if not for the plant, then for one of the smaller places. They were passing one now, the size of a big house, surrounded by docks and crab pots. A couple of women sat outside on a bench, smoking, clearly on break.

On the other side of the road from the bay, they passed fields of corn stalks, half-green, half-dry-and-brown. There was the Bay Your Way Salon, part of Estella Ramirez's house. Just after that, a garage that repaired cars, with several ancient-looking beaters surrounding it. People made a living however they could out here. She wasn't unique or special in her struggles.

"I should never have agreed to that plan," she said. "It's just, I needed the money. And I know you meant well. You were trying to be a good parent, that's all. Keep him safe."

"Trying to be some kind of a parent," Evan said.

"And anyway, he kind of did need babysitting, especially when he first got here." She lowered her window, looking toward the bay again. There were break walls of rocks that kept the waves from the road, spotted with pelicans and egrets. A loon let out its mournful cry, and then another returned it.

And then she spotted a flash through the trees. "Slow down!"

Evan braked.

"I saw something back there."

Evan turned the car and they drove back slowly. They both made out the truck at the same time, and Evan clicked into four-wheel drive and followed the barely visible tracks.

They both jumped out as soon as the police cruiser halted. Had Oliver wrecked here? Was he okay?

"Look who it is," came a slurry voice from the back of the pickup. "It's the coconspirators, come to check on me."

Avery hurried closer and saw that Oliver had spread a blanket and was leaning against the side of the truck bed. He wore the same jeans and T-shirt he'd been wearing yesterday, and his hair looked greasy, his eyes bloodshot. There were two cardboard fifteen-pack boxes of beer beside him, and the number of empties suggested he'd finished the one and was working on the second.

"Have you been drinking and driving?" Evan asked, coming up behind Avery, his voice stern. "And by the way, that truck is stolen."

"Just from my dear old dad," Oliver said. "And no, I only started drinking once I parked. There's no law against that, right, *Officer*?" He put a sneer into the last word.

This hadn't gotten off to a very good start. "What your dad means is that we were worried," Avery said. "And that we're really glad to find you safe."

"I guess you'd know what he means better than I do, since you're on his payroll."

Time to apologize. Avery drew in a deep breath. "I'm sorry about that," she said. "It was a bad arrangement, but it was done with good intentions. Especially on your dad's part."

"So you had bad intentions?" Now he was glaring at her. Even drunk, he didn't miss a trick.

She lifted her hands, palms up, and told him the simple truth. "I needed money. I barely knew you, but I figured I could keep an eye on you."

"And that's why you invited me to do things with you. I thought you were my friend."

Behind her, Evan cleared his throat. "Look, the whole thing was my idea, and it was a bad one. I'm sorry, Oliver."

Oliver looked away. "I came out here to be alone," he said. "I don't want company."

"I didn't know how to help you," Evan went on. "Thought maybe being around someone your age would help."

"Oh, so you were buying me a friend? Way to go, Daddy dearest. Look how well that turned out."

"Like I said, a mistake."

"And we're sorry," Avery added.

"Did you not hear me? I want to be alone."

Avery looked at Evan and saw the same resolve on his face. "Nope. We're not leaving you alone. We care about you too much."

"That's right. Come on."

"Let people live their lives," Oliver yelled at Evan.

Evan looked shaken, but he and Avery went over to the truck and half-helped, half-pulled Oliver down and toward the cruiser.

"You gonna put me in jail?" Oliver asked snottily but with a shade of real fear in his eyes.

"No. I'm taking you home to sleep it off, and then I'm going to Minestown," he said. "I have some police work to do at Price."

Avery could see that Evan was beating himself up for the whole thing, just as she'd been doing before. But now, seeing Oliver, she wasn't any longer, and she wanted to help Evan get to where she was. "Do you want me to hang out with him?" she asked Evan. "I'm willing to babysit for free."

Both men stared at her, and anger flashed into Oliver's eyes. "I can't believe you'd say that," he said.

"Look at yourself." She let her eyes skim over him. "You're drunk, you're dirty, you have no way home unless we drive you. You're acting like a child toward your father, who's trying to help you." She glared at him. "I have the misfortune of liking you, not that you deserve it, and not that you appreciate it. So why wouldn't I offer to babysit you?" Leaving the question hanging, she dropped Oliver's arm and climbed into the front seat of the cruiser. Let Mr. Indignation see if he could even get himself into the police car without falling on his face.

AFTER RETURNING FROM a frustrating and fruitless day in Minestown, Evan didn't feel like going home, either to his own place where he might encounter his hostile son, or to Cassie's, which felt too empty. So he strolled down to the docks.

The smell of a cigar led him to Rooker Smits's place. The old man sat in a chair on his dock, and he beckoned to Evan to join him and gave him a cigar.

They sat smoking for a little while, talking about this and that.

"Know anything about Teaberry Island?" Evan asked, because he couldn't help thinking about Cassie and her solo excursion.

"Nice place. Getting more popular." He studied Evan shrewdly. "Cassie Thomas is over there."

"She is." Evan stared at the older man, surprised.

"I can see the boarding dock from here." Rooker gestured to the left. "I like to watch the people come and go."

Of course. Rooker knew everything that went on in town. "She's due back tomorrow," Evan said.

"Good, hope she makes it before the storm. But she will. The ferry runs except in the worst storms." Rooker drew on his cigar. "Saw a funny thing yesterday. One of them, what do you call it? Guys who dress like girls?"

"Uh..." Evan didn't want to get into a discussion of gender fluidity with old Rooker.

Rooker must have spotted his hesitation. He waved a hand and puffed on his cigar. "I don't mean one of those transgender people. That's something else altogether. Have a great-niece who used to be a great-nephew." He frowned. "We used to call them cross dressers, but there's probably a more modern way to say it."

Evan tilted his head to one side and nodded. And reminded himself not to stereotype old people as being behind the curve.

"Anyway. This was a regular guy, wearing women's clothes. He parked his car on the street right over there—you can still see it, half behind those bushes—and I saw him putting on something like a swim cap. Thought he was going for a swim, but then he pulled on a wig and got out in a dress. Walked right down to the dock and got on the boat. Darndest thing."

Rooker went on to describe a couple of other characters who'd gotten on the boat, and then they moved on to more general topics. But as Evan strolled home, he felt increasingly uneasy.

Everything he'd discovered today in Minestown had pointed to the professor leaving town, leaving the state and going out west.

But a man dressing up as a woman and going to Teaberry Island...just where Cassie happened to be...it felt wrong. It couldn't be the professor, could it?

He could text Cassie and let her know she should be on the lookout, but she'd asked him not to get in touch. Think-

ing a cross-dressed man was the professor would not qual-
ify as an emergency, and it was likely to make her madder.

Anyway, she was coming home tomorrow. Best to just
wait until then, because what else could he do before that,
anyway? There was no other way over to the island, nothing easy, anyway.

He went home and went to bed, but sleep didn't come
easy.

CHAPTER TWENTY-FOUR

ON FRIDAY MORNING Cassie slept in, then decided to walk to the docks rather than taking advantage of the bed-and-breakfast's shuttle service. It was her last day, and she was proud, almost smug. From being afraid to spend a night at Victory Cottage by herself, with a dog in residence and Evan next door, she'd progressed to a point where she'd done a two-day trip to a strange place by herself.

Just that sensation of courage, of making a bold plan and executing it, had filled her with strength and confidence.

She wasn't ready to travel to Antarctica on her own—didn't want to do that—but now that she'd succeeded with this short island jaunt, she wouldn't hesitate to visit a city for its art galleries or take a weekend getaway for dramatic inspiration. There was a doll museum in Chicago she'd always wanted to see, and she decided she'd book a trip and go soon.

Pulling her suitcase, heavy and bulky with all her doll-making supplies, she walked along the rocky shoreline toward the boat dock. Morning fog swirled around her, a reminder that the cool nights of April contrasted sharply with the warmer days. Just knowing this was an island gave it a different feel than Pleasant Shores. There was no industry here to speak of. Very few vehicles except for golf carts. Terns and gulls held sway, their voices and the lapping of the water against the shore the only sound to break the morning's peace.

She kicked at stones and thought about the past few days. Mainly, about Evan.

He'd treated her as a woman, and then he'd pivoted and gone back to acting like she was his little sister again. She by far preferred the former. But maybe, by her own vulnerable behavior, she'd encouraged his coddling.

Or maybe it was a flaw in him, or in their potential relationship, that he couldn't see her as an adult.

He was strong and kind, caring about the community, thoughtful. He'd taken in Oliver with all his brattiness and donned the mantle of fatherhood without a complaint. Was doing a good job with it, as far as Cassie could see.

There was still an issue with his drinking; she knew that. He struggled with the desire for alcohol, especially when he was facing stress. He'd even succumbed, that one time. But he'd quickly climbed back on the wagon.

Gulls cried out and circled. The street was nearly empty, and with the fog, a little creepy. She turned in the direction of the dock, pulling her rolling suitcase, walking faster.

Someone was approaching her in the fog from behind. The heavy footfalls sounded like a man. Evan?

Her heart pounded. Maybe he'd come here to find her. Which would be maddening, and yet she couldn't help but smile at the prospect of seeing him.

Which wasn't good, was it? How could she stand on her own with overprotective Evan in her life?

And yet now, after a time of reflection, she felt stronger. Like she could stand up to him, insist on being her own person. Maybe, just maybe...

She heard huffing and puffing from the person behind her,

which meant it wasn't Evan. She turned and saw a heavyset woman she'd met last night at the bed-and-breakfast. The woman wore a long-sleeved dress and sensible shoes and carried a big overnight bag.

"I've been trying to catch up with you." The woman was breathing hard. "Can we walk together?"

"Of course we can. Looks like you're headed for the docks as well?"

The woman nodded. "This fog has me spooked. I've been paranoid ever since I lost my sister."

Cassie turned to continue walking as the woman reached her side, slowing her pace. "I'm sorry you lost your sister," she said.

"It was terrible. A car accident." The woman stopped, pulled a tissue from her pocket and wiped her eyes. "We visited Teaberry Island as children. I thought I could handle it, thought it might even be healing, but I was wrong. It's too hard. That's why I decided to leave early."

Cassie touched the woman's arm. "I'm sorry. That's so hard to deal with." And she got it about how a place evoked memories. Going back to Josh's apartment had been hard.

"You seem to understand," the woman said. "Have you ever lost someone dear to you?"

"As a matter of fact, I have," she said. She looked down at the gravel road, then glanced over at her walking companion. "I lost my brother."

"You being so young, he must have been young, too. What happened?"

Did she want to talk about it? Not really, but she did want to move past Josh's death in her mind, to really start living again, and part of that was being able to talk about it. "He was shot," she said.

"How horrible! Were you there?"

"I was," she said slowly.

"That must have been terrifying! Did you see the killer?"

Cassie frowned and nodded but didn't elaborate, not liking the avid tone in the woman's voice. This had happened a few times before: people wanted to know what it was like when a shooting happened. It was the same impulse that made people slow down and gawk at a bad traffic accident. Uncomfortable, but understandable.

To Cassie's relief, the docks came in sight.

"Did they catch the person who shot your brother?" the woman persisted.

"No." Cassie didn't want to keep talking to this nosy woman, so she sped up her steps a little. Hopefully, her companion would soon get too out of breath to talk.

But now the woman kept up. "I don't know why I feel moved to tell you this, but I do," she said. "You need to get on with your life. You can't dwell on the past."

"I'm learning that." They'd reached the dock now, and people were disembarking. Cassie would get on and sit away from the woman who'd latched on to her. With that in mind, she gestured for the woman to walk ahead.

As she watched the woman easily heft her overnight bag into the carrying rack, she frowned. There was something weird about her.

The hairs on the back of Cassie's neck rose. When the woman sat down on a bench on one side of the boat, Cassie sat on the other side, keeping her in sight, but not close enough to talk.

There was a static sound, and then the boat captain's voice came over the speaker. "Hurry up onboard, folks, and take your motion sickness medicine. It's choppy out there, and this is the last crossing until this one blows over."

Cassie studied the woman who'd followed her as she talked to the man next to her. She kept watching her surreptitiously while the boat launched into the choppy bay.

Something kept tickling her memory, making her uneasy. There was something about the woman.

Was it a woman?

That wasn't a woman, that was a man, who'd been asking questions about Josh's death.

Her heart pounding, she studied her phone, pretending to respond to messages, but instead, looking up the professor by name. She'd done so before, and the previous search results popped up, but now she was looking for something specific.

She scanned through the images: of him teaching, playing a pirate onstage, playing an old-fashioned founding father with a white, styled wig.

Playing a woman.

She looked across, holding up the image to put the two side by side, and all the blood left her head. She quickly snapped a photo and texted Evan.

The professor didn't leave the area. He's on the boat with me.

The photo was taking forever to send. *Please, please let there be cell phone service out here.*

She glanced up again and saw that the so-called woman was looking at her, not smiling. She, no, he, beckoned to her. *He knows I know.*

She shook her head and focused on her phone, stealing

peeks at him throughout the rest of the short ride. Each time she looked, he was staring at her.

Cassie tried to look calm and unconcerned, although her heart hammered.

How had he found her?

Surely, he wouldn't dare do anything to her here on the boat, with witnesses all around. But once they got off...

Who knew what a man who'd killed her brother would do to her? Especially when she'd just acknowledged to him that she'd seen Josh's killer?

She wanted to live. She had so much to live for. Her art, her new independence. Making Josh proud, making up for what he'd lost.

Evan.

She wanted to live, for Evan.

The boat pitched and lurched as the mainland dock came into sight. She drew in a slow breath against the panic that wanted to rise in her. Unbidden, an image of her mother rose in her mind.

Her mother had lost one child; she couldn't lose another.

She faced front and started to plan.

EVAN REACHED THE docks just as the boat pulled in. He'd panicked when he'd gotten the message from Cassie. He'd told Oliver and they'd both tried to find someone to take him out to intercept the boat. But there were small-craft warnings and not enough time, anyway. With that option off the table, he'd called his chief and let him know what was happening. Backup was on the way.

He watched the crew tie up the boat, scanning the small crowd of passengers. His phone buzzed. "Bad accident out on the highway," Earl Greene, his chief, told him. "Me and Daugherty are both here."

Boom, there went his notion of backup.

A car horn honked, and then Avery and Oliver climbed out of an old sedan.

He jogged over to them. "I want Avery out of sight. Seeing her is likely to set him off." He'd gotten Oliver to make a couple of calls for him, but he hadn't intended for his son to show up here.

"She heard me trying to get a boat to take you. When I said I was coming over, she wouldn't stay home. She drove me." Oliver pointed. "Is that him? The one in the blue dress?"

Avery looked toward the boat, her brow creased. "That's my professor, dressed up as a woman. With Cassie. Why is he with Cassie?"

There hadn't been time to explain the whole story to Oliver, and of course, Avery didn't know it all, either.

Evan looked at the professor's face and saw ruthless intent. The kind of ruthlessness he'd rarely seen before. Maybe once, when he'd been overseas, a rebel leader ordering kids to shoot, to kill. Another time when he'd worked as a cop back in the city, on the face of an arsonist who'd loved to set fires in occupied buildings.

It was a complete devaluing of human life, and something ignited inside Evan now, just as it had in those two occurrences.

He was born, meant, called, to stop this kind of evil. It was who he was, or at least, who he wanted to be.

The two biggest reasons for him to live into that calling were right here: his son, beside him, and Cassie, coming down the ramp with the professor behind her.

The motivation for putting the past to rest and cleaning up his life seemed to make everything click into place for him. He knew what he wanted, how he intended to live from here on out.

But there was no time. "Get back in the car," he barked at Avery, and strode toward the boat.

Cassie was walking off in front of the professor, abnormally close. Close enough that Evan could tell he had a gun on her. She saw Evan and her eyes widened; her steps faltered. On her face was a mixture of relief and fear.

He saw the moment when the professor's eyes lit up. He was looking in the direction of Avery's car, and Avery was...not inside. Instead, she stood arguing with Oliver.

Evan was the only barrier between three people he wanted to protect—Cassie, Avery and Oliver—and a crazy gunman who'd killed before and would kill again.

"He's too dangerous," Oliver yelled, and the professor's eyes moved. Evan glanced back to see that Avery was stepping away from Oliver.

The wind gusted, pressing her loose top against her. Her pregnancy was clearly visible.

Seeing Avery pregnant would set the man off.

Evan looked back at Halofax and sure enough, the joy on his face was replaced by rage. Both the professor and Cassie were off the boat ramp now, and he jerked her to his side.

The crowd dissipated, talking and laughing, unaware of the drama in their midst. Most walking over to a mini-bus that took people to the seafood processing plant.

The professor pulled Cassie along beside him. He was marching directly toward Avery. If he'd seen Evan, he didn't show it.

Oliver put a protective arm around Avery, and the professor's face broke into a snarl. And then everything happened at once.

Cassie looked over at Evan, met his eyes and nodded, and the communication was wordless.

We have to go for it.

He may kill you.

He may kill Avery and all of us. We have to go for it.

She was right.

He lifted an eyebrow to say: *Are you ready?*

She nodded again.

He did a flying tackle while Cassie shoved the professor away from her and toward him with all her might.

Oliver pushed Avery behind him. "Stay back!" he yelled, and ran at the professor.

As a backup cruiser squealed into the lot, the gun went off.

Evan landed on the professor and knocked him hard to the ground. Cassie screamed.

And Oliver went down.

CHAPTER TWENTY-FIVE

THE TRIP TO the ER felt surreal to Evan. He rode with Oliver in the back of the ambulance, which was good because he saw for himself, and heard the EMTs confirming, that Oliver had just been grazed and there was more blood than damage.

He'd wanted to stick by Cassie, but she'd shooed him into the ambulance. "Go, be with your son, I'm fine," she had said.

Another officer, the backup that had finally arrived, had driven Cassie to the hospital to get checked out. She'd tell her full story to that officer, who was thankfully female—he had the feeling that would be easier for Cassie. He'd called Bisky, who'd quickly offered to meet them at the hospital to provide support. It was one thing Pleasant Shores was known for—they took care of their own. And Cassie had quickly become part of the community. Avery was fine, mostly angry, so she'd ridden along with Cassie in the cruiser. She wanted to see Oliver and ascertain for herself that he was okay.

After he'd filled out the paperwork, Evan walked into the curtained cubicle. Seeing Oliver in a hospital bed, hooked up to an IV, his throat got tight. Partly from worry, even though his head knew Oliver would be okay. And partly from regret, that he'd never been there for Oliver's cuts and bruises and broken wrist and appendicitis, all of which he'd only heard about from afar.

Oliver was sleeping lightly while the doctor typed into a computer on a rolling stand.

The doctor looked up and smiled—she was someone he knew a little, from multiple visits to the hospital related to his work. "He'll be fine," she said. "He got lucky. There was a lot of blood but he was just grazed. If he has someone to go home with, to keep an eye on him, we can release him real soon." She stood and typed something into the computer on the push-around stand. "I'm prescribing a mild pain reliever, but he may not even need that."

Evan narrowed his eyes. "Not an opioid, I hope."

She flashed a glance at him. "I can do Tylenol if that's better."

"That's better." Then he looked at Oliver, whose eyes had fluttered open. "Sorry. It's for you to decide what kind of pain reliever you need." When a man threw himself in front of a woman to save her, he definitely was old enough to chart his own course.

To his surprise, Oliver didn't take offense. "Tylenol's better," he said, confirming Evan's words. Then to Evan, with a rueful grin, "I never got into opioids, but there's a first time for everything."

After the doctor left, Evan sat down in the chair beside his son. "You showed a lot of courage out there."

Oliver waved a hand like it was nothing, but Evan was getting to know him; he saw the telltale flush that meant the comment had pleased him.

"I'm not the greatest nurse, but I'll do my best," he went on, feeling his way. "I'm guessing that Avery can fill in when I'm working."

At the mention of Avery, Oliver brightened. "Man, she's

tough," he said. "I can't believe that professor thought she'd give him the time of day."

"She's a great girl. Woman, really."

Oliver looked down at his hands, then met Evan's gaze. "I want to try to make a go of things with her."

Evan nodded slowly. "Like I said, she's great. She's also pregnant."

"I know."

"You ready to fill in as a father?" Evan cleared his throat. "You sure didn't have a good role model in that area." Inside he was thinking, *if Oliver and Avery get together, I'll become a sort of grandfather to Avery's kid.*

Oliver shrugged. "I'd like to try. I'd definitely be the supporting actor, not the main parent, but I can learn and do my best."

The words startled Evan. *I can learn and do my best.* It was the most ambitious thing he'd heard Oliver say, and all of it motivated by love for a woman. Interesting.

The machines beeped around them. In the hall, a stretcher rushed past, surrounded by scrub-clad workers.

"And it's true. You weren't a good father, at least in person." Oliver said the blunt words without malice. "But you did pay child support and stayed in touch with Mom. Tried to pay for my college. I appreciate that."

"Well…good." It hadn't always been easy, had kept Evan on the low side of the savings and lifestyle scale, but he'd done it gladly. The fact that Oliver had noticed and appreciated it made the sacrifice even more worthwhile.

"And I see how you are now, and I wouldn't mind being a little bit like you," Oliver went on. "Including going to AA. I need to."

Evan blew out a breath. "I wondered. I can give you the

schedule of meetings, let you know which ones I attend. Which would let you either come to the same meetings or avoid them." He stood. Wished he could touch Oliver's arm, hug him, but they weren't there yet. So he did the next best thing. "You're welcome to stay with me, you know. I mean, if you want to. However long you want."

"Really?" The bald gratitude in Oliver's voice told Evan it had been the right thing to say.

"Really. Now, go to sleep. I'm going to doze over here until they kick us out." He sat down in a hard plastic chair in the corner of the cubicle.

He remembered the wonder of watching Ollie sleep, back when he was a baby. How he'd slip into his son's room and sit, just watching him breathe and feeling amazed that he'd helped create a child.

He shouldn't feel heartache right now. He should feel proud of what Oliver had done, and grateful that he was going to be okay. And Evan did feel those things.

But he'd missed so much of Oliver's childhood. Now, right before Evan's eyes, Oliver was turning into a man. He wanted to reach out and rewind the film, so he could take his time and savor it.

That wasn't going to happen, of course. He took the folded blanket at the foot of Oliver's bed and spread it, gently, over his son.

MIDAFTERNOON CASSIE CAUGHT a ride home from the hospital with Bisky.

When they reached Victory Cottage, Cassie thanked Bisky and got out of the car, every part of her body aching.

To her surprise, Bisky got out, too. "I'll walk you in, make sure you're okay."

"What?" Cassie stopped and stared at the woman. Behind her, the sun was incongruously bright, the seabirds swooping, the early-spring flowers releasing their sweet fragrance.

And it was a world where evil lived. Where a man could target one woman in order to get at another, where a man could kill a beloved, good person because he wouldn't comply with his wicked ways.

Cassie had always thought of herself as a good person, but she'd been, at a minimum, complicit in the harm that had resulted. Avery—pregnant, vulnerable Avery—had been put at risk. Oliver had actually gotten shot, because Cassie had decided she had to make a stand and be independent.

It was the thought of her mother that made her catch her breath and grab on to the porch railing. "I could've been killed. My mom could have lost her only living child."

"Don't let yourself spiral down." Bisky took her arm and led her inside, sat her at the kitchen table. She asked where Ace was, then ran over to Avery's to get him and brought him back. Bisky was smart to do that, because when Ace came in and jumped and licked Cassie, she started to feel marginally better.

"Let's take the dog," Bisky said. "Come on. We'll go down to my place and get the boat, take a little ride."

"Are you kidding me? Never again."

"Yes, again." Bisky was hooking up Ace's leash. "Get right back on the horse. You've got to be comfortable on the bay if you're going to be a part of this community."

Was she going to be a part of it? She asked herself the question as she dutifully followed Bisky back to the car, helped Ace climb in and then climbed in herself.

"What's going on in your head?" Bisky asked as she drove them across town. "You worried about Evan?"

"Is it obvious?" There had been no one Cassie had wanted to see more, when she'd gotten off that commuter boat with a gun jammed into her side.

And yet, she'd shown beyond doubt that she was too much of a screw-up, too weak, too just plain inadequate, to be in any love relationship, let alone one with someone as complicated and amazing as Evan.

Half an hour later they were in Bisky's crabbing boat on the bay. Ace's tongue hung out as he sat on a low seat on the boat, nose lifted, clearly loving the excursion. The soft salt air was warm, almost balmy. The rocking of the boat reminded her of the commuter boat and her terrifying ride from Teaberry only momentarily, and then it began to soothe her.

She loved it here, loved the bay. She wasn't going to let Professor Halofax steal that away from her.

"Want to talk about what happened?" Bisky asked from the back of the boat as she steered.

Cassie didn't think she did, but suddenly the words spilled out of her. As she told of her realization of who the woman was, of her fear for Avery, Bisky just listened and made sympathetic sounds. Ace moved over to lean against her, still panting and sniffing the air, and she put her arm around the big, comforting creature.

Bisky stopped the boat and they just floated. Only when she brought over tissues and a soda did Cassie realize she was crying.

Bisky patted her back and, crowded between the tall woman and her dog, Cassie started to gain strength. "He admitted everything," she choked out. "He killed Josh because Josh was onto him about his obsession with Avery and wanted to report him."

"Your brother died a hero," Bisky said firmly. "Just imagine if he'd continued helping that professor. What could've happened to Avery."

"I don't like to even think about it."

Ace whined and leaned his head onto her shoulder, and she rubbed his soft fur.

"He found me so easily, though," Cassie fretted. "He broke into Victory Cottage and read the note I'd left for Evan. I was stupid. Stupid, stupid, stupid."

"First of all, we're all vulnerable to being duped." She went into a roundabout story of rescuing pit bulls from a dog-fighting ring. "You can't hold yourself to a higher standard than anyone else. So you made a mistake. You're also doing a lot of good, with your dolls and your work with our teens. You came right into our community and got to work, and we love you for it." She paused, looked out over the bay and then back at Cassie. "You can't let one bad man stop you. There's important work still to be done."

They floated awhile longer before Bisky turned the boat back toward the shore. By the time they reached the docks again, Cassie felt almost human.

Bisky had something else to say, though. "Sit down while I tie up," she said. "Look, I don't know if I should say this, but I met your mom."

"When?"

"We were talking after Easter services," Bisky said. "She told me that you couldn't ever have a family. That you weren't well enough."

Hearing it pointed out like that, stark and real, made

Cassie lean her head back against the wooden shed. "That's right."

"No, it's not right." Bisky tugged a rope taut and then came over to kneel in front of Cassie. "That's a harsh thing to say to a young woman, and it's false. All kinds of people have families. Including people with disabilities, or health problems, or other issues."

Cassie wanted to believe the words, but a lifetime of listening to her mother's cautions couldn't just drift away. "She has my best interest at heart."

"In a way," Bisky said, "I'm sure she does. But on the other hand...man, I don't get it. I've always wanted my daughter—daughters, now—to be strong, to grow up thinking they can do whatever they put their minds to. Why would your mom try to hold you back?"

"She doesn't want me to get hurt."

"Well, sure, but...if you don't take a risk and explore whatever it is that you have with Evan Stone, then you'll be hurt in a deeper way. Because you didn't even try."

Cassie blew out a breath, suddenly exhausted.

"Come on, I'll take you home," Bisky said, standing and reaching out a hand. "Sorry to lecture you when you're at your weakest point, but... I always found that worked pretty well with Sunny, my teenager." She grinned.

Cassie smiled back at her. "I'll think about what you said," she promised. And she meant it.

CHAPTER TWENTY-SIX

THE DAY AFTER the whole wretched episode with Halofax, Avery hugged practically every person in their small church. For good measure, she hugged her parents, too, and her twin brother, Aiden, who'd rushed home when he'd heard of her narrow escape.

And then she took Oliver's good arm. "I'll walk home," she told her family. "To *my* place." She'd spent last night at her parents' house, but she didn't want that to become the new normal. Her independence was important to her.

"Only if you'll come over in a couple of hours for Sunday dinner." Mom, who wasn't usually demonstrative, gave her another hug. "I need to see you again, sooner rather than later."

"Sure, we will," Avery said, "especially if you're cooking scalloped potatoes to go with the roast."

Her mother gave her a sideways glance. "I was *going* to bake the potatoes, which is a whole lot easier," she said. "But for you, I'll scallop them. Especially since I can conscript your brother into peeling."

"Thanks a lot, Ave." But even Aiden gave her another hug before following her parents to their car.

She and Oliver strolled slowly through the town, still quiet before noon on a Sunday. Avery kept hold of his arm. "I wanted to say thank you, a real, private thank you, for how you literally took a bullet for me yesterday," she said.

"I'm totally using that for the rest of our relationship." He grinned over at her.

Avery felt something dance inside her at his words. Was there going to *be* a rest of their relationship? And was that happiness or nerves she felt? "My life's going to get more complicated," she warned him. "For one thing, I've sent a court request for a DNA test to Mike, the baby's father. I'm going to make him pay child support."

"That's fair," Oliver said.

"It means he'll be part of my life going forward," she said, "which I'm not thrilled about, but it's important for the baby and for our financial future. Hers and mine," she clarified, so Oliver wouldn't think she was making any demands or promises.

He stopped and took her hand with his good one, pulled her to face him. "That's okay," he said, "as long as you're not wanting to get back with him." He studied her face. "Do you still have feelings for him?"

She shook her head. "Annoyance, mostly. Which I sometimes feel for you, too, but mostly..." She tugged him closer and brushed his lips with hers. "Mostly, I like you a lot."

She just meant it to be a friendly kiss, short and sweet, but Oliver caught her by the waist. "Do that again," he said, softening the order with a crooked grin.

She leaned closer and slid her hand into his hair, pulling his face down to hers, and then he took over, splaying his hand across her back, touching her cheek, planting little butterfly kisses along her hairline.

And Avery felt something relax inside her for the first time since she'd discovered she was pregnant. She felt cared for, like she didn't have to be the only strong one. Felt like she could let down her guard a little. Felt like what had

gone all wrong between her and Mike didn't have to de-
fine her life.

She felt a flutter in her stomach, then another one and
then she smiled against Oliver's lips. "The baby's kicking."

He stepped back and blinked. "Did I hurt her? It's a
girl, right?"

She smiled. "It's a girl, and no, you didn't hurt her. I
think she likes you." She took his hand and held it to her
belly. "Maybe you can feel her."

He held his hand there, his expression intent, and when
the baby kicked again, his smile widened. "That's cool!"

"Most of the time, yeah."

Once her heart rate had settled and they were strolling
again, Avery decided she should tell it all. "I'm also going
to college again," she said. "At Bayshore. I sent in my application this morning."

He raised his eyebrows. "This morning?"

She nodded. "Adrenaline plus baby. I didn't sleep much."

"What made you decide to do it now? I mean, when
you're about to become a mother and all."

She shrugged. "Things aren't going to get easier for a
while now," she said. "I really, really want to be the person I was before all the craziness started happening. The
nerdy girl who loves to study. Who maybe, one day, wants
to become a professor."

Oliver made a face. "A good one, not…" He waved his
hand in the direction of the waterfront.

"Well, right, exactly." She looked over at him as they
passed the Catholic church, its doors just opening, spilling
people out into the April warmth. "But the biggest thing,
bigger than college or anything else, is I'm having a baby.

She's going to take a lot of time and commitment. Between that, and working, and going to school…"

"You won't have a whole lot of time for me. I get it." To her surprise, he didn't sound upset. "I'm going to be busy, too. Work, AA, EMT training…"

"AA?"

He nodded. "I need it. I've gotten myself in trouble for drinking too many times. What if I'd had an accident driving, hurt someone?"

"Serious stuff. What about the EMT thing?"

He ducked his head, looking shy. "I know it's all kind of new, but I was talking to the EMTs yesterday. I liked what they were doing, the way they were, so I asked about learning to be one. There's a big need," he said. "I don't want to go to college for a four-year degree, but for something hands-on, I think it might be good."

"You're definitely cool in a crisis," she said, thinking of yesterday. "Kind of like your dad."

He blew out a breath and nodded. "Yeah. I guess I am." He looked over at her. "So we'll both have a lot going on, but can we see each other in the spaces?"

She swung his hand. "I'd like that, but my spaces are probably going to have a baby with me, or in the next room napping."

"I like babies," he said. Then frowned. "I think. I've never been around them much. But for you, I'm willing to give it a try."

And that was all she could ask, she thought as they emerged from the downtown and headed toward Evan's house and her own place. Despite everything that had happened, for Avery, things were looking up.

PAINFUL. WONDERFUL. BITTERSWEET.

Visiting the hospital with Evan, a week after the awful episode with Halofax, was all of those things.

They were here to deliver a completed lookalike doll to a patient. The hospital didn't allow big groups to visit the pediatric oncology unit, so Cassie had planned to deliver the doll alone. But Evan had gotten wind of that from the teens and had quietly insisted on coming along, to drive her and film the event.

And although she hated to admit it, she welcomed his support. After the adrenaline of her risky venture had worn off, she'd found herself jumpy. Looking around for a threatening person, even though Halofax was safely in jail awaiting trial, having already been charged with felony murder and arraigned.

It was similar to how she'd felt after the break-in that had resulted in Josh's death, although this time the underlying sense was relief, not pain and grief.

Their half-hour car ride had been quiet, after a couple of bursts of polite conversation. Evan had asked after her mother, and had seemed genuinely happy that Mom had gained some closure and elected to stay in Ireland and finish the trip. She'd wanted to come home, but Cassie had insisted she was fine. And she was, mostly.

It was a huge relief to know that Oliver was recovering well and, in fact, was going to be able to work a short shift at the Gusty Gull tonight.

But now, as they walked into the small regional hospital, Cassie lost her easy distance. The smell of disinfectant, the soft pings of the elevator, the carefully modulated voices on the intercom, all of it brought back the scary years of her childhood.

Evan strode to the reception desk and told their business, got directions to the pediatric oncology floor. When he came back toward her, he tipped his head to one side and studied her. "You okay?"

"Yeah." She looked around. "Lots of memories."

Understanding crossed his face. "Do you want to sit a minute?"

"No, I'm fine," she said.

"Sit down." He took her arm and steered her toward a chair.

Even as she sank down into it, she was shaking her head. "I can walk. I'm fine. I was just here a week ago and I barely noticed my surroundings, so..."

"And everyone needs help at times. I'd be nowhere without my AA friends."

"I guess you're right." It did feel good to sit, take a break before continuing on their task.

"Besides," he said, "you don't want to approach a sick kid with that pale, upset look on your face."

"Good point." She smiled ruefully. "I remember some of the visitors I had as a kid. People who felt obligated but were totally uncomfortable with baldness and bandages." She looked around thoughtfully. "I've always known I got into this line of work partly to process everything that happened when I got sick as a kid. Usually, I'm fine delivering to hospitals. Wonder what's spooked me this time?"

"Trauma piles up," Evan said promptly. "You've just gone through a rough time on top of a rough time."

"Yeah, I guess." She stood. "And I'm over it. Let's go."

Once they'd checked in and gone to the child's room, Cassie forgot her own emotions. She approached the ten-year-old girl's bed. "Hey, Marisol," she said. "How are you doing?"

The child turned her face away.

A dark-haired woman came around the bed and shook Cassie's hand. "I'm Mom," she said. "She's a little depressed. I'm sorry. Marisol, say hello."

The child waved a hand and uttered a barely distinguishable "hi."

"It's fine," Cassie said, introducing herself and Evan. "Okay if I talk to her?"

"Yes, of course," she said, and nodded at Evan's request to video the proceedings for their social media.

"I have something for you," she said to the little girl, approaching the bed.

The child didn't look at her.

"It's a doll."

"I'm too big for dolls."

"Not this kind. Even grown-ups like this kind." She pulled the doll from its box and set it gently beside the child.

Marisol's mother made a little sound. "It's beautiful," she said with a catch in her voice.

Marisol turned toward the doll, a frown already on her face, and Cassie held her breath.

She looked at the doll, tilted her head to one side and looked again. Then she reached out and pulled it into her arms, and Cassie could breathe again.

"She's like me, but with hair," the child said.

Cassie nodded and pulled up her chair to the bed. "It's hard to lose your hair, huh? I hated when it happened to me."

"You have hair." Marisol's frown was back.

"I do now. I lost it all when I had cancer, though."

"You got better?"

Cassie nodded. "Sometimes it felt like I never would. But I did, and I have a good life now, with friends, and a little house, and a job I love, making dolls and visiting kids." It was true, she realized. She loved her job and was making new friends. The house was temporary, but with the money she was putting away, she'd be able to rent an apartment or small cottage. It was way more than she'd expected when she was a child.

They visited awhile longer and then headed out. "That was fun after all," Cassie said, relieved.

"And I recorded the whole visit. You were great in there, really great."

"Thanks! That means a lot." She strode briskly toward the car; she wasn't going to think about what she didn't have. A future, and a family, with a great guy like Evan.

And living next door to him was just too painful. She'd finished a good stage of the teen work now. "Mom's coming home from Ireland in a week," she said. "I think I'll go back to Minestown, meet her and make sure she's settled, and then find an apartment up there."

"What? Why?"

"I'm safe now," she said simply. "The big risk is gone." *The risk to my safety. The risks to my heart are bigger here.* "I'll have to be frugal, but let's be real—that's where my life is going to be, not here. I need to get started on it."

"Don't go yet." He took her hand, held it. "We never did our Josh Boat Launch."

"Our Josh... Oh." She remembered, now, that four months ago they'd talked about taking a homemade boat to Josh's favorite part of the shore and launching it. She'd forgotten, and she was surprised Evan hadn't.

302   FOREVER ON THE BAY

She tilted her head and studied him. There was something she couldn't understand in his expression. "I'll leave Saturday, so let's make it happen before then." *Before you break my heart in a million pieces.*

CHAPTER TWENTY-SEVEN

EVAN CLIMBED INTO the center seat of the rowboat at Duck's Cove and pushed off from the dock. He faced Cassie, who was seated in the rear of the boat, wearing a simple white sweater and jeans. Looking gorgeous. Ace balanced out the other end, his head raised to sniff the air. "You ready for this?" Evan asked Cassie.

"I guess?" She lifted a shoulder. "As ready as I'm going to be."

Evan wasn't ready himself.

He had been here, a couple of times, when he and Josh had driven down. That made the place a little emotional for him. Cassie had spent lots of time here with Josh in the summers. She was more likely to be really sad, but it was sadness they'd expected when they'd planned to do their own little memorial for Josh.

Evan was mostly nervous, because he was planning something more. Was he crazy to mix remembrance with romance?

He rowed them out through the wetlands, green with water lilies and seagrasses, until they reached the broad, open bay. Waves lapped against the boat, and gulls swooped and cried. The clouds moved overhead, the sun peeking through off and on. Ace snapped at a dragonfly.

Evan's heart pounded like a kid on the first day of school. He shouldn't feel that mix of excitement and nerves; he should be focusing on the memorial aspect of the day, on what they'd lost. A better man would have prepared a serious prayer to say, or brought an inspirational book to read from.

But he was here with the woman he loved. As long as he was with Cassie, his heart was going to race. That was how it had always been, and, he understood now, how it would always be.

He looked up at the scudding clouds and imagined he could see Josh there, hanging out with the angels, laughing. Watching over Cassie.

I'm sorry, man. I have to break my promise. But I think, if you were here to talk to us, you might be okay with it.

Cassie pulled out the wooden boat Josh had built long ago. She turned it over and over in her hands. Her hair blew in the wind. "I'm glad we got justice for him," she said, looking up at Evan, "but it didn't fix everything. It didn't fix the grief."

"No, it didn't. You'll always have that, you and your mom and to a lesser extent, all Josh's friends."

She nodded. "He would've said to go on living."

"Right, he would've punched us for moping around."

They looked at each other and then Evan rowed them a little farther out. "How's this spot?"

"Good." She nodded. "He'd make a joke about whether it was biodegradable. But he'd kind of mean it. He wouldn't want us polluting the bay."

"It won't. I checked."

They watched the little boat float out. It felt natural to move into the bottom of the boat, to scoot closer to her. He leaned on one hip and she reached for him and clasped his hand.

Ace flopped to the bottom of the boat and rested his head on his paws.

In his mind, Evan remembered what Josh always always used to say. *Life is short, man.*

Life *was* short. He thought of Oliver, already considering asking Avery to get engaged.

"Do you mind hanging out here for a minute?" he asked. "There's something I want to talk to you about."

CASSIE'S EMOTIONS WERE FRAYED, and Evan's request took them almost to the edge.

What did he want to discuss with her? Didn't he know that every moment they spent together meant more pain for her?

She'd fallen in love with him, that was why.

"Look, Cassie," he said as the boat rocked them, so very gently, "Josh made me promise something a long time ago. I think I mentioned it before."

"Yeah?"

"Yeah. Remember? He told me to leave you alone. To take care of you but leave you alone romantically. I didn't do a great job of either one."

Cassie straightened, pulling her hand away from his and propping it on her hip. "Okay, first, you *did* take care of me as best you could. And second, that is the most patronizing thing I've ever heard." She rolled her eyes. "I can't believe you took it seriously. If he were here, I'd yell at him."

"He had a point, wanting me to stay away. I was a terrible partner to Oliver's mom, and I have a drinking problem."

"You've been doing a lot of work on yourself. You're not the same mixed-up person Josh was worried about."

"I hope not," he said. "I was a bad risk, but people change. I like to think I've changed and grown, but I still have work to do. Learning to be a better father to Oliver, for one thing."

"If the kids get together, maybe you'll be a grandfather," she teased. Evan had told her that Oliver and Avery were getting serious, thinking about getting married.

"Grandpa Evan," he grimaced. "That's another thing. I'm too old for you."

"You're as young as you feel," she said automatically. Inside, she was thinking, *Wait. Why is he talking about being too old for me?*

"It's the alcohol, too," he went on. "I want to make sure I'm still on a good path. It's always going to be something I have to be careful about."

She looked at him and decided to just ask. "Why are you bringing this stuff up?"

"Because I care for you, Cassie. I don't want you to go. I want to…to be with you."

"But I can't have kids," she blurted out, her heart racing. "At least, maybe not. So if you're thinking to get involved…"

He touched her hand, held it. "I'm thinking to get involved," he said. "Hoping to. Seriously involved."

She opened her mouth to say she couldn't be in a relationship, that her health wasn't good, that she'd be too dependent. That no man would want to take her on.

And then she thought of what Bisky had said and closed it again. Because maybe, just maybe, Mom had been wrong about that for all of these years. And even more, maybe Cassie had been wrong to believe it.

She watched Josh's boat as it bobbed farther out into the bay.

Evan squeezed her hand. "Adoption, or helping teens, those are good ways to expand your reach, influence and help others. But that's getting ahead of ourselves. There's something we need to do first."

He rose to his knees and Cassie's heart started galloping, her chest sweating, her face hot. Was this…was he… she couldn't even articulate it to herself, because it was so far beyond her wildest dreams.

"I want to be with you the rest of my life," he said, his face, his dear, dear face, as earnest as she'd ever seen it. "You're an amazing woman, Cassie. I've loved you forever and I didn't think I could love you more. But lately, seeing your strength, your courage, how much you care for other people, my admiration and respect and love have only grown."

Her heart was fluttering madly, but a worry still nudged at her. "I… I'm overwhelmed and honored, Evan, but…"

"Wait," he said. "Don't say no yet. Take all the time you need to think about it. Just think about it, okay?" He paused. "Think about us getting married."

Hearing him say it—marriage—made her breath catch. "I want to be my own independent woman," she said when she got her wind back. "Do you—could you—see me that way?"

"Are you kidding?" His eyes widened, and he clasped both of her hands in his. "You're one of the strongest women I know. I guess it's because you've had a lot of troubles. You didn't let them make you bitter, though. You're still good. Warm and positive and good. And definitely independent,"

As he spoke, his eyes never left hers. She could see his sincerity. "You've faced a lot, too, and grown from it."

He shook his head, a rueful grin on his face. "I've had to be hit with a metaphorical two-by-four a number of times," he said. "And I probably still will. I'm nowhere near perfect, Cassie, but I'll try with everything I've got to make you happy."

"You're already making me happy," she said. She sucked in a breath and closed her eyes for a few seconds, then opened them again. "Happy enough to say yes."

The shock on his face made her burst out laughing.

Ace raised his head and let out a low-key "woof," then flopped back down.

Cassie's heart turned cartwheels in her chest as she tried to take it all in. "You really didn't think I'd say yes, did you?"

He shook his head. "I gave myself very low odds. But every once in a while, I get lucky. And this is the luckiest day of my life." He sat back and pulled her to him, secure between his legs, her back nestled against his chest. Together, they watched as Josh's boat bobbed off toward the horizon.

Cassie looked up at the sky, a Chesapeake sky, ever changeable, clouds scudding, the sun peeking through. "He's up there," she said. "And you know what? I think he's okay with this."

Evan looked up, too, and she felt his heartbeat, steady and strong. "I'll take good care of her, old friend," he said.

The words made Cassie's throat tighten, but there was

something she had to say. "And it goes both ways. I'll take care of him, too."

And as the sun emerged and sent its rays down on them and the bay, it felt like a benediction.

EPILOGUE

CASSIE WIPED HER hands down the sides of her jeans and opened the door of her new shop. The late-July air blew in, but at this time of evening, it was cool enough to prop the door open.

What a Doll had been operational for just two weeks, ever since a vacant storefront had unexpectedly fallen into her lap. Tonight was her first group event. Depending on how it went, she'd know whether this was a good addition to her business. She'd gotten off to a good start, since it was tourist season; especially on rainy days, lots of families came in to make dolls.

But tourist season was short. If she could get the locals on board, attract the girls' night out and kids' birthday party business, she'd know she could make a go of the shop year-round.

"Are we the first? I hope?" Amber half-walked, half-bounced through the door, followed by Erica. "Oh, how pretty it looks!"

"It's not too much?" Cassie had gone all out with crepe paper and balloons. The shop was practically drowning in pink and blue.

"No. She'll love it." Erica set down a big wrapped gift box. "How can we help?"

"Pour drinks and get people to sit down. We'll start even before the guest of honor gets here."

Two tables ran the length of the shop with wine bottles and lemonade pitchers at the centers. At each chair were the materials to decorate a simple doll.

The shop's doors jingled, welcoming in some of Avery's girlfriends from town.

Mary and Goody came in next, and then Bisky. Kayla the preschool teacher followed, now visibly pregnant.

"Where's our guest of honor?" Mary asked. She was the one who was throwing the last-minute shower, and she'd suggested Cassie's shop as a venue. Avery hadn't been allowed to do any of the planning, though she'd been consulted about the guest list.

"Her mom's bringing her." And right then, Avery and her mother walked through the door.

Avery's eyes lit up to see the decorations and the small group of smiling, cheering women. "You all came! This makes me so happy!"

Everyone gathered around her, asking how she was feeling, whether she'd stopped working yet. Clucked over her when they learned she intended to stay on the job right up to her due date. Then people started finding seats, sipping wine or lemonade or mocktails and choosing outfits for their dolls.

When Avery noticed the big stack of gifts, she threw up her hands. "I told you guys I don't want presents. This is supposed to be a party to benefit the hospital's pediatric ward, not an excuse for me to get gifts." Avery had resisted the idea of a traditional baby shower, and had only agreed to this when Cassie had assured her they could donate the dolls to the hospital.

"You can't *stop* people from bringing gifts," Cassie pointed out now.

Avery's mom patted her shoulder. "Believe me, you'll be glad to have some baby supplies."

"You both sit down," Cassie ordered. "You have to make dolls, too." And then she fluttered around from seat to seat, showing the non-sewers what to do, helping them choose the accessories and decorations they wanted.

When everyone was working, Cassie sat down and started putting together a doll herself. It was what she loved to do, and to do it in the company of all of these women was magical.

Josh would have been so proud.

They all sat making dolls, talking and laughing, and Cassie realized that she'd gotten her dream. She was independent, part of a community, making her own way. The fact that Mom and Donald had decided to move nearby was icing on the cake.

Evan, of course, was the sweetness itself, the true prize. She couldn't believe she was lucky enough to be his wife.

As everyone finished their dolls and started talking about getting home, there was a knock on the shop's closed door.

Cassie went over and there was Evan, Oliver at his side. "Incoming men, keep it clean," she called over her shoulder.

Oliver walked in, and Evan pulled Cassie into his arms. "How's it going? You're not working too hard, are you?"

"Stop." She pushed at him. "We're all fine. And if you're going to come in here throwing your weight around, we'll force you to make a doll."

"Or carry the gifts out to your truck and drive them back to Avery's place," Mary suggested, always practical.

Especially considering that one of the gifts was a crib, that seemed like a great idea.

"If you had fun, spread the word," Evan said as everyone left. "What a Doll is a great venue for all kinds of events."

Cassie nudged him and shook her head, embarrassed.

"What? I'm proud of you and I want you to succeed." He tossed his keys to Oliver. "Tell you what. You drive the truck home. I'll be over to help you unload after I help Cass clean up."

When they were alone, he pulled her close and she rested her head against his broad chest. "Seemed like it went well. This is going to be a big success."

"I hope so."

"And Amber and Avery will be good to run it during our honeymoon." They'd decided to get married in a small ceremony, quickly. It hadn't bothered Cassie. The delay in their honeymoon, so that she could get her shop off the ground during tourist season, was just one of many ways Evan was supportive.

"How was your meeting?" she asked him. Evan was attending AA meetings on a weekly basis, being open about it. He'd wanted to delay the wedding to make sure of his sobriety, but neither of them had been able to wait.

"Good. Oliver came, too."

Father and son had been attending the same meetings fairly often, and it seemed like it was strengthening their relationship. "I'm glad."

They locked up the shop and walked out into the moonlight together, heading home to the little cottage they'd rented on the bay.

Cassie had achieved the family she'd dreamed of and hadn't believed she could have. She leaned into her husband's side, lifted her face for his kiss and embraced the gratitude in her heart.

She'd tell him later what the doctor had confirmed today: she'd soon be needing a baby shower of her own.

* * * * *

Did you know there are free stories related to
The Off Season series? Gain access by joining
Lee's newsletter. To find out about the freebies,
as well as news about new releases and cute dog photos,
visit her website, www.leetobinmcclain.com,
and become a subscriber today!

Read on for a sneak peek at the first book in
Lee Tobin McClain's new Hometown Brothers series,
set on Teaberry Island, *coming this Fall!*

CHAPTER ONE

THE FERRYBOAT REACHED Teaberry Island just as the last bit of sun sank behind it, turning the bay into a flat, glossy, golden mirror.

Ryan Hastings considered himself a serious scientist, not given to surges of emotion. Nonetheless, as he stepped onto the small, isolated island, happiness washed over him like a gentle Chesapeake wave.

"Travelling light, are you?" The ferryman handed Ryan his single suitcase and accepted the substantial bonus Ryan had offered for the late-evening ride. "Got a place to stay?"

Ryan nodded, even though he wasn't sure of his welcome. "With Betty Raines."

"Oh, uh-huh. Shame about Wayne." Then he squinted at Ryan. "You're one of their foster kids. The genius, right?"

Ryan's face heated. "I lived here with them as a teenager, yeah."

The man shook his head. "Never thought the three of you would amount to anything. Shows what I know."

"You weren't alone." None of their social workers had expected much from the foster placement. It had been a last-ditch effort to isolate three near-hopeless teens so that at least they didn't influence or harm anyone else.

The three of them had arrived within a month of each other, broken, hurting, in trouble with the law. Wayne and Betty Raines had welcomed them into their rambling house on the shoreline, had provided them with good meals and warm beds and rules.

But most of all, there had been the bay, stretching all around them, a protective moat against their different but equally ugly pasts. There'd been a canoe and a rowboat and the freedom to spend endless hours exploring the marshes and wetlands, the sun baking their pain away, the lap of water against the dock's pilings soothing whatever nightmares each of them had faced in childhood.

Four years of that, and they'd all healed enough to make something of themselves.

As the boat chugged away, Ryan turned and lifted his head to sniff the salty, beachy fragrance of the small fishing port. He *was* travelling light. Was hoping this would be a short trip.

Get here, check on Mama Betty, get out. Hopefully within twenty-four hours.

Silvery moonlight lit his path as he walked the half mile from the docks to Betty's home. He glanced to his right, toward the island's tiny downtown, but saw few lights. Good. That meant the stars shone brighter, a welcome contrast from his home in Baltimore.

Betty's two-story clapboard house rose in front of him, circled on two sides by a wide porch where Ryan had spent plenty of time staring at the house—the girl—next door.

He didn't allow himself to even look in that direction now. Mama Betty was the focus, not himself and his childish, romantic dreams.

After ascertaining that there were a couple of lights on upstairs, Ryan climbed the steps and tapped on the front door. Arriving at 9 p.m., especially as a surprise visitor, could be considered rude, but Mama Betty wasn't an early-to-bed type.

And if he'd warned her he was coming, he was afraid she'd have declined the visit.

Getting no response, he tapped again, louder, and rang the doorbell, anticipating Betty's face when she saw him. No matter what dirt he and his brothers had acquired on his traipses through the marshland, back in their teenage years, no matter what trouble they'd gotten into, she'd always welcomed them with open arms.

He owed her everything: his sanity, his career, his life.

Ryan knocked and rang the bell again, worry tightening his stomach. Could Betty be away, visiting a friend? But no, she never left more than a tiny light on when she went out. Like most of the islanders, she was frugal, had to be. Likely she was caught up in a book from the tiny island library.

Ryan had always felt the most responsibility for Betty. They'd been very close, sharing an interest in books and learning, while Cody and Luis had connected more with their foster father. Since Wayne had died nearly three months ago, they'd all tried to call Betty often, but Ryan was the one who'd been in the most regular phone contact.

Not so regular lately. She'd stopped answering her phone most days. Just when he would start worrying, though, she'd send him a late-night text. *I'm fine. Just not in a talking mood.*

Even the succinct late-night texts had gotten less frequent recently, and he'd made the decision to come see her himself.

Where was she? She couldn't be *that* involved in the latest thriller or fantasy novel, could she? He sidestepped to the window, cupping his hands around his eyes to peer in.

There were signs of habitation—a stack of recent maga-
zines, an open crossword puzzle book by a chair—but no
Betty.

Tension knotted his stomach but he tried to ignore it.
No point giving in to emotions, regrets that he should have
come sooner. She was probably fine.

Other people would have had friends on the island they
could call to have them check on her, but Ryan didn't have
the best people skills and he hadn't stayed in touch with
the islanders.

He'd spoken to his brothers about it yesterday. They'd
agreed her silence was concerning, but they'd come to the
same conclusion: Ryan was the one who should come check
it out.

"You have to." Cody, just six months younger than Ryan,
had insisted. "My unit won't be stateside anytime soon, and
I used up my leave for Wayne's funeral."

"And I can't leave Dalia or pull her out of school," Luis,
a year younger, had said. "She's struggling enough with
her mom leaving us, and to be honest, I'm struggling too."

Ryan had quickly agreed to come. He'd wanted to. But
now, his throat constricted. If there was something wrong,
really wrong, one of his brothers would have been able to
handle it better.

Ryan glanced over at Mellie's house. Lights on there,
too, but no movement. If only he and Mellie hadn't parted
on such bad terms, he could have called her to get her take
on how Betty was doing.

Could Betty be hurt, or sick? He tried the doorknob.
Locked, but easily picked. He reached for his pocket knife
and knelt, studying it.

"Stop it right there. I have a weapon."

The female voice was pitched low, but Ryan would have known it anywhere. Static sparking up and down his spine, he dropped the knife, lifted his hands, and turned to face his would-be assailant. "Mellie. It's Ryan."

She went still, her features still hidden by moonshadows. "Ryan... Hastings?"

"It's me." Slowly, he lowered his hands and stood, but didn't move toward her even though longing tugged at him, strong as an ocean's riptide.

It was something he shouldn't feel.

A whole, healthy man would have moved on from his first love. Met other women, gotten married, started a family. But Ryan wasn't healthy or whole, not in his heart where it mattered.

For the first time her weapon registered: a baseball bat. He felt his lips twitch, even on top of his deeper feelings. Mellie had always been a great hitter, driving balls way into the marshland when it was her turn at bat.

She could have packed a wallop if he had been a real intruder.

A dark figure moved behind her. "Mom? What's going on?"

"Everything's fine, hon." She reached out and put an arm around a young boy, maybe ten. "Go back to bed."

"Who's he?" The boy pointed at Ryan, yawning, leaning against Mellie.

"This is... Mr. Ryan." It was the island's respectful, slightly southern way kids were taught to address adults. "Ryan, this is my son, Alfie."

Ryan's image of Mellie reconfigured to include this new information. She had a son?

HE CAN'T FIND out the truth about Alfie.

Mellie Anderson stared at Ryan, her body going from hot to cold and back again. Of all the people breaking into her neighbor's house, Ryan was the last one she'd expected. He hadn't been back to the island for several years, and before that, his rare visits had been planned. She'd made sure she and Alfie were away.

Even in the dim moonlight, she could see his brown hair, a square jaw, and muscles. He'd filled out since his teenage years. Grown up. Gotten sophisticated.

A light flicked on upstairs. A window opened. "Who's there?" Betty called, her voice nighttime-scratchy.

"It's me, Mellie." Her own voice came out shaky and she consciously relaxed her shoulders. "Thought I heard something. Everything's fine."

"Hi, Miss Betty," Alfie sang out. "There's a—"

"You okay?" Mellie called up to the window, silencing Alfie with a firm hand on his shoulder. Her son was sweet-natured and adored their older neighbor, but he tended to be a blurter.

"Fine. *Trying* to sleep."

"Sorry. See you tomorrow."

"Good night." The window creaked down and banged shut.

And then she beckoned Ryan away from the porch, play-acting calm. "Come on, she doesn't sleep well. If you show up unexpected, she'll be up all night. If it's not an emergency, you can talk to her tomorrow."

"It's not." He picked up his valise. "This was a bad idea. I'll walk into town and stay at the inn."

"Is it open this late?" Alfie, who'd inherited her care-taker gene, looked worried.

"Not likely." She double checked the time. No way was

he getting a room this late. The inn's proprietor closed down once the last ferry had come and gone. Nobody showed up after that, anyway.

Well, unless they had the funds to pay for a private charter and a reason to arrive at night.

Mellie should just go back inside and let him and Betty deal with it. She didn't have to shoulder every burden, take everything on.

Except, where would Ryan stay if she didn't help out?

Concern for him outweighed her worries that he'd learn the truth. "Too late for the inn. And you weren't wrong to check on Betty." She sucked in a breath and said what she did *not* want to say. "Come on over. You can sleep on my couch."

AFTER SHE'D GOTTEN Alfie back into bed, Mellie took deep breaths and wrapped her arms around herself, standing outside the door of her son's room.

Ryan was *here*. In her house. Spending the night.

Why, oh why had she let her impulse to help and protect Betty send her out into the night, there to encounter the man who'd broken her heart and kicked it aside on his way off the island?

And given how much he'd hurt her, why had she invited him to sleep on her couch?

Every minute he stayed made it more likely he'd find out the truth about Alfie. The possible consequences of that tried to push their way into her mind, clamoring for attention, but she firmly shoved them back into the dark cellar where they usually lived.

Then she straightened her shoulders and walked down the stairs to face Ryan.

He'd remained standing and was looking at the pictures

on her mantel. He'd always been intense and focused, even when, as now, he was doing something mundane like looking at family pictures. "Em had a baby?"

Mellie forced a smile, nodded. "Not a baby anymore. John Junior's three."

"They live off-island?"

She nodded. "Both Em and Angela. Em's in Baltimore, so I see them some. Angela's in Sedona finding herself." She smiled to make him think she didn't worry about her youngest sister, although she did.

The normal thing. She needed to do the normal thing so he wouldn't see her agitation and start to wonder about the cause of it. "What can I get you to drink? Coffee? Tea?"

"A cup of tea would be good. Thanks, Mellie. I really appreciate this."

She fixed the tea and put slices of leftover pound cake on a plate. A plain snack, but the best she could do for unexpected company.

Especially when her hands were shaking.

How could Ryan be here? Wasn't he supposed to be doing research overseas? He'd missed his foster father's funeral for that reason. And it was important research too. He'd gotten grants and made discoveries; Mama Betty had framed a magazine cover with him on it, when he'd won a "young scientist of the year" award.

He was brilliant, she'd always known that. And, unencumbered, he'd gone from the island and made something of himself. A lot.

Now this famous scientist whom she'd once thought she loved was in her living room. And she had a big secret to keep from him.

She carried in the plate and set it and the tea on a table

beside the big, comfortable recliner. She cuddled up in her rocker, herself. *Act normal, act normal.*

He studied her in that precise, scientific way he had. Precise, and scientific, and intense. "You look good, Mellie."

She looked down at her T-shirt and sleep shorts. "I didn't exactly dress for visitors."

"You didn't know you'd have one." He took a bite of the pound cake and smiled. "This is good. Thank you. You always did like to feed people, just like Betty." Then his cheeks flushed a little.

Was he remembering the picnic when they'd fed each other strawberries?

He cleared his throat. "Tell me about Betty," he said. "She didn't sound like herself. Is she all right?"

"Sure." She was glad of the change of subject. "I was thinking of calling you guys. I'm in touch with Luis occasionally, but I didn't want to bother him. And Cody's back with his unit overseas."

"And you didn't call me? You know I'd have come." His brow wrinkled.

"Well," she hedged, "I thought you were over in Europe somewhere. Besides, Betty says she talks to you, so I figured you were aware."

"I'm back in the States for good, to start a lab. And I knew something was wrong, but not what. That's why I'm here." He leaned forward. "What's going on with her, Mellie?"

Mellie sipped tea. "She's depressed. Which of course you'd expect, since she just lost her husband three months ago. Not even. But it seems more than normal. Like, she often won't leave her house for days."

He propped his chin on his hand, frowning. "Is she able to run the market?"

"No. She won't go to work. I'm doing it for her. Which is okay for now, but there are decisions only the owner can make. She needs to get involved again." As she described Betty's issues, her overactive mind hummed with worry.

If she portrayed to Ryan how badly Betty was coping, he wouldn't feel okay about leaving. Knowing him, he might even stay and try to help her get out of her funk.

Whereas if she downplayed it, he'd probably leave tomorrow, to get back to his important work.

"Thank you for doing that for her. She's lucky to have you as an employee and friend."

"I'm happy to help her. She's helped me plenty." Betty had always been her go-to babysitter for Alfie and her supportive friend when she was struggling with motherhood.

In fact, Betty had been a wonderful neighbor ever since Mellie had been a child. How could she even think of hiding the extent of her problems from Ryan, who might be able to figure out how to help her? "The depression seems like it might be serious," she said reluctantly. "And another thing. Her house is bad."

He must have heard the concern in her voice, because he looked at her with a penetrating gaze. "How so?"

"It's a mess. Really, really cluttered. I wouldn't call it a hoarding situation, but Wayne didn't like to throw anything away. She needs major help cleaning it out."

He frowned. "Would a cleaning service be useful? Because I would be glad to pay..." As Mellie shook her head, he trailed off.

"That's a nice idea, but I don't think she'd let strangers into her house. And the truth is, she needs more than a cleaning service. She needs counseling, most likely, but I'm almost positive she won't accept it."

"So no strangers, and no counseling. That doesn't leave a lot of options."

"Maybe one of your brothers could come stay with her for awhile. I know Cody's overseas, but maybe Luis and his daughter—"

Ryan shook his head. "They're having a hard time right now. I don't think Luis should separate Dalia from her friends just after her mother dumped them." He frowned, looking at the floor, then nodded decisively. "I can talk to my board about a research leave before starting up the new lab. I have a grant to write, and just a little field work to do. If it's necessary, I can do it here."

"Oh, I'm sure she won't want you to stall out your career." Ryan couldn't stay here. She couldn't keep the agitation she felt from showing on her face.

He misunderstood the cause of her upset. "Don't worry. If I did come, I'd stay at Betty's. Not here."

"Right," she said faintly. Even having him next door would be way more than she could handle.

Because if he stayed close by, how could she keep him from finding out that he was Alfie's father?

Don't miss the first book in this new spinoff series
by Lee Tobin McClain!

ACKNOWLEDGMENTS

I have so many people to thank for helping me to bring this book, and this series, to life. My editor, Shana Asaro, Editorial Director Susan Swinwood, and agent, Karen Solem, have been incredibly smart and helpful at keeping me on the right story path. The art, marketing, and sales teams at Harlequin do amazing work creating gorgeous covers and getting books out into the world, even during the pandemic. Thanks, too, are due to my sharp and detail-oriented assistant, Annette Stone, and my enthusiastic release team.

I get terrific support, literary and emotional, from writer friends Rachel, Dana, Sandy, Jo and Michelle, from my Wednesday morning writers' group, and from all my colleagues at Seton Hill University. For professional advice, I am indebted to the one and only Susan Mallery.

Closer to home, I am grateful to Sue, Ron, Jessica, Bill and most of all Grace, who keep me grounded, sane and laughing.

Finally, I want to thank my readers who have stuck with me throughout all six books and two novellas of The Off Season series. Your kind messages, letters and emails provide the encouragement that keeps me writing.

The brick building that housed the county Division of Family
Services always brought back a myriad of emotions for Emery
Guthrie. As she stood on the sidewalk on a too-warm day in May,
the memories came back stronger than ever.

Absently, she reached to pet her service dog, Zeb. The
chocolate-brown labradoodle understood that touch and he moved
close to her side. He grounded her to reality, to the present. She'd
been rescued.

Rescued. She drew on that word. She'd been rescued. By this
place, this building and the people inside. They'd seen her father
jailed for the abuse that had left her physically and emotionally
broken. They'd placed her with a foster mother, Nan Guthrie, the
woman who had adopted her as a teen, giving her a new last name
and a new life.

But today wasn't about Emery. It was about the two young girls
whom Nan had been caring for the past few weeks. They'd lost
their parents in a terrible, violent tragedy. They'd been uprooted
from their home, their lives and all they'd ever known, brought to

Pleasant, Missouri, and placed with Nan until their new guardian could be found.

That man was Beau Wilde. A grade ahead of Emery, Beau had spent their school years making her life even more miserable with his bullying.

He'd taunted, teased and humiliated her.

She shook her head, as if freeing herself from the thoughts she'd not allowed to see the light of day in many years. Those memories belonged in the past.

Just then, a truck pulled off the road and circled the parking lot.

Emery hesitated a moment too long. Beau was out of his truck and heading in her direction. He nodded as he closed in on her.

"Please, let me." He opened the door and stepped back to allow her to go first. "Nice dog."

"Thank you," she whispered. She cleared her throat. "His name is Zeb."

Don't miss
Earning Her Trust *by Brenda Minton*
wherever Love Inspired books and ebooks are sold.

LoveInspired.com

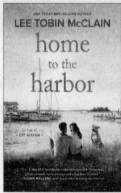

Get 4 FREE REWARDS!

We'll send you 2 FREE Books <u>plus</u> 2 FREE Mystery Gifts.

Both the **Romance** and **Suspense** collections feature compelling novels written by many of today's bestselling authors.

STRSMAX22